THE WHITE WOLF OF WISHING MOON BAY

HARMONY RAINES

The White Wolf of Wishing Moon Bay

The Bond of Brothers

Book One

* * *

All rights reserved. This book, or any portion thereof may not be reproduced or used in any manner without the express written consent of the author or publisher.

This is a work of fiction and is intended for mature audiences only. All characters within are eighteen years of age or older. Names, places, businesses, characters and incidents are either the product of the author's imagination or are used in a fictitious manner. Any resemblance to real persons, living or dead, actual events or places is purely coincidental.

© 2022 Harmony Raines

Sign up to the Harmony Raines Newsletter by going to:

http://www.harmonyraines.com/newsletter-sign-up/

Never miss a new release!

You'll also receive the EBOOK 'A Bond to Bear'

Just to say thank you!

Created with Vellum

SERIES ORDER

1. The White Wolf of Wishing Moon Bay

2. The Horse Shifter's Mate
3. Her Fae-vorite Bear
4. Fae-ted to the Bear
5. The Snow Leopard's Love
6. The Dragon Shifter's Desire

US LINKS

Website and Newsletter: harmonyraines.com

Facebook: facebook.com/harmonyrainesauthor

Amazon Author Page: amazon.com/Harmony-Raines/e/B0090Q3DWM

Bond of Brothers Series Page

On Amazon: amazon.com/dp/B08T6JF1QZ

On My Website: harmonyraines.com/all-books/bond-of-brothers-series

UK LINKS

Website and Newsletter: harmonyraines.com

Facebook: facebook.com/harmonyrainesauthor

Amazon Author Page: amazon.co.uk/Harmony-Raines/e/B0090Q3DWM

Bond of Brothers Series Page

On Amazon: amazon.co.uk/dp/B08T6JF1QZ

On My Website: harmonyraines.com/all-books/bond-of-brothers-series

THE WHITE WOLF OF WISHING MOON BAY

THE BOND OF BROTHERS

Book One

A second chance shifter romance

He has a reputation for being a grumpy wolf. But when his mate arrives in town with her adorable son, he'll do whatever it takes to make her stay.

After a devastating tragedy left him orphaned, white wolf shifter, Logan, was adopted by Valerie and raised in Wishing Moon Bay, a town like no other.

Most of the inhabitants have supernatural powers. Shifters live alongside witches and vampires, usually without any trouble. But when Logan's mate ends up in town—not an easy feat for a non-magical person—trouble soon follows.

With the help of his adopted brothers, Logan promises to keep them safe. Whatever the cost.

Newly dumped and divorced, Penny is traveling to her sister's house when her car breaks down in the middle of nowhere. Only it's not the middle of nowhere. A road sign to a town she's *never* heard of, and is not on any map, looms out of the darkness. As her car makes sounds no car should ever make, she has no choice. Penny makes a lifechanging decision and drives toward Wishing Moon Bay.

Soon, Penny is caught up in otherworldly danger.

Her shock at learning the supernatural is just plain *natural* in Wishing Moon Bay soon disappears as she falls for Logan, the man who says he's her mate.

But even the grumpy white wolf shifter might not be able to save Penny from the danger that stalks her.

And then there's the weird feeling that she's visited Wishing Moon Bay before...

1

PENNY

"Oh, no. No, no, no." Penny stared at the flashing light on the dashboard which didn't stop no matter how many times she *no-ed* it.

"What's wrong, Mommy?" Milo's small, scared voice came from the back seat where he was buckled in safely with his toy wolf tucked under his arm.

"Nothing." The flashing light said otherwise but there was no use worrying her son. Not yet at least. Maybe the light didn't mean an emergency. Maybe it just meant, *get me to a garage at your earliest convenience*. But cars weren't polite in that way. As if to confirm this, something clunked under the hood.

"That didn't sound like nothing." Milo squirmed in his seat and sat up straighter so that he could see out of the window. Not that there was anything to see, darkness surrounded them on all sides. Deep, penetrating darkness.

"We're okay. The car is still running." She closed her eyes briefly as they kangaroo-hopped down the narrow country road. They were in the middle of nowhere, heading for her sister's house.

After the breakup of her marriage, Penny was practically destitute, thanks to the lying, cheating man she thought she loved. But what love she had for him was gone after her jerk of a husband ran off with an older woman. When you hit forty, your husband was supposed to run off with a young, nubile woman. Not a woman ten years his senior.

She let out a small sob and quickly covered her mouth with her hand. Her confidence was at its lowest ebb, she was a failure, forced to go beg her sister to let her and Milo stay until she got herself back on her feet.

Penny focused on keeping the car on the road and refused to think that at least the headlights were still working in case they heard her and gave up, too. Not that it mattered if they were working or not if the engine failed. There were no towns, no houses for a hundred miles in either direction. No one to see them, no one to come to her rescue. Not according to the map.

Wishing Moon Bay 2 miles

She read the sign as the car bounced along the road like Milo when he had the hiccups. Her forehead creased. Penny had driven this route before and was certain there had been no sign for Wishing Moon Bay the last time she'd followed this road to Helena's house. As for the map... Wishing Moon Bay wasn't on the map.

Perhaps it was a new town. One that had been built recently. Too new to be on any map.

Wishing Moon Bay 1 mile

The car lurched forward, and Milo grabbed hold of the door while clutching Mr. Wolfy even tighter. "Is it going to stop?"

"I hope not." She meant the car, but she suspected Milo meant the bumping and clanking that seemed to have combined into a steady rhythm like an acapella group waiting for someone to start singing. Penny was not in the mood for singing.

Wishing Moon Bay 1/2 mile

The singing started anyway. A small whine from under the hood which she suspected was steam escaping from the radiator.

"What are we going to do?" Milo asked the question that had been beating in her head in time with the clanking.

"We're going to take a detour and find a garage to fix the car." Penny peered into the darkness, looking for the turnout to Wishing Moon Bay. It had to be close and she couldn't risk missing it. The car was barely capable of driving forward let alone reversing.

"We're going to Wishing Moon Bay?" Milo's hopeful voice gave her confidence.

"Yes, we are. It sounds like a good place, doesn't it?" Any place was better than breaking down on the side of the road in the dark.

"Do you think we could make a wish if we go there?" His hope cranked up a notch.

"I don't see why not."

"There's the turnout, Mommy!" Milo pointed and Penny turned the wheel sharply.

The turnout was almost hidden between the trees on the left side of the road. It would be so easy to drive past and never see it at all. But they had seen it and now they were driving along the narrow road. With no hope of turning around, the car seemed to have toned down its cacophony of noises and only emitted a small hiccup every now and again.

The temptation to back the car up and drive back toward the known world, the safe world, was almost too much. However, every time she even looked for a suitable place to turn around, the car reminded her it was in control, it could stop any moment.

Then they reached *THE TUNNEL*.

"Shit!"

"Don't swear, Mommy." Milo reached for the back of her car seat and leaned forward to look out of the windshield. "Spooky."

Let's just hope we get through the other side. She kept that thought firmly in her head as they entered the darkness. The headlights hardly penetrated the absolute darkness and Penny shrank back, gripping the steering wheel tightly. "Shall we sing a song?"

"What kind of song?" Milo was invisible in the dark of the tunnel.

"'Twinkle Twinkle Little Star?'"

"That's a baby song," he insisted.

You will always be my baby, she told him in her head, knowing he would protest if she said the words out loud. "Then you pick a song."

"I can't think of one." He pointed ahead, his hand touching her ear in the dark and she nearly screamed. "I see a light."

Get a grip. It's not Halloween.

"I see it, too." She let out her pent-up breath and relaxed her hands on the wheel as the light grew bigger and brighter.

"It's the moon."

"It can't be." Her brow furrowed.

"*That* is the moon," Milo insisted.

"I guess it is." There was no point arguing with her son. The light at the end of the tunnel was the moon, it hung in the sky just above the horizon, although she had no idea how since on the other side of the tunnel there was no moon.

Only last night she'd stood outside of their house, with all their belongings packed in the car ready for their next adventure, and stared at the sliver of moon that hung in the sky. She'd stood and thought how appropriate that the moon would be fully waned by the time they began their journey to Helena's and that it would grow bigger and brighter, as she hoped their lives would when they put the past couple of months behind them.

In the distance, tall mountains were silhouetted against the sky. Mountains that were no more on the map than the town itself.

But as the car lumped and bumped down the road toward the collection of houses bathed in moonlight, she was too relieved to care about the impossibilities of the moon or the rest of her surroundings.

"What if we can't find a mechanic?" Milo asked. "Won't they all be in bed?"

Penny glanced at the clock on the dashboard. "It's not very late. I'm sure they won't be in bed, but they probably have already closed down for the night." The car jolted and lurched forward, letting out a loud bang.

"I think if they were in bed, we would have just woken them up." Milo seemed to be enjoying this far too much, although it was better than him being afraid.

"You might be right. But if we don't find a mechanic this evening, we can always find a hotel for the night and ask for directions to the nearest garage in the morning."

"A hotel!" For Milo, the day was just getting better and better.

For Penny, it was getting more and more expensive. She had barely any money and what she had was supposed to support them for the next few weeks. Car repairs and hotel rooms were not within her meager budget.

"There." Milo pointed out of the window as they rolled past a large, illuminated sign that read, *Frank and Dennis Car Repairs*.

"Good spotting." She steered the car into the parking lot, relieved that one of the large sliding doors that guarded the entrance was half open. As she came to a halt, the engine spluttered its last breath and died. Much like her marriage and her old life.

"Can I come, too?" Milo had already popped his seatbelt and shuffled to the edge of his seat. "I don't want to stay in the car on my own."

"Sure." Penny had no intention of leaving her son in the car on his own. However, she suspected that whereas she was worried about leaving Milo alone in a strange town, Milo was excited to get out of the car and check out his new surroundings. The boy sure had an adventurous head on his shoulders. Even if their adventuring up until now had been exploring the concrete jungle more than the mountains and forests that surrounded Wishing Moon Bay.

Cracking open the door, Penny got out of the car and stretched her legs, grateful for the chance to walk around, even though the cost of the car repairs might just empty her bank account.

The clear air hit her first. A breeze, swept down from the mountains, caressed her skin and she shivered at the threat of snow carried down from the highest peaks. If she got stranded here, she might not be able to cover the cost of the hotel and the car repairs. Yet, as Milo threaded his hand into hers, she had no choice but to get the car fixed, she could only hope it was a quick fix, a cheap fix, and then they could be on their way.

"I can hear someone whistling," Milo whispered as they neared the entrance to the garage workshop.

"Me, too." Penny gripped his hand tightly. This scene had all the makings of a horror movie. An unarmed woman and child lured into a backwater town and never seen or heard from again. "Hello!"

She stopped walking and stood in the pool of light spilling out from the garage. Not that there was anyone else around to see them. A quick glance over her shoulder confirmed there was no one else in sight.

"Hello." A cheery face accompanied the cheery voice.

Yep, way too friendly. Or maybe they were just desperate for business. How many car repairs could there be in a small town like Wishing Moon Bay?

"Our car broke down." Milo grinned at the guy who approached them as if they were the luckiest people alive. He had the sunniest nature and a way of setting people at ease. Despite his age, Milo was great with people, young or old.

"I heard." The guy looked past Penny and cast a critical eye over her ten-year-old Ford. "We can take a look at it if you want?"

"Now?" she asked hopefully. If it was just a loose connection or a nut that needed tightening, she might be on her way within the hour and still get to Helena's tonight.

"In the morning." The guy smiled brightly. "We were just about to close."

"Oh." She looked over her shoulder at the town with the moon hanging low over the mountains that seemed to cradle Wishing Moon Bay. "Is there a hotel?"

"A hotel?" The guy nodded. "Sure..." He did not sound sure.

"Is it far?" Milo asked.

"No, not too far. Just follow the street and you'll find it. It's called Wishing Moon Hotel." He nodded and stuck out his hand, which was washed clean of all dirt and grime. "I'm Frank, by the way."

"Penny." She put her hand in his and shook it.

"I'm Milo." He offered his hand to Frank.

"Good to meet you, Milo." Frank smiled widely.

"We should go and get an overnight bag from the car and then I'll drop the keys back to you." Penny turned around and hurried back to the car. "What do you need?"

"I already have Mr. Wolfy." Milo patted the head of his favorite cuddly toy. "PJs, a toothbrush..." He watched as Penny quickly sorted through their luggage. She soon had two backpacks with everything they needed for a night in a hotel. With a sigh, she checked that everything was secure before she closed the trunk and headed back to the garage.

"Thank you so much. Can you look at it first thing in the morning? We're supposed to be staying with my sister. She's expecting us tonight." She gave an apologetic smile. Soon she'd have to make a phone call to Helena.

"Sure, I'll take a look at it first thing in the morning," Frank assured her before she gave him the keys.

"So the hotel is straight along the street?" Penny didn't want to be wandering around at night, in a strange town, trying to locate a place to sleep

"Straight down the street." Frank sliced his hand through the air and nodded. "Tell Logan that Frank sent you."

"Thanks." With a backpack on her shoulder and her son's hand in hers, Penny turned her back on the garage, walked past her car, resisting the urge to kick it, and headed straight down the street, trusting that Frank was pointing them in the right direction in the town which didn't really exist.

What else could go wrong?

2

LOGAN

"I just need to get some air." Logan pushed open the back door that led from the kitchen out into the small, paved area where the trash cans were stored. The door bounced back at him and he cursed himself for nearly taking the damn door off its hinges. He did not need more maintenance work at Wishing Moon Hotel.

Sucking in the cool night air, he strode away from the small patch of light that streamed out of the kitchen and opened the back gate which led onto the street. The distant mountains called to him, he longed to go home, to leave behind the noise and the chatter that seemed to permeate every part of the small hotel he'd agreed to run for a couple of weeks.

How could he say no when his adoptive mom, Valerie Kelts, who owned the hotel, was recovering from an operation on her knee? If anyone else had asked, he'd have said no. Logan was not a people person and despite his best efforts, he didn't seem able to empathize with all the guests who were staying at the hotel.

One particular guest seemed hellbent on making Logan's life a misery.

So what if the hot water cut out halfway through your shower? Cold water washed the soap away just as well.

His wolf chuckled. You're going to need a cold shower to cool that temper of yours.

I'm not angry. Logan sighed and stared at the mountain peaks that lay beyond the borders of the town. *I just want to be free. I'd forgotten what it was like to be surrounded by people all the time.*

Valerie needs us, so we're going to suck it up and get the job done. His wolf was always the practical one.

Logan sighed. His wolf was right. They were both missing their cabin on the edge of the woods that fringed the mountains, where they spent most of the time hunting and fishing. Living off the land meant he could drown in silence and he only came to town a couple of times a week to trade in his furs and the fish he'd smoked himself.

And to see his mom and his brothers, five other shifters who Valerie had also adopted when they were kids. All grown up now, they all kept in close contact with the woman who had showered them with love and understanding. They owed her so much.

They also loved each other and were there for each other. If ever one of them needed help, he knew he could rely on the others to be there. Logan's brothers often visited him at his cabin where they sat and drank beer under the stars. They would sit and talk, reminiscing over their happy childhood days, and dreaming of their futures. And their mates. Who none of them had been lucky enough to meet yet.

Where are we going? his wolf asked. We can't just abandon the hotel.

We're not. I just had the urge to get out of there. Logan stopped and sniffed the air. *Can't you feel it?* There was something different about Wishing Moon Bay tonight. *The air smells different.*

Snow, we're going to have snow. Just think, all those people snowed in at the hotel. He chuckled as Logan grimaced. His wolf liked people. Or he didn't dislike them as much as Logan.

You don't dislike people, his wolf told him. You just don't always understand them. They confuse you.

Logan shook his head from side to side. They don't seem to be the thing that is confusing me now. There's something...

Here... His wolf stood up, his head raised, his mouth slightly open as he tasted something in the air.

What is it? The hairs on the back of Logan's neck stood on end as he stared into the distance. The streetlights lining the road were not exactly bright, but he could see something approaching them. Something on foot. A beast about to attack?

His wolf itched to be free as he prowled the edges of Logan's mind, but he didn't sense danger. He sensed something else. Something he could not name.

Logan's pace quickened. He needed to see what the thing was coming toward them. It had a long and a short body. He tilted his head to one side. If that was right, it was walking sideways.

Two. There are two of them. His wolf's excitement ratcheted up a notch. *Go.*

What?

Go.

Do you mean run away? What kind of devil would make his wolf want to run away?

No, go to her. Go to them.

Logan stopped walking. Cold sweat on his forehead chilled him and he shivered. He didn't need his wolf to tell him anymore. He knew what he was facing. The biggest threat he'd ever faced.

Our mate, his wolf finally said.

Our mate. Just what we need.

Exactly what we need, his wolf agreed.

I was being sarcastic.

I was not. His wolf chuckled but Logan didn't find it amusing at all. No matter how often he'd dreamed of having a mate, he didn't think he was ready.

And a child, his wolf added.

And a child. Logan's heart hammered in his chest. His mate was here in Wishing Moon Bay with a child by her side. They must need his protection. The urge to offer her his protection was overwhelming.

They might just be visiting town, his wolf told him as Logan began to walk again, his legs stiff and his mind numb.

And out for a moonlit walk? Isn't it late to be walking the streets with a young child?

It's not that late, his wolf replied, although he also felt the need to protect the two people in front of them.

Slowly they closed the distance between them and his mate.

Where is she going? Logan took a couple of running steps forward as his mate suddenly turned toward the houses on her left, dragging the child with her.

You've scared her off and we haven't even spoken to her yet, his wolf chastised.

All I was doing was walking down the street, Logan objected as he broke into a run, following her trail. If she thought she could lose him, she must not know much about shifters.

Maybe she doesn't know anything about shifters, his wolf pointed out.

Then what is she doing here in Wishing Moon Bay? The only people who cross the border are those who...

Are supposed *to.* His wolf bristled with excitement as they caught the scent of their mate. Her hand had touched the tree on the corner of the front yard between two houses. He could smell her, he could hear her breathing, whispering to her child that it would all be all right.

"Hello," Logan called out, his voice low so as not to scare them.

Too late, his wolf sniffed the air.

"I'm not going to hurt you."

Said every axe murderer ever.

"I'm from the hotel."

Lame. But his mate's breathing slowed, and she inched toward him. He could see the outline of her body, he could see the small child's silhouette against the huge moon that hung in the sky over the ocean.

"You're from the hotel?" she asked. "How did you know we needed the hotel?"

"I..." A truck in the distance caught his attention. The tow truck. Frank was on his way home. It was late. "Frank."

"Frank told you to come and meet us?" She took a couple of small steps toward him, holding onto the small boy's hand tightly, although the child didn't look scared. His eyes were curious, to him this was an adventure, but his mother was guarding him, protecting him as mothers should.

"Yes. I thought I'd come and meet you. Help you carry your luggage." He sounded wooden, his tone stilted. Logan wasn't a practiced liar.

She sighed and came all the way out of her hiding place. "Frank didn't say he was going to call you."

"I'm Logan." He thrust out his hand.

"Logan." The name seemed to soothe her fears. "Frank did say you ran the hotel."

"Temporarily." She hadn't taken his hand. He wanted her to take his hand. He needed her to take his hand. It was as if once she put her small hand in his, he would own her on some level. They would be connected. Yet when she finally slipped her hand into his and he closed his fingers around her warm skin, he realized he did not own her, but she owned him.

His life would never be the same again.

Her eyes flashed in the moonlight as a jolt of recognition passed between them. "I'm Penny." Her voice cracked and she coughed to clear her throat before she placed her hand on her child's head and said, "And this is Milo."

"Hello, Milo." Logan stared down at the little boy. He couldn't be more than six or maybe eight. Logan wasn't good with ages. People were people. When he looked at them, he didn't define them by age or height, but by the way they behaved.

"Hi." Milo held up a plush toy that was well-worn and well-loved. "And this is Mr. Wolfy."

Logan's wolf nearly choked as he stared at the soft fluffy creature thrust into Logan's face. There was irony there. Fate sure had a sense of humor. He'd never believed it until now.

"Hello, Mr. Wolfy." He kept his voice even and low.

"Is the hotel far?" Penny asked as she adjusted the straps of her pack and stepped out of the front yard where she'd tried to hide from him. She didn't offer any excuse for why they had left the street and hidden from Logan and he didn't ask.

"Not very far." He smiled like a fool as they reached the road and turned toward the Wishing Moon Hotel. "Here, let me carry your bags."

"Oh, I can manage." Her fingers tightened on the strap. She was still wary of him. Or perhaps she was wary of all people. They might have more in common than he'd hoped. "But you could carry Milo's backpack." Her tone and body language softened.

"You can carry me." Milo tugged free of his mom's hand and held up his arms.

"Milo, I can carry you." She stepped forward as if to protect the child.

"He is safe with me." Logan scooped the boy into his arms and the child instantly wrapped his thin arms around Logan's neck and rested his head on his shoulder.

"It's been a long day." Penny's toe caught on the ground and she stumbled forward. "A very long day."

"Our car broke down," Milo told him sleepily. "Mommy was worried we'd get stuck in the middle of nowhere. But then we saw the turnout and the tunnel. It's Mommy's birthday next week. We need to get to Aunt Helena's so that she can help me choose a present."

"Is it?" Logan glanced sideways at Penny. "I'm sure you'll get her a present in time."

"I'd never seen the turnout before and the town is not on the map." Penny changed the subject and fell into step with him, at least she tried but his strides were too long, and she kept having to jog a couple of steps to keep up.

"No, we keep ourselves to ourselves here. So far we've managed to stay off all maps." He shortened his stride so she could keep up.

"Really?" She let out a breath and a cloud of vapor surrounded her face. "I thought that was almost impossible these days unless you live on an isolated island somewhere." She glanced up at the huge moon that shone across the bay.

"Mommy also said the moon is in the wrong place." Milo lifted his head off Logan's shoulder. "Did someone move the moon?"

"No, the moon is exactly where it's supposed to be." He chuckled. "Wishing Moon Bay is like being in another world."

"I thought maybe it was a new town. But I can tell by the

buildings it's old. Very old." She turned around and walked backward, her attention fixed on the library building, with its gargoyles perched on top watching them with suspicion as they passed.

"It is very old." He pointed up ahead. "The hotel is just along the street." This conversation was getting awkward. He didn't want to get into the history of the town tonight. Penny and Milo were tired and tired brains tended to protest information differently than an awake, alert mind. The last thing he wanted to do was scare them. Not on their first night.

Not on any night, his wolf said firmly.

But there were things in Wishing Moon Bay that were scary. And if they were going to stay, then they'd have to learn about them.

If they are going to stay? his wolf asked.

We can't force them, Logan said as he placed his hand tenderly on Milo's back to stop him from sliding out of his arms. The child was asleep. Drifting off into the land of dreams where anything was possible. In the town of Wishing Moon Bay where the impossible was not a dream, but a reality.

Like us finding our mate, his wolf said before he rested his head on his paws and joined the boy in his dreams.

3

PENNY

Don't talk to strangers. That's what her mom had always told Penny and that was the same warning she'd passed onto her son. Yet here they were in a strange town with a strange man carrying Milo in his arms. She only had his word that he was Logan from the hotel. For all she knew, he could be taking them anywhere. But what choice did she have? None right now. It was too late. The time for making choices was when she'd seen the man prowling down the street.

Her first instinct was to run. There was something about Logan that unnerved her. With the huge moon behind him, there had been something otherworldly about him.

Otherworldly. Another warning her mom had given Penny and her sister when they were small children and Helena was convinced there was something hidden in her closet. Most mothers would have told her not to worry because there was no such thing as monsters. Instead, Penny's mom had hung a talisman in the closet along with a bunch of herbs that would ward off all manner of nasty beasties.

"Here's the hotel." Logan pointed to a turreted building set back from the road.

Yes. Turreted.

"Quirky." There was no other way to describe it. The building looked as if someone had plucked a medieval castle out of their imagination and shrunk it in size so that it would fit on the corner plot on the street.

"Like its occupants," Logan murmured under his breath.

"You must get a lot of visitors to the town." Penny followed Logan as he strode up the short driveway to the large wooden door, hung on massive iron hinges.

"Enough." His tone actually said, *too many*, but she wasn't going to push him on that point.

"How long have you owned the hotel?" She twirled around as she climbed the marble steps, looking up at the building as she traced her hand over the handcrafted stone.

"Oh, I don't own it. I'm...hotel sitting...for my mom. She's out of town for a few weeks while she recovers from an operation on her knee." He pushed the door open. There was no creak or squeak, the hinges were well oiled, and as they entered the small reception area, the smell of beeswax polish and pine gave her the impression the hotel was well-loved and well cared for.

"Looking after a hotel. You must be a good son." She relaxed a little. The hotel was real, Logan was doing a big favor for his mom, all was well. There were no monsters in the closets.

"I owe her a lot." He went to the reception desk and slid around the polished wooden counter. "Hi, Sophie."

"Hi, Logan. Is everything all right?" A tall, slim, attractive blonde cast a dismissive glance over Penny before fixing her blue eyes on Logan. She was probably in her late thirties, but Penny found it hard to get a fix on her age.

"Everything is fine." Logan grabbed a key off the hooks

behind the reception desk. "Penny's car broke down and she and her son need somewhere to stay for the night."

"Oh, shall I sign them in?" Sophie didn't make eye contact with Penny as she tapped the keyboard of the reception computer.

Logan slipped back around the reception desk. "No," he said quickly. Too quickly. "We can figure all that out in the morning." His hand on Milo's back was light but secure and a lump formed in Penny's throat. If only Milo's dad was half as loving toward his son. "This little man needs his bed."

"Thank you." Penny's voice cracked and she looked away as she blinked back tears.

"Come on, I'll show you to your room. It has an amazing view across the bay." He was tall, well over six foot, his broad shoulders encased in a blue shirt that would not ward off the winter chill outside, and yet when they had shaken hands, he'd been warm, very warm.

A hot-blooded male. She stopped that thought in its tracks. *Sworn off men forever,* she reminded herself. Yet, already forever seemed like too long.

"Thank you." She gripped the strap on her backpack as her emotions swelled inside her like a stormy sea.

"My pleasure." And oh, did his eyes promise so much pleasure as he stared down at her. Not in a leering male kind of way. But there was something in his soft brown eyes cracked with amber that enveloped her like a warm blanket under which they could make slow, passionate love.

"I'll give your hotel five stars on TripAdvisor." She laughed awkwardly to break the moment and shatter it into a million pieces.

"TripAdvisor?" His brows furrowed together.

"Nothing." She shook her head and looked away from him.

"This way." He turned around and headed toward the

sweeping staircase that rose from the reception area. Before the hotel, the building must have been someone's well-loved home. Penny could imagine ladies in long dresses and men in suits and cravats coming down the elegant staircase to dinner.

"This place is amazing." She clutched the handrail as they climbed the stairs, noting the small animals carved into the wooden spindles.

"I suppose it is." Logan looked around as if seeing the place for the first time.

"Milo would love to explore it." She touched her son's hand, draped over Logan's back. "It's a shame once the car is fixed, we need to leave."

"So soon?" His sharp tone caused Milo to stir and he rubbed her son's back until he settled back down.

"Yes. We're traveling to my sister's. I'm between houses. And jobs." She sighed, unsure why she felt safe confiding in Logan. "My marriage fell apart and I have nowhere else to go."

"So you're staying with your sister while you figure things out?" They reached the top of the stairs and he took a left.

"Yes, uprooting Milo from all of his friends, from everything he's ever known..." She brushed her thumb against the gold band of her ring finger. It wasn't there. She hadn't worn it for weeks, but she often forgot. "It hasn't been easy."

"And...Milo's dad?" Logan stopped outside the door at the end of the corridor. Room eight.

"Milo's dad." Her bottom lip trembled.

"Sorry, it's none of my business." But he didn't open the door, and instead, half-turned to look at her as if it was his business.

"No, it's fine. Milo's dad is the reason we're here." She pressed her lips together as she fought to keep control of her emotions. The events of the night had caught up with her.

From their car breaking down to her worry as to how she was going to pay the repair bill and the hotel bill, to her fear of Logan when she saw him in the street... Yet how could she be afraid of the man before her? He was gentle and kind.

"You don't have to tell me."

She inhaled deeply. "There's no mystery." She forced herself to smile, to brush off her situation as if it didn't matter. "Milo's dad, he had an affair with an older woman. Somewhere along the way he also managed to squander everything we saved and then some. The sale of the house just about cleared the debts."

"Ahh." Logan sounded sorry, but also relieved.

"Which is why we're temporarily homeless." She held out her hands. "And I'm going to be straight with you. We don't have a lot of money."

"Don't worry about it." He unlocked the hotel room door and carried her son inside. Laying him gently down on the bed, he stepped back before he turned to her.

"I do worry about it," she whispered, hanging back by the door. "If the car repair is too expensive." She dragged her hand through her hair. "I'm sorry, this is my problem." She let out a low laugh. "Although, it might be your problem if I can't pay the hotel bill."

"We'll figure something out." His concern was evident as he stared at her. Whether his concern was for her or her potential unpaid bill, she couldn't figure out.

"Why don't I bring you something to eat?"

"No." She waved his offer away. "I really can't afford room service."

"Call it an early birthday gift." He ducked his head and held her gaze. "Please."

She nodded. "Thanks. Maybe I can pick up a shift in the hotel or something, to repay you." Her forehead wrinkled. "I am not trying to get you to hire me."

"Just eat and rest. We can figure things out tomorrow." He stepped sideways, skirting around her as he headed toward the door. "I'll be back in a few minutes with something for you to eat."

"Thank you." His kindness was enough to bring her to her knees. She'd been so scared of the future, but the kindness of this stranger gave her hope.

He nodded and left the room and Penny dropped her backpack on the floor before she went to the bed and slid Milo's shoes off his feet. Unbuttoning his jeans, she carefully removed them before digging his PJs out of his pack and putting them on his little legs. Cradling his head against her, she carefully removed his coat and sweater. He could sleep in his T-shirt for the night.

After dropping a kiss on his forehead, she picked him up and slid him under the bedcovers. Stepping back, she stared down at her son. He was the most precious thing in the world to her. As long as they were together, it didn't matter where they were.

A light knock at the door signaled the arrival of Logan with a trayful of food. She smelled it before she even opened the door and her mouth watered while her stomach rumbled in appreciation. She'd bought takeout for Milo on the journey but had been too anxious about the trip to eat herself.

"That's too much," she protested as Logan carried in the tray. There was a plate of chicken, potatoes, and vegetables, with an herby sauce just begging to be savored. Next to the plate were a couple of desserts. One was a cheesecake, her favorite, while the other was some kind of chocolate cake smothered in a silky sauce. Not what she'd been expecting from a smalltown hotel.

"The kitchen is about to close. So think of it as leftovers." She didn't quite believe Logan, but she wasn't going to argue with his generosity. She would hate to insult his hospitality.

"You've been so kind." She followed him across the room as he set the tray down on the small table for two in the corner by the window.

Penny hadn't taken much notice of the room, she'd been so concerned with getting Milo into bed that the furnishings and decor had remained unnoticed until now. Each piece of furniture looked handmade, certainly nothing like the furniture found in modern hotels. The small table was made of solid wood, as was the dresser which graced one side of the room, next to a built-in closet, with intricately carved handles. The drapes adorning the windows were thick, the kind that would be a pleasure to pull across the window when a storm raged outside. Only there was no storm.

Penny stared at the moon. It hadn't moved since she'd arrived in town. Or perhaps it had, and it was Penny who had moved and was looking at it from a different angle.

"Maybe tomorrow, I could show you the bay." Logan's inviting tone made her nod as if she had no choice but to say yes.

"Won't you be busy?" she asked.

"I can find an hour or two to take you and Milo down to the beach." He turned to face her, the moonlight catching his eyes making them crackle. She could stare into his eyes all day. And all night.

"I'd like that. Frank is looking at my car in the morning. I said I'd meet him at the garage, but I'm sure it'll take him a couple of hours to fix the car."

"A couple of hours," he murmured.

"Yes, then I have to leave. Helena will be worried enough already that we're..." Her eyes widened, and she reached for her phone. "I haven't called her to tell her we won't be arriving tonight." She took her phone out of her pocket and checked for a signal. A couple of bars. That should be enough. "Thanks for everything."

"Enjoy your food. I'll see you tomorrow." It was a promise, one she doubted he would break.

"Tomorrow." She nodded and watched him leave before she pressed dial on her phone and waited for Helena to answer. "Helena. It's me."

"Penny, are you all right?" Helena always seemed to pick up on her sister's mood, even over the phone.

"My car broke down," Penny explained.

"Oh, no, are you and Milo okay?"

"Yes, we're fine. I made it to a town called Wishing Moon Bay. The car is at the garage and they'll take a look at it in the morning."

"Where are you sleeping tonight?" Helena was well aware of Penny's financial situation. "You're not sleeping in the car, are you? I know Milo would see it as an adventure, but still…"

"No, we're not in the car. We're in a hotel."

"Do you need me to send you some money?" Helena had offered to help Penny out financially when she heard about her money troubles. Up until now, Penny had said no. This small detour might have to make her reconsider.

"We're fine for now. Thanks for the offer. I'll let you know if I need anything."

"Please do, Penny. Don't let your pride get in the way." Helena paused. "Keep me updated on what the garage says about the car. Get here when you can."

"I will."

"And if you have to stay a few days, then enjoy it. You and the little man need a break. Maybe this is fate's way of telling you to slow down and take a couple of days off. Enjoy the moment."

"I need to get Milo settled and find a job, I don't exactly have time for a vacation."

"Which is exactly when you need one." Helena gave a short laugh. "You know what Mom always said."

"Life doesn't always give you what you want, it gives you what you need, even if you don't know it yet." Penny missed her mom with all her heart. Even if there were times when her behavior was a little strange. "I love you, Helena."

"I love you, too. Sweet dreams and don't worry."

"I'll try not to." Penny ended the call and picked up her fork. There was nothing she could do to change the current situation. So she might as well take Helena's advice and enjoy the moment.

As she took a mouthful of the wonderful food, she realized that was a good, simple plan.

A very good plan.

4

LOGAN

He had to convince her to stay. Logan went to bed with those words circling around in his head and when he woke up, they were still there. With no apparent solution short of going over to Frank and Dennis Car Repairs and ripping the wiring out of her car.

A little over the top, don't you think? His wolf stretched leisurely, seemingly untroubled by their mate walking into their lives and then right back out.

No, I don't think. Penny is supposed to go and live with her sister. Do you think she'd change her plans and stay here with us just because we asked her? He ground his teeth together as he slid out of bed and went to the bathroom.

Stepping into the shower, he switched on the water, it was cold, just as he liked it. Why the guy in room one had to keep complaining was beyond him. But then the guy was older and a non-shifter. Logan didn't need to use his senses to know the guy was a warlock. He'd been very open about that information when he'd arrived. It was as if the guy thought it made him special or would get him better service.

It wouldn't. Everyone was equal to Logan. He'd learned that lesson from Valerie.

Logan's mood hadn't improved by the time he'd showered and dressed. As he went downstairs, the first rays of dawn were creeping through the window and the call of the outdoors was stronger than ever. Only this time he wanted to take his mate and her son with him. If only he could scoop them up into his arms and run away with them to his cabin in the mountains. There he would persuade Penny to stay.

However, his duty to Valerie prevented him from doing just that.

Good, because nothing would scare our mate more than being kidnapped and taken to a remote cabin, his wolf said drily.

Penny and Milo might love the cabin. Logan raked a hand through his hair. There was no point thinking about whisking them away, he had to stay here at the hotel. He'd promised Valerie he would, and he wasn't about to break that promise.

His first stop was the coffee pot. The first person into the kitchen in the morning always made a fresh pot, it was one of Valerie's unwritten rules and one he obeyed. Everyone worked better after their first cup of coffee.

"Morning." Ivan, one of Logan's brothers and also the hotel chef, was next into the kitchen. He always arrived as the coffee was ready. Logan was certain Ivan had a sixth sense, not only for when the coffee was ready. Ivan was an alchemist, with the natural ability to turn the simplest of food into delicious meals.

"Morning." Logan poured coffee into two cups and handed one to Ivan.

"You look rough." Ivan's people skills were better than Logan's, but the guy said it like he saw it.

"Thanks." Logan ran his hand through his still-damp hair. "I had a restless night."

"Anything to do with the new arrival?" Ivan sipped his coffee, his eyes twinkling as he watched Logan. "You know, the one who got *your* dinner last night."

Logan ground his teeth together. "She'd had a traumatic experience."

Ivan arched an eyebrow. "As have most of our guests. You do know you're supposed to keep them all happy and make sure their stay here is hassle-free and peaceful. Mom always says the customer is always right."

"I'm not Mom." Logan drank his coffee, his senses fixed on his mate who was still in bed. *Sleeping*. His chest rose and fell in time with hers and a sense of peace descended on him.

"I think we all know that." Ivan chuckled. "Just remember Valerie has spent years building up the reputation of this place... You know, after the last owner..."

"*Rad the Bad.*" Logan shook his head in disdain. "Who calls themselves that?"

"The kind of guy who thought the town needed a Gothic-themed haunted hotel." Ivan rolled his eyes. "Warlocks."

"Exactly. Warlocks. They think they're above the rest of us."

"But the warlock in room one is still a paying guest. Which means, if the shower goes cold, we apologize and figure out the problem." Ivan fixed Logan with a look. A look that said he needed to do better.

"I'll take a look at it today. Again," Logan relented. "Although, I have no idea why the shower in room one has to behave any differently than the showers in the other rooms."

"The house has a will of its own." Ivan went to the coffee pot and poured himself another cup. "A refill?"

"No, I'm good, thanks. I want to get all my chores done, I offered to take Penny and Milo down to the bay and show them around." Logan placed his cup in the sink.

"Penny and Milo." Ivan turned to face Logan. "Is she *the one?*"

Logan nodded absently, his head reverberating with one question—how did he convince her to stay?

"Lucky you. Maybe she might put a smile on your face."

Logan frowned. "I know how to smile."

"Maybe you should practice it a bit more." Ivan carried his coffee to the fridge and pulled it open. "I'll get breakfast started. There are more guests arriving today. There are no vacancies after tomorrow night." He didn't lift his head from the fridge as he reminded Logan of this news.

"I'll figure something out." His eyes lifted to the ceiling and he focused on Penny. She was stirring. Milo was awake.

"Yes, you will," Ivan assured him. "If you need any help, let me know."

Logan's attention jolted away from his mate and fixed on Ivan instead. "I could offer them Valerie's room in her apartment. But I think Penny might find that weird." Valerie's once large apartment, where she'd raised the six boys had been converted into a smaller two-bedroom apartment. The remainder of the rooms had been converted to allow the restaurant area to grow as Ivan's cooking skills brought in more diners.

"Asking your mate to move in with you on the first day? Just a little. But if they are really stuck, they can have my apartment and I'll bunk here with you."

"Thanks, Ivan. I didn't expect you to offer up your apartment."

"I am a believer in true love. If Penny found her way here, then she's meant to stay." Ivan placed a slab of bacon on the counter. "Call me a romantic."

"If you have any ideas on how I'm supposed to make that happen, I'm all ears."

Ivan chuckled. "Don't say that in front of room one. As a warlock, he might make that happen for you."

"He wouldn't dare."

"Oh, I think he would." Ivan lowered his voice and approached Logan.

"I'll go take a look at his shower."

"You do know why he gets the cold shower, don't you?"

Logan's brows bunched together. "No."

"The house hates warlocks." Ivan nodded knowingly.

"The house hates warlocks." Logan let out a shuddering breath. "There I was thinking you were being serious."

"I am. Rad the Bad was a warlock. He used to perform spells on the house. He made the staircases move, the doors disappear..." Ivan thumbed his chest. "I was told by a guest who stayed here back then that the house hated it."

"The house... The hotel... You're saying it has feelings?" Logan asked.

"How would you like to have all your insides twisted around?" Ivan chuckled as he fetched the heavy frying pan from where it hung on the wall. "Believe me or not. But there is a reason the water runs cold for the warlock."

"Then there's no way I can fix it?" Logan narrowed his eyes. "Or are you making the whole thing up?"

Ivan chuckled as he put the bacon in the pan. "That, brother, you will have to figure out for yourself."

"Great, a dragon shifter with a sense of humor."

"A sense of humor and a huge talent for culinary skills. I'd say my parents would be proud, but I'd be lying." His laughter followed Logan out of the kitchen and into the reception area. He really should go up to room one and check if the water was okay. But what he really wanted to do was wait here until his mate came downstairs. Even if it meant standing there for hours. Or eternity.

She is worth waiting for, his wolf sighed.

Logan went to the bottom of the stairs and looked up, then he stepped onto the first stair, then the second. It was as if she was reeling him in, pulling him toward her with an invisible irresistible force.

"Logan." Room number one's door flew open and the guy, Jeremy Barnes, stood there in a robe, his hair wet and glistening with shampoo. "The water is cold. *Again.*"

Penny is coming down the stairs, his wolf hissed, distracting Logan from Jeremy and the cold shower.

"Logan!" Jeremy snapped.

"What?" Logan turned toward the stairs and watched as his mate appeared with the dinner tray in her hand.

"The water."

"Can't you just take a cold shower?" Logan smiled as his mate saw him.

"We went over this yesterday. I want a hot shower." He folded his arms across his body. "There must be a loose connection or something. One minute it's hot and then the next it's freezing. It's not good enough."

"I'm busy right now, I'll get to it later." Logan swallowed nervously as Penny came toward them.

"Later isn't good enough. I have shampoo in my hair and an appointment at ten o'clock."

"I'm busy," Logan ground out.

"Busy staring at one guest while ignoring another one," Jeremy replied bluntly.

"Is there a problem?" Penny reached the two men and smiled brightly.

"My shower is running cold, again, and Logan refuses to take a look at it," Jeremy said quickly.

"I didn't refuse..." Logan sighed heavily. "I'll come and take a look at it now."

"Thank you." Jeremy stared at Penny for a long moment. Too long a moment. "I don't think we've met." He held out a clean hand.

"I arrived last night. Logan very kindly found me a room after my car broke down and I found myself unexpectedly in Wishing Moon Bay." She juggled the tray into one hand and shook the warlock's hand.

"*Unexpectedly.*" Jeremy's eyes narrowed and his attention switched briefly to Logan. "How about that?"

"I'll check out the shower." Logan ushered Jeremy inside and turned in the doorway to speak to Penny. "Ivan is in the kitchen, he'll get you a tray of breakfast and some coffee. I hope you and Milo slept all right."

"We did, thanks." She looked past him into the room where Jeremy hovered just behind his shoulder. "I'll leave you to your work."

Logan nodded like a fool and then shut the door firmly. "Right, let's take another look at this shower."

"*Unexpectedly,*" Jeremy repeated. "That doesn't happen."

"I know." Logan should have gone and gotten his toolkit before attempting to fix the shower, but he'd wanted to put a barrier between this warlock and his mate. There was something about the way the guy looked at Logan's mate that he did not like. He did not like it one bit.

"So why is she here?" Jeremy followed Logan to the small, connected bathroom that contained a toilet, sink, and shower. Eyeing the offending shower, he recalled what Ivan had said about the hotel not liking warlocks. Logan didn't like them much either, not when they were this interested in his mate and why she was in town.

"Because she's supposed to be here." Logan switched on the shower and put his hand under the stream of water that cascaded out. Sure enough, it was freezing cold. He waited, while Jeremy stood next to him with his arms still crossed as if he was trying to put up his own barrier.

"Why is she supposed to be here?" Jeremy was persistent, that was for certain.

And annoying, his wolf added.

"The water is running hot." Logan kept his hand under the running water as it heated up. "Scalding hot." He turned the temperature down until it was hot but not burn-your-skin-off hot. Once the water reached the desired temperature and stayed there, he stood back. "Perfect. Try it."

Jeremy sidestepped Logan and put his hand under the shower. He waited and waited, his eyes fixed on the wall while the water ran. "Maybe there was air in the pipes."

"Maybe." Logan backed toward the bathroom door. "Have a nice shower."

"Why is she here?" Jeremy pulled his hand away from the hot water and squared up to Logan.

"She is my mate."

"Oh!" Jeremy's eyes flashed with humor. "Wow, she lucked out, didn't she? I mean you have such wit and charm, and you are so amenable."

"Do you have a point?" Logan's wolf wanted to leap out and claw Jeremy's face.

"My point is, what has she done to deserve such a grumpy, backwater hillbilly?" Jeremy arched an eyebrow.

"That is a very good question." Logan wagged his finger at Jeremy and then turned around and left the bathroom, pulling the door closed behind him.

Stalking across the bedroom, Logan yanked open the door leading back into the corridor, cursing the warlock under his breath. As the door closed behind him a shout of, *cold water,* reached Logan. He ignored it and kept on walking. Penny might not deserve Logan as a mate, but Jeremy Barnes deserved a cold-water shower, whether it was sent by the house or not.

5

PENNY

"Welcome to Wishing Moon Bay." The chef leaned back against the counter and sipped his coffee while the bacon sizzled in the pan. He was looking at her with an intense curiosity, like she was a newly discovered species. "I'm Ivan."

"Thanks, I'm Penny and it's good to be here." Her brows knitted together as she spoke the awkward sentence. What else was she supposed to say? Arriving in the dark and walking down the street to the hotel hadn't exactly given her a glimpse of anything other than neatly tended front yards and the hotel with turrets. "I like the hotel. It's very unique."

"It is unique. Like most things in town." He smiled and sipped his coffee. "Do you intend to stay long?"

"No, I'm traveling to my sister's. Milo and I are going to live with her for a few months while we get back on our feet."

"You're homeless?" Ivan sauntered over to the coffee pot and poured her a cup.

"My marriage broke down and she offered us a place to stay." She didn't see the need to hide her circumstances since she'd already told Logan all this.

"Is that what you want?" Ivan handed her the coffee cup and went back to his sizzling pan.

"What I want." Penny shrugged. "I recently figured out that you don't get what you want. If I did, I'd still be married, and my son would still have a father he could count on."

Ivan looked up from his pan and stared at the doorway. There was no one there. "You could stay here for a while. This is a good town."

"I believe you. But I can't afford the hotel," Penny explained. Even though Ivan's suggestion was tempting. Very tempting. Penny had no idea why. She loved Helena and welcomed the chance to spend time with her. But there was something about Wishing Moon Bay that made her want to stay. Or maybe it was her kind, handsome rescuer that made her feel like this was home.

"Logan will figure something out for you, won't you, Logan?" Ivan grinned as Logan appeared in the doorway. Had he heard him approaching or had Logan been hiding outside the kitchen listening to their conversation?

"No, I should go to my sister's. I need to register Milo for school there. And then look for a job." Who was she trying to convince?

"Milo's dad. Is he in the picture?" Ivan asked.

"No, we've hardly seen him since the divorce." Penny had nothing to hide but Ivan's questions were beginning to feel like an interrogation of sorts.

"Divorce." He nodded at Logan who shot the chef a warning look.

"I should go back to the room. Milo is awake and I told him to stay put until I got back, which is not easy for a boy to do when he's in a place like this." Penny backed away toward the door.

"Wait." Ivan held up his hand and then reached for a plate. "I made this for you."

"Oh." Her shoulders slumped forward. Ivan had made her breakfast. "Are you sure?"

"Yes, help yourself to whatever you need." Logan went to the fridge and pulled out a pitcher of orange juice. "There are glasses on the counter there."

"You're gonna need your strength," Ivan said as he piled another plate with bacon and eggs. And pancakes. The smell was enough to make her mouth water.

"My strength?" she asked as Logan quickly put everything onto a tray and handed it to her.

"Logan is going to show you around while your car is being fixed. Isn't he?" Ivan's eyes shifted from Logan then back to Penny. "It's a beautiful day and maybe once you have seen the town, you might decide to spend a little more time with us."

"I... I really need to get to my sister's." Penny looked down at the tray. "Thank you for breakfast." She glanced up at Logan. "Do you have time to show us around? Once I've been to the garage, I'll have some idea of how long we'll be here. Hopefully."

"I'll be finished here by nine. I can drive you to the garage and then we can take a tour of the town."

"Nine it is." She glanced down at the tray. "Thanks again for the food and if you need me to do some chores around the hotel, just let me know."

"I will." Logan swallowed nervously as Ivan watched them both, his eyes dancing with humor.

Penny turned around and headed back toward the stairs. The guy from room one was coming out of his room once more, this time he was dressed but the expression on his face said he was not happy. "Morning. It's a beautiful day."

"It would be a whole lot better if my shower worked properly," he grumbled then his eyes widened at the tray full of food. "At least the food here is good. Unlike the hotel manager." His eyes darkened.

"Logan has been very kind to me." Penny figured it was time to keep on walking.

"Of course he has." Jeremy brushed past her and went downstairs to the dining room, leaving Penny perplexed by his meaning.

Something definitely seemed off about the hotel and the people in it. Although she could not fault Logan's kindness, there was something odd about him. Last night she'd put it down to their unexpected arrival, now she wasn't so sure.

Carrying the tray of food up to room number eight, she opened the door and went inside to find Milo had pulled one of the chairs across to the window. He was standing on it staring out at the bay. "I love this place."

"Do you?" Penny set the tray down on the table and joined her son at the window. "It sure is an incredible view."

"I saw a tiger walking along the street."

"Did you?" Penny looked down at the empty street. "It's gone now." Milo was still young enough to enjoy make-believe.

"It ran off toward the mountains." Milo pointed into the distance toward the mountain range that had also not been on the map.

"Okay, well, we need to eat and get dressed and then go find out what is wrong with the car. While it's being fixed, Logan, the guy who carried you to bed last night, has offered to give us a tour."

"Great, he might know where the tiger went." Milo slid down off the chair and dragged it back to the table.

"Careful, buddy. This furniture looks antique. We don't want to break anything or damage the floor." Penny helped her son put the chair back next to the table.

"Do you think the hotel is haunted?" Milo climbed onto

the chair and sat down but his focus was on the ceiling with its carved edges rather than on eggs and bacon.

"I don't know. It all certainly looks old." She blinked, reminding herself that she was supposed to tell her son that there were no such things as ghosts. "But I doubt it's haunted."

"Why not?" Milo picked up a fork and began to eat the food she'd put on his plate.

"If you were a ghost, wouldn't you have better things to do than hang around a hotel?" Still not telling her son there were no such things as ghosts. She needed to work on teaching her son reality skills. But they had both had enough of reality the last few months. Reality consisted of losing your home and not seeing your dad.

"I don't know. It would be kind of cool to scare people." Milo was imagining being a ghost and what he'd do. Penny could always tell when he was thinking up great plans and schemes by the way his eyes went out of focus.

"I don't think I'd go around scaring people. I think I'd go around making people laugh." Penny forked up her eggs. "This food is delicious."

"I guess that might be pretty cool, too," Milo conceded and picked up his fork.

"I think it'd be hard work. I mean it's easy to scare people, but making people laugh, that's a skill." She watched her son as he thought it over.

"I want to make people laugh." He sat up straighter and ate his breakfast now that his decision had been reached. Penny loved watching him learn and grow, it was the most rewarding job in the world.

She sighed and glanced toward the window. A real job was what she needed. Staying with Helena was not a long-term plan. For now, Penny planned to take any job she was offered just so she and Milo could have some independence. They needed to stand on their own two feet.

Which meant finding childcare, too. She swallowed down the lump in her throat. She loved caring for her son, she loved picking him up from school and listening to his excited chatter as he told her about his day. Milo was not one of those children who kept it all bottled up inside. He liked to share his thoughts on all aspects of the world around him.

"The pancakes are good." Milo's small voice brought her back to the hotel room. The concern on his face made her heart squeeze in her chest.

"Ivan is a great chef," she enthused, putting a smile on her face as she picked up a pancake. "When we go downstairs, we should go thank him." Penny took a bite of her pancake and her eyes rolled back as the buttery soft texture melted in her mouth. "These aren't just good, they are the best."

"I could eat these every day." Milo watched for her reaction. He wanted to stay here in town. He wanted to live in the hotel. But he was going to be disappointed, there was no way they could move here.

"I'll ask Ivan for his recipe and maybe get him to teach me his magic." She took another pancake and ate it, while Milo did the same.

"I think he must know magic," Milo agreed.

"We're going to be all right," Penny didn't know where the burning need to reassure her son came from, but the words just fell out of her mouth before they had even formed in her head.

"I know." He smiled at her with all the innocent belief of a child who trusted their mom implicitly.

Penny just hoped she wouldn't fail him. Milo deserved better.

6

LOGAN

"Hi, Milo." Logan met Penny and Milo in the reception area as they came down the stairs. "Here, let me take the breakfast tray." He held out his hands and his mate passed over the tray which contained nothing but empty plates. "I see you enjoyed your breakfast."

"The food is wonderful, we were going to say thank you to Ivan if he's around."

"He's in the kitchen. Come on, I'll take you through."

"Thanks." Penny held out her hand and Milo took it without objection. He was a good kid.

"Did you sleep okay?" Logan led them to the kitchen.

"Yes. Thank you for carrying me up to bed." The boy smiled up at Logan. "I like the hotel. We think it's haunted."

"*We* don't think it's haunted, *you* think it's haunted," Penny replied.

"*I* think it's haunted." Milo looked up at the ceiling. "I'd also like to live here but Mommy says once the car is ready, we have to leave."

"Sorry. Milo has a habit of saying exactly what is on his mind. I don't want you to think that I've primed him to say that. We are leaving once the car is fixed. And I will pay the hotel bill..." She hesitated and clamped her hand down on her purse. "If I have enough money left in the bank."

"Don't worry about the money." Logan shot Ivan a warning look as they entered the kitchen. "And Milo is not the only one who has a habit of saying exactly what is on his mind with no filter from his brain to his mouth."

"He means me." Ivan put up his hand which was covered in soap suds. "I don't like anyone else washing my pans."

"Ivan means he doesn't *trust* anyone else to wash his pans." Logan set down the tray and began loading the dirty plates into the dishwasher.

"Well, I am grateful for what you cook in those pans," Penny told him. "I don't think I've ever tasted food like it." She put her hands up. "I mean in a good way. A really deliciously good way."

"Thanks. I appreciate your kind words." Ivan bowed his head.

"Can you teach my mom how to make pancakes the way you make them?" Milo asked.

"Sure, if you decide to stay in town longer, it would be my pleasure." Ivan turned back to his work.

"Thanks, Ivan. I didn't know if you had a secret ingredient."

"No secrets. Just hard work and a little experimentation with the consistency of the batter." Ivan finished drying the pans and carried them across to the stove.

Logan closed the dishwasher and went to the sink. "I'll just be a couple of minutes and then we can go." He washed off the tray and set it down on the drainer.

"What happened with the cold shower guy?" Penny watched Logan work. "He seemed a little on edge this morning."

"It was working fine. When I left him, it was working

fine, at least. Then, as soon as he gets under the water, it goes cold."

"I told you the hotel was haunted," Milo said. "There's a ghost in the room who turns the water to cold."

"I like your way of thinking." Ivan pointed a soapy cloth at him.

"There's probably something wrong with the pipes," Penny said, changing the subject. "Milo has enough of a vivid imagination without any encouragement."

"I think you know magic."

Logan dropped a plate into the dishwasher and all the other plates clattered disgruntledly. "Ivan doesn't know magic."

"I think there's magic in your pancakes because they are so good." Milo licked his lips and Logan smiled gently at the young boy. He sure had a wonderful imagination.

"Unfortunately, I do not," Ivan told the boy. "However, I have learned to cook through trial and error. And a few YouTube videos."

"Mommy needs a new job, maybe you can teach her all about cooking."

"We are not going to be here that long, Milo. You know that." Penny smiled apologetically. "You've both been so kind to us already."

Ivan cracked an egg into the frying pan, and it sizzled on the stovetop. "If you have time when you get back from your grand tour of Wishing Moon Bay, I can give you some tips."

"Thanks. Although, I don't think the kitchen is where my future lies." Penny looked at the large clock hanging on the kitchen wall. "We should get going. If you're ready? If not, we could walk to the garage and wait for you there."

"No, I'm ready." Logan grabbed his jacket which was hanging behind the kitchen door. Checking that he had his keys, he ushered Milo and Penny toward the back door. The last thing he wanted to do was go out through the front and bump into Jeremy. He was not in the mood for yet another debate over the cold shower. As far as Logan could tell, there was nothing wrong with it.

It runs cold. If there is nothing wrong with it then why does it do that? his wolf asked. Because he is a warlock? Do you really buy into the idea that the house doesn't like him?

I don't believe the house does it on purpose. Logan led his mate and her son out onto the street. He'd seen enough magic and mayhem in his time to believe anything was possible, but the hotel being magic was going too far. *Of course, there is one way to test that theory. He could swap rooms.*

Good thinking. His wolf liked that idea, he also liked the idea of spending the day with Penny and Milo.

"This is me." Logan fished his keys out of his pocket and unlocked the truck.

"Is this a *monster* truck?" Milo asked as Penny helped him climb inside.

A monster drives it, Logan's wolf laughed.

"No, it's just a normal truck. The big wheels help me drive up the mountain roads." Logan stood still and peered into the distance. "There." He pointed to a clump of tall pine trees halfway up the mountain. "That is where I live."

"Wow! Can I come and visit you?" Milo asked. "It must be like living on the top of the world."

"Let's get your seatbelt on, Milo." Penny helped her son into his seat and then climbed in beside him.

"I'd like to show it to you." Logan inserted the keys into the ignition and started the engine. He'd also like his mate and her son to live with him. But he needed to take things one step at a time. First, he needed to persuade them to stay in town. Then he'd persuade them that he was the man to care for them and protect them.

"Maybe we can come back sometime. After we've settled

down somewhere." A nervous edge to Penny's voice alerted him. Things were not good in his mate's world.

All we have to do is figure out what she needs and then give it to her. Then she'll stay, his wolf said.

I can give her everything she needs, Logan replied. *But I doubt whether she would just take what I have to offer. She needs independence.*

Or she needs us to persuade her it's okay to rely on others, even after you have been let down so badly. He stretched and flexed his claws. If I could get my claws and teeth on that ex-husband of hers.

Violence won't make this any easier, Logan reminded his wolf.

Pity, he replied.

"Can we come back soon?" Milo asked.

"If we get a chance, yes."

"Promise?" Milo asked.

"I said we'd try but I don't want to make a promise we can't keep. We talked about this before we left the house. I don't know what the future holds for us. But we said we would treat it as an adventure, didn't we?" Penny placed her arm around her son.

"This is the start of our adventure." Milo stared out at the mountains in the distance.

"Why aren't the mountains on the map?" Penny swung her head around to face Logan.

"I don't know." He stared at them, trying to think of a plausible answer. "Perhaps they are hidden from the road outside of town."

"In all the years they have been making maps, they have found the remotest of islands, but they have never seen those mountains?" She gave him a hard stare. "Google Maps sees everything. But not those peaks or this town."

His wolf lifted his head and chuckled. Wait till Penny finds out what else Google doesn't know about.

"I have no idea." Logan decided to keep it simple. He

wasn't exactly lying to his mate. He really didn't have any idea as to why Wishing Moon Bay and the surrounding area were hidden from human technology. He guessed it was some kind of cloaking spell. Although, the town occasionally let people in who possibly didn't belong there. Penny and Milo being two of those people.

Jeremy's question of why came back to Logan. Had the town let Penny see the signs, had it revealed the tunnel to her simply because she was his mate? Or was there another reason? A reason that might mean she wasn't supposed to leave. A reason that might mean she would need his protection before too long.

Logan drove the truck to Frank and Dennis Car Repairs and parked outside. He got out and waited around the front of the truck for Penny and Milo to join him. "Is this your car?"

"That's it." Penny held Milo's hand and walked over to her car. "I wonder if they've had a chance to look at it yet."

"Do you want me to go ask?" It was still early, Logan doubted that Frank or Dennis had started work before nine and since it was only a quarter past now, the car was probably untouched.

Or it was a quick fix and Penny is going to drive out of our lives right now. His wolf was always telling Logan things he didn't want to hear.

"I'll talk to them." She smiled in thanks as she went to the half-open door leading into the garage and poked her head in. "Hello."

"Ah, there you are." Frank appeared from somewhere inside and came out into the light. "What a beautiful morning." His eyes narrowed as he saw Logan. "Ah, I see you found your way to the hotel then."

"Oh, yes, thanks for calling ahead. Logan met us on the road and helped carry Milo and our backpacks."

"Calling ahead?" Frank tilted his head as he looked at Logan.

"Yes, so that I knew to go meet Penny and Milo." Logan hoped Frank would go along with it.

Even though you haggled over your repair bill last time you were here, his wolf said drily.

"Penny and Milo." Frank looked at mother and son and then his eyes wandered across to the car. "I haven't had a chance to look at the car yet."

"Okay. Well, Logan has offered to give us a tour of the town. Perhaps you could call my cell phone when you have looked at the car and let me know what is wrong." Penny bit her bottom lip as she followed Frank's gaze to the car. "Hopefully, it isn't too expensive."

"It sure did make a racket when you drove it in here last night." Dennis came out of the garage to join them. "Logan."

"Dennis." Logan backed away toward the truck, he wanted to make the most of his time alone with Penny and Milo and not stand around talking. "Why don't we leave these guys to look at your car? It gives us more time to explore the town."

"Good idea." Milo broke away from Penny and ran back toward the truck.

"Thanks." Penny followed her son. "I'll wait for your call."

Frank and Dennis stood side by side and watched Logan as he backed up the truck and pulled back onto the road.

"I get the feeling I am not going to be leaving any time soon." She sighed and leaned her elbow on the truck door.

"Maybe Aunt Helena will get tired of waiting for us and we'll have to stay here," Milo said brightly.

"Don't you like your Aunt Helena?" Logan asked even though it was none of his business.

Did you actually say that? His wolf was in mock shock.

"I love my sister. Although, we're different in a lot of ways. She focused on work and her career and I got married and settled down. I don't really have any other family. I never knew my dad and my mom died over ten years ago. Milo's dad lives in Spain now and we barely see him or hear from him."

"Ah, I see." Families sure were complicated. Even more complicated outside of Wishing Moon Bay.

"After everything that happened, I need to be with someone who I know cares for us..." Penny slid her arm around Milo and hugged him. "Genuinely cares for us."

"Then stay here."

The silence stretched out between them. Even Milo didn't speak. He tilted his head back and stared at his mom but what was going through his head was obvious by his wide-eyed expression.

"We have plans."

"Plans change," Milo argued. "That's what you told me."

"Thanks for that, Milo."

"He's right, plans do change. The hotel is so busy, I could always use an extra pair of hands." Logan glanced at Penny, not daring to hope that getting her to stay would be as simple as asking her. Of giving her an offer of a job.

"But where will we stay if the hotel is full?"

"You can have my room and I can..." What would he do? Sleep in the storage closet? Perhaps he could drag a mattress into the storeroom and sleep on the floor. He couldn't leave the hotel, not when Valerie depended on him to care for the guests. Maybe he should mention Ivan's offer of loaning Penny and Milo his apartment. But Logan hated the idea of Penny not sleeping under the same roof as him. What if she needed his protection?

"I can't kick you out of your bed," she protested.

Yes, you can, his wolf answered.

"Logan offered." Milo shuffled in his seat as if he had ants in his pants.

"And it was very kind of him to offer. But..." She shook her head. "Oh, I don't know..." Penny rubbed her forehead as she looked out of the window.

"Let's go take a look around town," Logan suggested. "Maybe once you see the bay and walk on the beach, you might find it easier to decide."

"I will keep an open mind."

Penny has no idea how open, his wolf replied drily.

We have to make this work, Logan replied. This was it, no second chances, no do-overs. In the next couple of hours, while Frank worked on the car, he had to find a way to persuade his mate to stay. Without putting too much pressure on her. It seemed an impossible task but one he had to rise to. If not, his life would crash and burn.

They sat in silence as he headed back along the road heading into town. Past the library where Logan had spent endless days as a child hidden away in among the books, discovering worlds beyond the borders of Wishing Moon Bay and yet never wanting to leave. He'd had his fill of life outside of town.

This was his home, a place of sanctuary. A place where he could help Penny raise Milo. He'd thought parenthood had escaped him. When he reached forty, he'd figured it was too late for him and he'd grown acquainted with the disappointment which lived in his heart. With no mate, he had accepted his life. Perhaps that was what had pushed him to the outer edges of the community. Watching people he'd grown up with find their mate and settle down and raise kids had left him with a deep-rooted sadness.

Not that he wasn't happy for those who were lucky enough to find their mate. Envious perhaps but he'd celebrated with them. He rejoiced in their happiness.

You're going to have to tell them about shifters and everything else that lives in town, his wolf warned him. There's a reason only certain people ever find the town. There are secrets here that not everyone understands and accepts.

And what if Penny doesn't understand or accept what she sees? Logan's stomach clenched. He had never been this scared. Not even when faced with a marauding vampire.

That's because this isn't something we can fight off with teeth and claws. There is no monster to slay. No villain to kill. Instead, we must figure out how to enable Penny to accept what is. Even when, up until now, the things that live in Wishing Moon Bay were only make-believe.

His wolf had summed the situation up succinctly. There was no way to brute force the situation. Instead, he would have to get to know Penny and Milo and figure out how to deal with human emotions and reactions. For a man who had shied away from all emotions for the last few years, this might be close to impossible.

7

PENNY

*P*enny's sense that there was something weird about Logan and the whole town wouldn't shift. After dealing with a deceptive husband, she'd developed a sixth sense where the truth was concerned, or lack of it. Yet there was something familiar, almost comforting about the ride through town. There were certain buildings, odd landmarks that she swore she'd seen before. How was that possible when this was her first visit to Wishing Moon Bay?

"Okay, I'll park the truck and we can walk down to the beach." Logan, who had descended into a brooding mood, steered the truck into a parking space. The small parking lot was situated alongside a stone wall that ran along one side of the bay and had likely been built to protect the houses set back from the beach. If a high tide were coupled with a strong wind, the area would easily flood without the protection offered by the wall. Just like any other town with beachfront houses.

Perhaps the stress of her divorce and losing her home had messed with her head. Add in the car breaking down last night and was there any wonder she was seeing and believing things that weren't real?

Throw in a dose of living alone with a child with a vivid imagination and it was no wonder she was halfway to crazy.

"I'd love to live by the beach." Milo glanced sideways at his mom and gave her his irresistibly cheeky smile.

"It is beautiful." Penny sat staring at the sparkling ocean that filled the bay. Even in winter, the water looked inviting.

"Shall we get a closer look?" Logan asked, his hand on the truck door but not opening it. He was unsure of her and how to react. Why her reaction meant so much to him, she could not fathom.

"Yes." Milo stood up, leaning over the truck seat as he shuffled toward her. "Please."

"I guess there's no harm in looking." She opened the door and slid down to the ground, her feet hitting the asphalt harder than she expected and she hung onto the door to keep herself upright. "I forgot it was a long way down."

"Need a hand?" Logan was behind her in a flash. He'd moved so fast, impossibly fast.

"I'm good, thanks." Although her brain could not resist teasing her with thoughts of what it would be like to feel his hands on her waist. To hide the pink flush that spread across her cheeks, she focused on Milo and reached up for him. "Come on, buddy."

"I can do it. On my own." He hung back inside, peering over the edge of the seat.

"Okay. Just hold onto something." She stepped back and allowed him to try it on his own. Milo was a determined young man, and she loved his fight for independence, but she would always be there for him, ready to catch him with open arms if he failed.

"I've got this." Milo turned around and grabbed hold of the door with one hand and the seat with the other and lowered himself down. With his feet dangling a foot above the ground, he looked down and then finally let go. "Here I come." He bent his knees and landed on the balls of his feet before springing upwards and clapping his hands. "I did it!"

"You sure did." Penny's heart swelled with pride. She loved this little guy more than anything in the world and her actions and decisions had to revolve around him for the foreseeable future. When she caught Logan grinning at Milo, she got the feeling that this stranger was on the same wavelength. She had no idea why, but for the first time since she discovered her husband's infidelity, it truly felt as if she was not alone, there was someone by her side who would look after them.

And catch them if they fell.

"Can we go onto the beach?" Milo jumped and skipped around Logan and his mom as she shut the truck door.

"Sure, if Logan thinks it's okay. We have to remember that we don't know this place well and sometimes the tide and currents can be dangerous."

"Why?" Milo slipped his hand into hers.

"Because sometimes even the most serene-looking water can hide a riptide. If you get caught in a riptide, you might get swept out to sea." She glanced at Logan. "Is the beach safe?"

"There are no riptides here," he confirmed but didn't go as far as agreeing the beach was safe.

"Okay, let's go." Penny started walking toward the steps leading down from the parking lot toward the beach, but Milo didn't follow. Instead, he twisted around and held out his hand to Logan. "Can you hold my hand and then I can swing?"

"Swing?" Logan flexed his fingers but didn't immediately take hold of Milo's hand.

"Yes. If I hold Mommy's hand and I hold your hand then I

can swing." He wriggled his fingers at Logan who finally took the offered hand. "Now, hold tight and then lift me up when I swing, like this."

Milo fell back a little and then took a couple of quick steps forward and lifted his feet off the ground. Penny raised her arm and Logan mirrored her movements, sending Milo high enough into the air to elicit an excited laugh. Logan laughed along with him and was happy to repeat the movement over and over again until Penny's arm felt as if it might drop off.

"Okay, one more, and then we're going to walk down the steps to the beach."

Milo hung back and then ran forward as fast as he could before launching himself into the air. "Whee!" he called out at the top of his voice.

"You sure know how to have fun." Logan laughed as Milo breathlessly planted his two feet squarely on the ground, let go of Penny's and Logan's hands, and ran off toward the steps.

"Walk down the steps," Penny called after him.

"I will." Milo slowed to a walk at the top of the steps and then carefully walked down them, his hand on the wall to help him balance.

"I like hearing him laugh." Logan watched Milo as he reached the third step from the bottom and jumped.

"It's a good sound," Penny agreed. "My favorite sound."

"And his dad left him?" Logan asked quietly as if he couldn't fathom how a father would leave his only child. A thought Penny had pondered once too many in recent months.

Penny had reached the top step but didn't go down to the beach. Instead, she turned and faced Logan. "He decided to make a new life with another woman."

"And he was okay with making you give up everything

you knew, everything you owned?" Logan's eyebrows met in the middle as if he were trying to figure out a puzzle.

"He didn't really care." She looked over her shoulder to where her son was running around as if he were chasing his own tail.

"How could he *not* care?"

"Because he'd moved on. In truth, I don't think he ever really wanted to be a father. Milo was...an accident."

"An accident?"

"Yes." Her cheeks were tinged with pink and she dared not look at Logan. "You know, he wasn't planned. He just happened. Kelvin, Milo's dad, wasn't totally on board with me keeping him. Not at first." She recalled the discussions but refused to be pressured into not keeping the child growing inside of her. "As Milo grew bigger inside me, Kelvin came around to the idea of being a father. But the dream was not as easy as the reality. Children take up a lot of time and energy."

"Children are a gift."

She cracked a smile and met Logan's eyes, witnessing the honesty there. "I think so, too. And Milo has been the best thing to ever happen to me. Seeing things through a child's eyes is incredibly humbling."

"You like being a mother."

"I *love* being a mother." Her bottom lip trembled. "Although, there are times when I think I might not be the best mother for Milo. He's been through so much and here we are starting over again. We're homeless. I just hope he's happy at Helena's, she lives in an apartment building in a busy city and, as you can see, Milo likes open spaces where he can run off his endless energy."

"Penny, you have a home here. If you want it." The truth shone in Logan's eyes and her eyes misted with tears. All she had to do was reach out and accept his offer and they would have a home here in Wishing Moon Bay. But was that the right thing for them?

"I don't understand."

"Which part?"

"I arrived in town yesterday. We don't know each other." She inclined her head slightly. "You don't exactly have great people skills...no offense...but here you are asking me and Milo to stay. That sounds kind of...shifty."

"Shifty." His head snapped back.

"Sorry, I didn't mean to insult you. You have been nothing but kind. But don't you see how strange it seems?"

"No stranger than you going to live with your sister. You don't sound too enthusiastic about where she lives."

The air left her lungs in a whoosh. "Wow."

"Sorry, I was being honest."

"And you are probably right. But I have no choice."

"I'm giving you another choice. One where Milo will be welcomed."

"Wait." She held up her hand. "We don't know each other. I can't just agree to stay."

"There's a job and somewhere for you to live right here. Milo would have all the freedom he needs to run and play. That is better than where you are heading." He really did want her to stay. Worse, his arguments were starting to sound more plausible.

"Mom!" Milo called her from the beach, and she turned away from Logan and went down the steps without answering. His words pierced her heart and even though she knew he wasn't being unkind, she was wounded by the truth that he laid out before her. She was taking Milo to Helena's, even though she had her reservations about where they would live. But her sister loved them and would help them. Penny could depend on Helena. Staying here would be a leap of faith. "Mom!"

"Coming." Penny reached the bottom of the steps and her feet sank into the soft sand. With an effort, she waded forward onto the harder sand. Milo was farther down the beach and for a moment she was scared he'd gotten stuck in the wet sand or perhaps gotten wet in the tide. But as she drew closer, she saw him pointing at something swimming in the ocean. "Do you have sharks here?" Panic bloomed in her heart, there was something in the water.

"No," Logan said as he joined her. "No sharks."

"It's a dolphin." Milo turned an excited face toward her. "A real live dolphin."

"There are dolphins here?" Okay, she was sold. If dolphins liked to visit Wishing Moon Bay, then it must be a good place.

"Okay, there's probably something I should tell you." Logan ran forward and positioned himself between Milo and Penny and the ocean.

"I want to see the dolphin," Milo protested and ducked around Logan to peek at the creature swimming toward the shore.

"It's going to get stuck on the beach." Penny dodged to the right of Logan as he went left to try to grab hold of Milo.

"He's not going to get stuck," Logan assured them as he tried to shield them from the dolphin who was in the shallows and definitely about to get grounded on the beach.

"What the hell!" Penny staggered backward as the air around the dolphin shimmered and it just kind of disappeared.

"Where did it go?" Milo stopped and put his small hands on his hips. "There is magic in Wishing Moon Bay. I knew it."

"It's a man." Where a dolphin had been only seconds before stood a man, his feet in the shallow water as the waves lapped around his ankles.

"Logan." The guy nodded and then grinned before he set off down the beach at a run.

"The dolphin turned into a man."

"Cool!" Milo exclaimed.

Cool was not exactly the word circling around Penny's head. But some words were not for the ears of a small child.

8

LOGAN

"What just happened?" Penny turned on Logan as her mind tried to figure out exactly what she'd just seen. "Was that some kind of a joke?"

"No joke."

"It was magic. I knew there was magic," Milo said happily.

"There's no such thing as magic," Penny told her son firmly.

"There is, we just saw it." Milo ran to Logan and grabbed hold of his hand. "It was magic, wasn't it?"

"Sort of magic, yes." Logan looked down at the small child at his feet. "The dolphin was a shifter, a person who can change from a human to an animal and back again."

"Like a werewolf?" Milo made his hands into claws and growled.

"No, werewolves only turn when there's a full moon. Shifters can shift from animal to human whenever they want." His anxiety spiked as he watched Penny's expression turn from shock to anger.

"Don't." She held up her hand to Logan before she reached for Milo's hand. "Come on, buddy, we're leaving."

"I'm not going," Milo insisted and yanked his hand out of hers.

"Milo, we can't stay here."

"Yes, we can. There's magic in Wishing Moon Bay and I want to learn all about it." Her son crossed his thin arms across his small body, looking vulnerable next to the huge Logan who towered above her son.

"There is no such thing as magic. Logan just played a trick on us."

"How?" Milo asked, looking up at Logan with uncertainty.

"I don't know. Special effects of some kind." She turned in a circle looking for a projector or a camera, something that would help explain what had just happened.

"It was real. I wouldn't play a trick on you and I wouldn't lie to you," Logan insisted.

"That wasn't real. Things like that do not happen." Penny eyed her son, he could see the uncertainty on her face. She was scared of losing the boy who she loved so much and it broke Logan's heart to be part of the cause of such pain for the person he wanted to protect above all others.

Show her, his wolf told him.

"I can prove it's real," Logan stuttered.

"How?" The challenge flashed across her eyes. "How are you going to prove it's real?"

"I'll show you." His heart hammered in his chest as he took a couple of steps away from her. "But you have to promise me you won't run."

"Run?" She looked around. "Where are we going to run to? We're stuck in this town with no car, remember?"

"When you see..." He paused, not sure if he should tell her why she might decide to grab her son by the hand and run as fast and as far away from Logan as she could. Or whether to simply shift into his wolf with no warning. Either choice might be a bad one. Either choice might lead him to losing his mate.

"When I see what?" Her hands were curled into fists as she leaned forward, a fierce mother who was ready to fight to protect her child.

"Are you an animal, too?" Milo's question was simple, and his tone held no fear.

"Oh, no." Penny shook her head. "Is that what you're about to do?"

"Yes."

"Cool."

"Not cool." Penny reached for Milo and wrapped her arms around him.

"I'm a wolf. Not a werewolf, a shifter. I can change at will and I want to show you that there is nothing to be afraid of." He also wanted to get down on his knees and beg her to stay. Logan would do anything not to lose her. For a man who had steered clear of most people these last few years, this was huge. He actually wanted to share his life with others.

"A wolf." She pressed her lips together and he wasn't sure if she thought he was making the whole thing up or if she thought he was a freak. "You're going to do what the dolphin man did and change from one thing to another?"

"Yes."

She sighed, the color in her cheeks rising as her heart beat rapidly in her chest. "Go ahead then."

"And you promise not to run?"

"Only if you promise not to eat us," Milo giggled.

"This is not funny, Milo."

"It's exciting. Logan is going to change into a real live wolf. I wish I could do that. I could run over the mountains." He looked up at her mom and stopped talking at her warning look.

"I don't understand what is happening," Penny put her

shaking hand to her forehead. "But if you want to show us, I guess we can watch. And we won't run."

Logan eyed her nervously, unsure if she planned something else, but his wolf was too excited to be contained for much longer, he wanted to be free, he wanted to meet Penny. *She is our mate. I want to feel her fingers in my fur.*

"Okay. Stay there. Right there." He looked around to check that there was no one else close by. If Penny screamed, he didn't want to draw a crowd, but it was early in the morning and no one else was down by the beach.

Penny tightened her hold on Milo as Logan took another couple of steps backward. He rolled his shoulders and tried to relax. He didn't want to mess this up.

When have we ever messed up shifting? his wolf asked.

There's always a first time and with so much riding on this, I just want to make sure we get it right. Logan stood still, his eyes fixed on Penny and Milo as he finally let go of the world around him.

His wolf wasted no time taking his place, but Logan still feared that in the split second they were gone, his mate would disappear into thin air. Which was not being overdramatic when a world of magic surrounded them. If they had been followed down to the beach, if someone decided to mess with him...like a certain warlock who didn't like cold showers, then his mate might be gone.

She is here. His wolf stood on four paws, his head low as he waited for the shock to register on Penny's face.

"You're a white wolf." Penny seemed more surprised at seeing his snowy white wolf pelt than just the fact that he was a wolf.

"He's adorable." Milo's reaction wasn't quite what Logan was going for, but he'd live with it. "Can I pet him?"

Milo tilted his head back and looked at his mom. "I'm not sure. Wolves are dangerous animals."

"But this isn't a wolf. This is Logan. Can't you see the wolf and Logan have the same eyes?" Milo stepped toward the wolf, but Penny tightened her grip on him and held him close.

Logan's wolf stepped forward and then waited. Then he took another step, leaned forward, and sniffed the air, taking in the scent of his mate and her son. He so wanted them to touch him and pet him and maybe he could even roll over and play in the sand with the boy.

"Mom, we have to say hello." Milo threaded his fingers through Penny's and pulled her forward.

"If you hurt him, I will hunt you down and skin you alive," Penny said as she shuffled forward to meet the white wolf.

The wolf gave them a quizzical smile. They had no idea he would rather die a fiery death than hurt either of them. But they would know. Soon, they would know exactly what they were to him.

Maybe one slow step at a time, Logan said. Finding out about shifters is one thing, finding out that you are bound to one for all eternity is another. Humans are used to free will.

Logan had no free will.

Milo petted the wolf's head, burying his fingers in the soft fur. "He's real, Mom."

Of course I'm real, the wolf said.

They can't hear you and I guess they might have thought you are just a projection. We grew up knowing about shifters the same as everyone else in Wishing Moon Bay. But Penny and Milo had no idea we were real.

"Be careful," Penny warned.

"It's safe. He won't hurt you, will you, Mr. Wolf?"

The wolf shook his head.

"You can understand what we're saying?" Penny asked.

The wolf nodded and stretched forward to nuzzle her

hand. Penny froze for a moment and then relaxed and opened her hand so he could sniff her. She smelled divine.

"This is amazing." Milo let go of Penny's hand and dropped to his knees. With a sigh of contentment, he stretched out his arms and buried his face in the wolf's soft fur while clamping his arms around Logan's middle.

"He's not a toy," Penny warned. "You have to be careful and not hurt him."

Logan's wolf rubbed his muzzle on Penny's thigh and nudged her. She petted him lightly, running her fingers along his neck. This couldn't have gone any better and both sides of Logan were relieved.

"I wish I could ride on his back." Milo sat back on his heels and stared at the wolf. "He's nearly as big as a pony."

"No," Penny said firmly, even though the wolf could easily have carried the boy and would have done so gladly. But their mate didn't know that.

There is time for that later, Logan told his wolf as he pondered how he could tell Penny that it was okay for Milo to sit on him. *Baby steps, remember?*

"Okay, I think we need Logan back here so we can talk about...shifting." Penny took hold of Milo's hand and backed up. "You can change back again at will?"

"Yes," Logan answered when he replaced the wolf.

"Great." She chewed the inside of her cheek. "How does it work?"

"Shifting?"

"Yes."

"I don't know. It's part of me, part of my genes." Logan had never thought too much about how he shifted, it was just something that happened when a shifter reached puberty.

"Can you teach me?" Milo asked excitedly, straining to break away from his mom.

"No, sorry, Milo. I was born this way. Unless one of your

parents is a shifter, then it's not something you can learn to do."

"Oh." Milo's disappointment was tangible but there was no point getting his hopes up. Shifting was in Logan's blood. It was not in Milo's blood.

"Is everyone in town a shifter?" Penny's next question threatened to open up a whole can of worms.

"Not everyone is a shifter, no." Logan winced, he was holding back on her. It wasn't as if he was lying, he was just not telling her the whole truth.

"This is just the weirdest thing I've ever seen." She put her hand on her cheek and shook her head. She looked pale and for a moment Logan worried she might faint but then she sniffed loudly and sighed. "So what now?"

"What now?" he asked in confusion.

"What's the point in showing us all this? What's the reason you keep asking us to stay?"

"I think you would be a good fit for the town," Logan told her.

Lame, his wolf complained.

"A good fit for the town." Penny tightened her hold on Milo. "I think it's time we went back to the hotel and collected our stuff."

"No," Milo complained.

"We're going to see if the car is fixed and we're leaving," Penny said firmly.

"You're my mate," Logan blurted out.

"Your mate. And what exactly does that mean?"

"It means that we're meant to be together. That you and I..." His gaze slid down to Milo and he clamped his mouth shut, this was not a conversation he wanted to have in front of the boy.

"Meant to be together." Her face paled and he was sure she was going to cry but she held it in.

"It's a fate thing. One true mate. That kind of thing."

"Fate." She covered her mouth with her hand and looked out to sea. "And you believe that?"

"Yes. It's what I've grown up believing, it's what I've seen with other shifters. It's real." He wanted to go to her and hold her. Logan had no idea why this piece of information hit her so hard.

As she stood gazing out to sea, Milo turned to her and hugged her around the waist. "Don't be sad, Mommy. This is where we belong."

The sound of her phone ringing broke the silence between them. "Hello?" She listened to the caller and then said, "Thanks. We'll be right there."

Logan ran his hand through his hair. "Frank?"

"The car is ready." She put the phone back in her pocket and leaned down to pick Milo up.

"We're not leaving," Milo said firmly.

"We have to go pick up the car," Penny told him. "I have to go pay Frank for the work he's done."

Logan followed her up the beach like a condemned man. When she met his wolf, he thought it was all going to be okay. Now he was not so sure, and he had no idea what he'd said to blow the situation.

After unlocking the truck, he waited while they got themselves into the passenger seat and then went around to the driver's side. He couldn't just drive them back to the garage and let them pick up the car and leave.

We could hold their luggage prisoner. His wolf's idea was not helpful.

We have to let them go, Logan said miserably. *If that's what Penny wants, we have to let them go. We might not have a choice over who we love but she does. She was married and raised a child with another man. Maybe she still loves him.*

That idea nearly wrenched his heart out of his chest.

Penny might be his fated mate, but she might believe her ex-husband was the man for her. She might still be in love with the father of her child.

He knew she was wrong. But he had no right to tell her that.

Of course you do, his wolf said heatedly. You have every right. Don't start being polite now. It doesn't become you.

As Logan started the engine, he was ready to fight for his mate. Whatever it took.

9

PENNY

Penny had nothing to say as Logan drove away from the beach. Her mind was racing, there was so much to process. Too much to process.

Logan had two sides. A human side and a wolf. How was that even possible?

Then to tell her they were fated mates who were meant to be together. It was the craziest thing she'd ever heard. Okay, second craziest to him being able to shift into a wolf.

"Mommy." Milo threaded his fingers through hers and looked up at her, searching her face.

"I'm okay, buddy." She leaned forward and dropped a kiss on the top of his head, hating to see the worry on his face. He'd seen her at her worst since his dad left. He'd seen her broken and vulnerable and that was not a face she wanted him to see again.

"Are we really going to leave?" he whispered as they drove toward the garage.

"I don't know." Her eyes went to Logan's face. Was she just running away, afraid that this man might hurt her just like Kelvin had?

He'd said they were meant to be together forever but that was what Kelvin had promised her on the day they were married. She needed time to think things over. Time to come to terms with what Logan had shown her and what he'd told her about them being mates. Yet she didn't have the luxury of time. She would have to decide whether to stay or leave very soon. Once she picked up the car from the garage, she would have to go back to the hotel to get their luggage. But what then?

As they neared the garage, the thought of continuing their journey to Helena's felt wrong. There was no other way to describe it. Wishing Moon Bay gave her a sense of coming home. It was as if she belonged here. Hadn't the town opened itself up to her, revealed the way in when normally it remained hidden? If she left, there might be no way to return.

Logan parked the truck outside of the garage and they all got out. Frank was at the door leading from the workshop before they'd had a chance to close the truck doors. In his hand, he held a wrench, and for one long moment, Penny worried he was about to whack Logan over the head with it. But then he cracked a smile. "This was your problem." He brandished the wrench at them, but he no longer looked menacing.

"A wrench?" Logan asked.

"Yes, someone must have left it on the engine, and it fell through, luckily it didn't do any real damage. Just pulled out a couple of wires which told the car it had no fuel, which made you bump along the road." Frank looked at the wrench and then handed it over to Penny.

She took the wrench with a bemused expression. "No one has worked on the car for months."

Frank shrugged. "I'm just telling you what I found."

"A wrench." Logan side-eyed Frank who nodded.

"Yep, we've been laughing about it since we found it. Someone really did throw a wrench in the works." He chuckled along at his own joke, but Penny didn't find it amusing at all.

"Is this a joke?" She held the wrench up and Frank sobered as he saw her expression.

"No, that's what we found. I figured you had the car checked over before you started your journey, and someone was careless about picking up their tools." He shook his head at her. "No?"

"No. Not unless it's been under the hood since I bought the car." She didn't add that she hadn't even checked the oil and water before their journey. She didn't need a lecture from Frank about caring for an engine.

The mechanic shrugged. "That's what I found. We repaired the wiring and drove the car around town to check that it's all working. You are good to go."

"I don't want to go," Milo said mutinously.

"Do you have the bill?" Penny was not going to have this conversation here in front of Frank.

"Mommy," Milo pleaded.

"Why don't you go back to the hotel with Logan and I'll meet you there?" Penny looked from Milo to Logan and back again.

"Sure! Come on, Logan." Milo grabbed hold of Logan's sleeve and pulled him toward the truck, but the broad-chested man just stood there. "Logan, don't let her change her mind."

Logan looked down at Milo and then nodded. "I'll meet you back at the hotel."

She nodded and followed Frank into the garage. She must be crazy letting her son go off with a man who could shift into a wolf, but she trusted Logan in a way she could not fully understand.

"How do you like our town?" Frank asked as they headed for his office.

"I like it a lot," she admitted truthfully.

"Does that mean you are going to stay?" He went to a desk filled with paperwork and invoices and sat down.

"I don't know. We have plans. We have somewhere we're supposed to be." Penny took out her wallet and slid out her bank card.

"Somewhere you are supposed to be or somewhere you want to be?" Frank put on a pair of thick-rimmed glasses which magnified his eyes.

"I'm responsible for Milo. I can't just act on a whim."

"Whims are some of the best things to act on." He placed the invoice down in front of her.

"Is that all?" Relief flooded her veins when she saw the token bill.

"The work only took us an hour. I only charge for my time. I'm an honest man." He smiled up at her. "And you look as if you need a break."

Penny smoothed her hand over her hair. "I look that good?"

"Listen, you have a wonderful son. I can see the way he respects you. And the love between you is obvious." He paused as she handed over her card. "You could both be happy here."

"And if we're not?" She waited for him to process her card.

"If you're not then you have just delayed leaving." He smiled at her kindly. "But if you are then you could both be wonderful assets to the town." He smothered a smile. "There are not many people who can put a smile on Logan's face."

"He's not so bad," she replied, sticking up for the man who had helped her so much and who had also trusted her enough to show her and Milo a secret side of himself.

"No, he's not. And I think you know he has your best interest at heart. You and the boy." He handed her the card and receipt. "Don't leave because you have plans. Not if you don't think it's the right thing to do. Sometimes we only get one shot at happiness and when we get that chance, we have to grab hold of it and hang on no matter what our sensible brains tell us we should do."

"When you have a child, isn't your sensible brain the one you're supposed to use?"

"That depends." He stood up and she headed back outside. "Sometimes we must listen to our hearts, and I think this might be one of those times, don't you?"

"I can't afford to get this wrong, Frank. I can't jeopardize my son's future." She still had hold of the wrench as they reached her car.

"It must have taken a lot of courage for you to get here. Why not take a leap of faith and stay?" Frank opened the door for her and held onto it while she got into the driver's seat.

"I don't know if I have any faith left," she admitted.

"Think of it another way," Frank held onto the car door. "Someone put a wrench in the works and that's how you ended up here. If you haven't had your car serviced, then how did it get there?"

"You are trying to tell me that the wrench appeared under the hood of my car just so that I would come to Wishing Moon Bay?"

"Do you have a better explanation?" Frank closed the door and walked away before she had a chance to reply. As she watched the mechanic go back inside, she stared after him, not really knowing what her next move would be. What she did know was that Milo wanted to stay and after all he'd been through, after all the times he'd done as she'd asked without question, leaving behind his friends and his old life, perhaps it was time he got his own way for once.

Penny leaned forward and rested her head on the steering wheel as tears stung her eyes. She'd tried not to see the tears as Milo took down the dinosaur posters from his walls and packed away his toys. But they'd been there.

Rolling her shoulders, she sat up straight and started the engine. Logan had talked about fate. It was fate who said they should be together. Some kind of shifter thing, from what she recalled. So what if fate had put the wrench under the hood? It might have already been there when she traded in her newer model car for this old one because she needed the cash. It might have sat there all hidden and secure until they reached Wishing Moon Bay and then boom!

"Boy, we are in trouble," Penny told herself as she backed the car out of the parking space and headed for the road. "The more time you spend in this town, the more you sound like your mom."

Her mom, who had believed in monsters in the closet and dreams and premonitions. She'd have believed in fate, too.

"A leap of faith." Penny looked at her reflection in the rearview mirror. She'd taken every other leap these last couple of months so why not a leap of faith?

Although, she wasn't ready to leap too far. She might agree to stay in town, but she certainly was not ready to leap into bed with a wolf shifter just because he said they were mates. Oh, no, she was still sworn off men at least for the immediate future. Logan was a complication she was not ready to add into the mix right now. If they were meant to be together forever, then waiting another couple of months or more would be easy.

As she drove into the small parking lot out back of the hotel and got out of the car, it was as if a weight had shifted off her chest. A weight she hadn't realized was there until it was gone. The plan to stay with Helena had been like another nail in her coffin, another kick when she was down. It had been a choice of necessity. Penny was tired of not being able to decide her own fate.

Pulling her phone out of her pocket, she scrolled through until she found Helena's number and pressed dial. She waited for the ringtone, her heart hammering in her chest as if she were about to do battle with a dragon. "Helena."

"Is that you, Penny? The line is terrible." Helena's voice crackled as she spoke.

"I am just calling to tell you we have decided to stay in Wishing Moon Bay for a few days. If you're sure you don't mind."

"No, not at all." Helena's voice crackled as she spoke. "Take your time, Penny. The world isn't going anywhere."

"Are you sure?" Was Penny hoping for an excuse not to stay? It was time to take back control of her life. "It really is beautiful here."

"I want you to be happy, Penny," Helena insisted, the line clearer now. "And whatever you think happiness is, I'm there for you. I know you had reservations about moving in with me. Believe me, I have reservations about my life here all the time."

"You do? You've never said."

"That's because I'm the sensible one. The grounded one." She gave a short, humorless laugh. "Sometimes I just want to tear it all down."

"Helena, honey, I had no idea."

"Ah, forget I said anything. I don't know where that came from." Helena was trying to smooth things over, push down her feelings, and put her sensible, reliable head back on.

"Maybe you should break free, too, Helena."

"One day." She sniffed. "You take your time. If things don't work out, then my offer still stands. And if you need some money, don't be too proud to ask. You would do the same for me."

"I love you." Penny sobbed.

"I love you, too. And Milo. I admit I was looking forward to having the little guy around."

"Maybe if things work out here, you could come visit. Once we have a place of our own."

"I'd like that." There was a long pause and muffled voices in the background. "I have to go."

The call ended and Penny shoved her phone back in her pocket.

"So, you are staying?" Ivan was leaning against the wall outside the front door of the hotel drinking coffee.

"I might be." Her head spun when she realized what she'd just done.

"Come on. I'll get you something to drink, you look as if you need it." Ivan inclined his head toward the door.

"Where's Milo?" She hurried after Ivan. Logan's truck was parked outside of the hotel but there was no sign of either him or her son.

"He's with Logan. They are in the restaurant. We're just about to start serving lunch." Ivan entered the kitchen and went to one of the cupboards high on the wall. "This is my secret stash. I trust you to keep my secret." He flashed a smile at her as he took a bottle of amber liquor from the cupboard. "Do you want to grab a couple of glasses?"

"Drinking before lunch. This is a slippery slope." Despite her words, she went to the cupboard Ivan indicated and took out two glasses.

"I think you deserve it. I know I do." He splashed the liquor into the glasses, picked up one, and raised it to her. "Here's to your new start."

"I must be crazy."

"What's wrong with being a little crazy sometimes?" he asked.

"So what are you?" Penny asked as she swirled the liquor around in her glass and gave it a sniff before taking a gulp.

"A dragon."

She nearly sprayed her drink across the kitchen. "A dragon."

He chuckled. "Is it a stretch to believe dragons are real when you've seen Logan shift into a wolf?"

"Wolves are a real thing in the real world. The world outside of Wishing Moon Bay. Dragons are not. So yes, it is a stretch."

"Do you want me to show you?" His eyes twinkled with mischief.

"Not right here." She stared at him for a long moment. "A dragon?"

"Yes." He chuckled. "Are you sure you want to settle for a wolf?"

"I'm not settling for anything or anyone." Her eyes narrowed. "So you don't have a mate?" The word sounded foreign on her tongue. There was so much she didn't know about shifters. Or the town she's decided to make her home.

"No, I do not." Sadness wrapped itself around him like a shroud before he shook it off. "Logan is lucky to have found you. The question is, are you lucky to have found him?"

"You don't know anything about me, so how do you know he is lucky?"

"You're here, aren't you?" He was teasing her, and she warmed to him.

"I am. Although, I have no idea where here really is." Penny downed the rest of her drink and warmth flooded through her. "But wherever we are, the liquor is good."

"It's made with honey and just a little magic." He winked and picked up the bottle. "Refill?"

"No, thank you. I need to keep a clear head if I'm going to figure out what I'm doing."

"In that case, I suggest you have another couple of glasses. A clear head is overrated when it comes to making decisions." He put the bottle away and placed both the glasses in the dishwasher. "Okay, I have to get the lunches served. My kitchen staff will be here at any moment."

"Is that your way of telling me to get out of the kitchen?" Penny backed away toward the door.

"It's a polite way of telling you to get out of my kitchen." He grinned. "At least for now. If you're staying, we're going to be seeing a lot of each other."

"I can't wait." She spun on her heel and left the kitchen. As she entered the reception area, she hesitated, unsure of where her son was. She should have gone and found him as soon as she arrived. Perhaps she'd wanted to test Logan and his ability to care for a small child for twenty minutes.

"There you are!" Milo pulled open the door to the right and came running across to her. "We thought you had left without me." He launched himself into her arms and she wrapped him in a motherly hug.

"I did but the car broke down again and refused to leave without you."

"Really?" Milo pulled his head back and looked at her.

"Yes." She kissed his cheek. "So I had to come and get you."

"You didn't really try to leave without me." Milo shook his head at her.

"You know I wouldn't do that." She shifted his weight, so he sat on her hip. "So, here we are. Now what?" She aimed her question at Logan, half expecting him to not have an answer.

"Your room is still free for the next two nights. After that, we'll have to juggle things around. I'll find you both somewhere to stay..."

"And what about work?"

"Work." He pressed his lips together as he watched Milo hanging onto her. "You don't have to work. I can support you while you and Milo get used to town..." He stalled as he saw her reaction. "Or I can work out some shifts for you here at the hotel."

"Enough to cover our room and food at least. I have enough in the bank to buy whatever else we need until we figure out something more permanent." She held out her hand to him as if they were about to strike a deal. "It's nonnegotiable."

Logan leaned forward and grasped her hand. A jolt of electricity shot up her arm and her eyes widened with recognition. There was a connection between them, one she could not ignore even if she could not understand it. "Then we have a deal."

As he held on to her hand longer than necessary, Penny couldn't help feeling she had just sealed her fate.

10

LOGAN

His gaze rested on their joined hands. What he thought might be impossible when they were on the beach was now a reality. His mate had agreed to stay.

"Can we get the rest of our things in from the car?" Milo asked.

"I suppose." Penny tugged her hand out of Logan's.

"Sorry." He should be helping in the kitchen, but he didn't want his mate to slip out the front door and out of his life.

She's agreed to stay, his wolf reminded him.

What if she was just saying that and once she goes back out to her car, she changes her mind? Logan couldn't help worrying that something would go wrong. He'd waited so long for his mate, it seemed too good to be true. Why him, why now?

You need to think of your glass as being half full, not half empty, his wolf told him bluntly.

"Do you need a hand?" Logan followed Penny to the door.

"We can manage," she insisted. "Milo has big muscles."

"I do." Milo curled his arm and patted his biceps.

"And I think you're needed in the kitchen. Or the restaurant." She nodded to the dining room. "You're busy."

Penny was dismissing him. She wanted time away from him. His primal shifter needs nearly overrode his common sense that told him to give her the time she needed. This was all happening so fast and she didn't feel the same way about him as he did about her.

Give her space to breathe, his wolf advised.

"If you need anything, just give me a shout." He backed away. "And if you are hungry, come into the dining room, or I can arrange for a tray to be brought up to your room."

"Sure." She reached for Milo's hand. "We'll get our gear in first."

Milo grinned and gave Logan a thumbs-up before they left the hotel, with Logan staring after them. Not that he lost contact with them. He pushed his shifter senses to follow them as they went to the car then he held his breath as he waited to see if Penny would bundle Milo into the car and leave town. She didn't. Instead, he heard her pop the trunk.

They are staying. His wolf practically jumped for joy.

"Hey, is there any service around here?" Rift came into the reception area and caught Logan staring at the wall as if he had X-ray vision.

"Rift. What are you doing here?" Logan asked gruffly.

"I got a call from Ivan. He said you might need help kidnapping your mate so that she doesn't leave town. But by the look on your face, she has decided to stay." Rift was a snow leopard shifter who had also been lucky enough to be adopted by Valerie. He was a couple of years younger than Logan, but they had grown up as brothers.

"Has Ivan been calling everyone?" Logan asked as he turned his back on his mate but kept his senses firmly fixed on her.

"Oh, that is a loaded question and one I am not going to answer. You know he's only got your best interest at heart." Rift hugged Logan. "Congratulations. I am so happy for you."

"Thanks. It's a little surreal," he admitted.

"Was that Penny?" He nodded toward the entrance. "I passed her in the parking lot, the lady with the young son?"

"That's her." His expression clouded. "She's not from town and had no idea about shifters or any of this."

"But she managed to find her way into town."

"Because a wrench got stuck in her engine." Logan arched an eyebrow as Rift's eyes widened. "It doesn't sound as if she is here by chance, does it?"

"And that worries you?" Rift asked. "You can't accept that she might have wound up in town because it was time for you to find a mate? Or because she needs you? Ivan said she's on her way to her sister's."

"Ivan has been doing a lot of talking." There weren't many secrets between the men Valerie had adopted. Mainly because if you told Ivan anything, he had a habit of sharing it with the others.

"He's excited for you." Rift held up his thumb and finger about an inch apart. "And more than a little jealous. Between us, I think he believes you finding your mate might just break the curse."

"Curse?" Logan asked.

"Yeah, if you hadn't noticed, none of us have found our mate. You never wondered if we were cursed?" Rift asked thoughtfully.

"I never did." Logan spun around and headed for the dining room. "Penny is coming back inside. She wanted to empty her car on her own. I need to look busy."

"Then get me something to eat, I'm starving." Rift followed Logan into the dining room.

"I'm glad you can still think of your stomach at a time like this," Logan said drily.

"Hey, I ran all the way here when I got Ivan's call. The least you can do is feed me." Rift headed for a table. "If you want, you can ask your mate to join me and I'll tell her all your secrets."

"I don't have any secrets worth knowing." Logan handed Rift a menu.

"Is that so?" Rift rose to the challenge. "Does she know how you came to be in Wishing Moon Bay? You're not the only one who wasn't born here."

"We haven't exactly talked much. All she knows so far is that I can shift into a white wolf and I'm looking after the hotel for Valerie." He put his hand on his hips as he sensed her coming back into the hotel with Milo.

"Ivan said she also knows you are lacking in people skills. Something about a warlock and a cold shower."

Logan rolled his eyes as he spotted the warlock entering the restaurant. "Thanks, you just summoned him." He left Rift and headed over to Jeremy. "Hi, how are you?"

Jeremy eyed him suspiciously. "Why do you want to know?"

"Do you want me to show you to a table?" Logan smiled, trying to look friendly which only deepened the warlock's suspicions.

"I think I can manage to find one myself." Jeremy pushed past Logan and went to a table near the window.

Rift was half-hidden behind a menu, his shoulders shaking as Logan approached. "People skills."

"The guy hates me."

"A cold shower in the morning has that effect on some people. Mainly those who don't have hot shifter blood running through their veins." Rift lowered his menu and glanced at Jeremy. "He looks kind of familiar."

"I've never met him before." Logan looked up at the ceiling. Penny and Milo were in room eight dumping their stuff. Now they were going back out into the corridor and down the stairs.

"Hmm. I have a good recall for faces," Rift was continuing. "I'm sure I've seen him before."

"Okay, it's getting busy." Logan was not really listening to Rift anymore. "Let me or one of the servers know what you want, and I'll charge it to your account."

"Sorry, what was that? You said it was on the house? Whatever I want?" Rift hissed so that only Logan could hear him.

Logan ignored him and started taking orders and organizing the servers so that no one waited too long to give their order and receive their food. As he kept his senses tuned to his mate as she emptied her car, he also kept the diners happy. Even Jeremy seemed in a better mood by the time he'd eaten Ivan's specialty steak.

"How was the food?" Logan asked Rift as he removed his empty plate.

"So good I nearly licked the pattern off the plates." Rift leaned back in his seat. "Who knew a dragon shifter could possess such a skill. It's like alchemy. He turns the ingredients of each meal into something amazing."

"Maybe you could keep that to yourself, too." Logan balanced the dirty dishes on his arm as he backed away. "Ivan already thinks he's the greatest chef in the world."

"He's not wrong." Rift frowned. "Not that I've been all over the world."

"Yeah, but his head is already so big it only just fits in the kitchen." Logan left Rift sitting alone and took the dirty dishes through to the kitchen. He timed it just right, Penny and Milo were coming down the stairs. "How are things going?"

"We are all done." Her eyes slid sideways toward the dining room.

"Do you want to eat?" Logan asked.

Penny nodded. "I will work off all the meals and the room."

"Don't worry about it, the meals are a perk of the staff who work at the hotel." Logan headed into the kitchen with Penny following and then groaned when he sensed Rift approaching. "This is Rift," Logan said without turning around.

"Who? Oh." Penny caught sight of the man stalking her. "Hi."

"You must be Penny. Ivan has told me so much about you. While Logan has told me nothing." Rift inclined his head toward Penny and then his attention switched to Milo. "And you must be Milo."

"I am." Milo seemed shy of Rift and closed the space between him and his mom. "Do you work here, too?"

"No, but I used to live here."

"In the hotel?" Milo's interest was piqued.

"Yes. We all lived here when we were younger," Rift said.

"You and Logan are brothers?" Penny asked.

"Yes. Well, sort of. Valerie, who owns the hotel, adopted us." Rift's comment got Penny's interest.

"She raised us as her own," Ivan added.

"I had no idea." She glanced at Logan. "You were all adopted?"

"Why do you think I squander my excellent culinary skills on a small hotel?" Ivan asked.

"Oh, here we go," Rift rolled his eyes at Penny who smothered a smile.

"Yes, here we go. Do you know why the hotel is so popular?" Ivan asked.

"They have heard about Logan's excellent customer service. *The guest is always an inconvenience*," Rift said drily.

"They certainly don't come and stay because of the house comedian," Logan bit back.

"They come back for the food." Ivan shook his head and told Penny, "You can see how underappreciated I am."

"I can and your food is wonderful," Penny told him.

"And that is why we are in your kitchen." Logan put his hand on Ivan's shoulder and squeezed it. "Penny and Milo are hungry."

"Why don't you come and join me in the restaurant?" Rift asked. "I was about to order dessert, but I could eat another meal with you."

"Another meal?" Ivan asked.

"Yes, you should serve bigger portions," Rift told him.

"Come on, let's leave Ivan to what he does best." Logan ushered them all out of the kitchen. "Do you want to be flame-grilled?" he asked Rift.

"You know he doesn't mean it." Rift winked at Milo. "Don't worry, we're always like this. I like to keep Ivan's feet on the ground."

"What he really means is he likes to wind Ivan up. Just like he did when we were younger." Logan escorted Rift to his table. "Please don't antagonize him. The hotel is fully booked in a few days. If he throws a fit and quits, I'm in trouble. Which means the hotel is in trouble."

"Which means Valerie is in trouble." Rift held up his hands in surrender. "I promise to behave myself."

"I wish I had a brother or sister," Milo said as they sat down next to Rift. "It must be fun."

"I'm not sure I would call it fun," Logan grumbled with one eye on Jeremy who was staring over at them with great interest.

"We had fun growing up together. Once we got to know each other." Rift became serious. "I don't know what would have happened to us if Valerie hadn't opened her door, and her heart, to us."

"She sounds like an incredible woman." Penny's eyes

lingered on her son. As a mother, she would empathize with Valerie and her need to nurture the children she'd cared for.

Valerie is an exceptional woman. An exceptional mother. I believe our mate has some of the same characteristics. The same big heart. His wolf was right. Logan could see certain aspects of the woman who had taken in a strange group of boys and given them a home. There was a strength they both shared, coated in kindness and love.

"She is exceptional." Rift locked eyes with Logan. "She'd do anything for us. And we'd do anything for her." His mouth curled up at one corner. "At least that was the case. Now that Logan has you, his loyalty lies elsewhere."

Penny's brow furrowed. "Surely there is room for the love of a mate and the love for other people in your life?" Her hand rested on the back of Milo's neck. "What if a shifter has children?"

Rift arched an eyebrow at Logan, putting him on the spot. "I have no idea what I'm talking about. So why don't you tell us since you actually have a mate."

Logan's jaw tensed, his heart wanted to rule his head and tell Penny she was everything to him. And more. But Rift was wrong, there was love enough to go around. "The...love...for a mate is different. It's stronger and all-consuming. But there is certainly more than enough love for the others in our lives." His attempt to be diplomatic was met by a questioning look from Rift and a concerned one from Penny. "And, since there will never be a time when I have to choose one over the other because my mate realizes there is room in my heart for more than her, it's a question best left unanswered."

Rift pointed at him. "That is a non-answer."

"It's also the only answer you're going to get." Logan glanced around the restaurant which was starting to empty after the lunchtime rush. "I'll be back for your order in a few minutes. Don't take too long, Ivan will want to close the kitchen."

When the conversation about choices between a mate and the other people in his life ended, Logan began clearing the empty tables, while trying to reconcile the mix of emotions swirling around inside him. Would this be his life from now on, or would he one day sort through them and find his equilibrium again? Finding his mate was both incredible and incredibly confusing in equal measure.

11

PENNY

"That was a delicious meal. Again." Penny helped clear the table while Rift took Milo out into the hotel gardens to show him the pond and the goldfish that lived in the pond. The same goldfish from when he and Logan were children, which fascinated her son.

"I'll tell Ivan."

"Will you?" she asked.

"Probably not." Logan chuckled, he seemed in a better mood now that she had agreed to stay.

"He's right to be proud of the food he creates." She glanced around the now empty restaurant. "In my world, he would be a top chef in an expensive restaurant. No wonder people come to the hotel for the food."

"He enjoys creating a good menu and then executing his plan to tantalize people's tastebuds." He piled the dirty plates on a table and then went to collect more.

"Could he leave here? If he wanted to?" Penny had so many questions bursting inside of her head. As she'd listened to Rift talk over lunch, she'd begun to see the wonders of the world around them. A new world, an exciting world, but also a dangerous world. There were elements of Wishing Moon Bay and the surrounding area that were strange and unpredictable. Her need to keep Milo safe from those dangers had threatened to make her change her mind about living here. But she'd agreed to stay for a while, and she would stick to her promise. But after that, if Logan was her mate and she wanted to leave, would he come with her or would he let her go?

"He could leave if he wanted to. Anyone can leave." He came back with more dirty plates and added them to his stack, which was getting dangerously high. If he dropped them, there might be a shortage of plates for Ivan to place his precious food on. "But not many people do. Or, if they do, they don't stay away for too long."

"And for a dragon shifter like Ivan, it must be tougher. I mean if you lived out there then you could shift and run where wild wolves run. But a dragon shifter does not have the same luxury." She nodded and grabbed the empty wine glasses from another table. "Have you ever lived outside of the town?"

"I live on the side of the mountain," he reminded her.

"You know that's not what I mean." Was Logan avoiding her question, was he embarrassed at never having left Wishing Moon Bay?

"I lived out there before Valerie adopted me." The plates clattered as he picked them up and carried them toward the kitchen.

Penny darted ahead and opened the door for him. Standing back so that he didn't trip over her feet, she waited patiently for him to continue. But as he entered the kitchen, he did not elaborate. Perhaps he didn't want to talk about it in front of Ivan. There was a rivalry between the two men, that much was clear, and Logan might not want to show his vulnerable side in front of the dragon shifter.

"We were busier than I expected." Ivan put his pans away and dried his hands. "If we keep filling the restaurant, we might have to extend."

"That's a decision for Valerie to make." Logan set the stack of plates on the counter and Penny opened the dishwasher and began loading it up.

"Where does she make the most money?" Penny asked.

"The rooms," Logan said.

"The restaurant." Ivan poured three cups of coffee and leaned back against the counter as he drank his. "If we ate into some more of the space on the ground floor or converted one of the bedrooms upstairs that look over the gardens, we would earn more money. Plus there would be fewer complaining guests."

"And less work for Valerie," Logan mused.

"Yes, at least with the restaurant, you close up and don't have to worry about anyone needing something in the middle of the night. How many times does Valerie get woken up at night because someone has lost their key or because something is not working?"

"I don't think I've ever been woken up," Logan shut the dishwasher and pressed the buttons to start the wash cycle.

"That's because your face says *do not disturb*." Ivan's eyes twinkled as they met Penny's.

"Is this how you've always talked to each other?" she asked.

"Isn't this how all brothers talk to each other?" Ivan asked.

"I don't know, I only have a sister and we do not talk to each other like that." A twinge of guilt about her earlier phone call with Helena left her uneasy. She had made plans to stay with her sister and perhaps she should have stuck to them.

"We have a healthy relationship that revolves around us each trying to be better than the others," Ivan stated.

"A healthy relationship?" Logan asked. "And you guys are always trying to prove who is the best. I have no part in that."

Ivan sipped his coffee thoughtfully. "You're right. You just want us to all get along."

"Which hardly ever happens," Logan told her.

"But you obviously love each other. I like that." She picked up her coffee cup and took a sip. "Oh, wow, even your coffee is good."

"What can I say?" Ivan held his cup up.

"So the two of you work at the hotel?" she asked. "But the others don't?"

"Yes."

"What do you want me to do?" Penny looked from one to the other. "I'm only willing to stay if I work."

Ivan's eyes narrowed as he looked at her. "The question is, what are you good at?"

"Ivan," Logan warned defensively.

"No, it's okay. Ivan is right, there's no point in you asking me to do something I am not good at." She covered her face with her hand. "I have no idea what I am good at."

"You're a good mom," Logan said supportively.

"And some of our guests behave so immaturely they might need a babysitter," Ivan added.

"Okay, I can make beds, I can change sheets, I can clear the tables and I can do laundry as long as you show me how to work the washer. I can clean." She shrugged. "Surely a hotel is just like keeping a house, only the guests pay instead of freeloading."

Ivan laughed out loud. "Oh, I like you, Penny." He stood up straight, drained his coffee cup, and placed it in the sink. "I'm going to go for a run and get some fresh air before dinner. You two have fun, get to know each other, and figure out the shifts."

"See you later, Ivan," Logan called after him.

"See you later." Penny drank the rest of the coffee and set the cup down. "Do you want to show me around while Rift is keeping Milo occupied?"

"Sure." Logan headed back toward the reception area. "This is where guests book in. Sophie works here on most days. Hey, Sophie."

"Hi, Logan." Sophie smiled brightly and then went back to looking at her computer screen.

"Sophie, this is Penny. I didn't introduce you properly last night." Logan moved closer to the desk.

Sophie looked up again. "Hi, Penny."

"Hello, Sophie." Penny felt kind of awkward as Sophie looked at Logan as if trying to figure out what he wanted.

"Sophie deals with the bookings online and…"

"You have the internet here?"

"This is Wishing Moon Bay, not the moon," Sophie laughed, not unkindly, but there was an edge to her tone.

"I just wondered. If the hotel is on the internet, don't people from out there in the real world try to book a room?" Penny knew she was missing something, something that was probably obvious to anyone who had lived in the town all their life. But she needed to learn about the town and how it worked.

"It's a different part of the web. Like the dark web, only lighter," Sophie explained. "You don't know it's there unless you know it's there."

"Right, that makes perfect sense." Penny would have to figure it out but maybe she would ask someone else to explain it to her. Sophie gave off a weird vibe, one Penny couldn't quite figure out.

"Hello, Mr. Barnes." Sophie's tone totally changed as the guy from room one entered the reception area and approached her desk.

"Shall we move on?" Logan guided her toward the restaurant, which she'd already seen when she ate lunch, but she suspected Logan saw it as a place to make a quick getaway from Jeremy Barnes.

"What is up with you and that guest?" she asked, not ready to let Logan off the hook. "You really should figure his water out for him."

"I did. This morning. Then when he gets in the shower, it starts acting up. Ivan thinks it's because he's a warlock." Logan moved away from the door and kept his voice low.

"A warlock? Like a male witch?" She caught up with Logan as he strode to the large window overlooking the gardens.

"Just like that. Ivan said the house doesn't like warlocks."

"The *house* doesn't like warlocks." She gave a short laugh. "He thinks the house is alive?" Logan didn't seem to be joking as he stared out of the window to where Rift was kneeling by the side of a large pond with Milo by his side. "You're not joking." Cold dread wrapped its fingers around her spine, and she shivered as she looked around the restaurant. If the house didn't like you, what else could it do? Wait, that was ridiculous. The house, or hotel, was made of bricks and mortar, it was not alive, it didn't have a heart or a brain.

"The house used to be owned by a warlock who, allegedly, cast spells on it to entertain the guests, Ivan thinks the house still harbors a grudge." Logan smiled as he watched Rift and Milo.

"You didn't tell me about your time outside of the town." She came to stand next to Logan and watched her son as he giggled as a frog hopped from Rift's hand into the pond.

"My time outside of the town wasn't a great experience." Logan half turned to face her. "My parents lived here in Wishing Moon Bay. They had a house on the edge of town. My dad was a wolf shifter, and my mom was a piano teacher."

"People learn to play the piano here?" It seemed such a normal thing to learn.

"Yes, it's not the kind of thing you can cast a spell for," he said in all seriousness. "Sure, a spell can help you learn the notes but putting them all together and playing well takes time and patience."

"I'm not sure if that is more surprising than you telling me the house is alive." So much to learn and none of it particularly intuitive.

"She was a good teacher, from what Valerie tells me. She was a normal woman who my father met while he was outside of Wishing Moon Bay." His eyes darkened as he continued. "My father was fascinated with the rest of the world and my mom liked to visit the places she'd known before she moved here. And so a couple of times a year, they would go on a vacation."

"You don't have to go on if it's too painful," Penny said gently.

"It was all a long time ago." Logan's sad smile showed the memories were still raw. "They were killed in a car accident. It was on a lonely road somewhere out in the wilderness and the other vehicle didn't stop. I was only a baby, just coming up to my first birthday."

Penny covered her mouth with her hand. "I'm so sorry."

"I don't remember them. Valerie has shown me photographs." He put his hand in his pocket and took out his wallet. Flipping it open, he showed her a photograph of a couple holding a baby. Mother and father looked so happy, so carefree.

"They look so happy." She ran her finger across the photo. The child in their arms, Logan, was chewing on his fist, he must have been close to a year old. It was hard to believe that the happy family in the photo had been ripped apart so soon after posing for this family snap.

"They were happy. They loved each other. They loved me." He pushed the photograph back inside his wallet and closed it.

"What happened? How did you get back here?"

"I didn't. Not for another five years." He turned and looked out the window. "I was found by a pack of wolves. I can only think that they smelled the other side of me even though it wasn't there yet. It wasn't fully formed."

"A pack of wolves?" It was the most incredible thing she'd ever heard. "They actually took care of you?"

"They did. I was one with them until some hunter found me and took me to a local town. I was taken in by social services. They found me a foster home, which I hated. Not because they were bad people but because I just wasn't used to living in a house. It was like a prison with four walls and a door, when I was used to running free through the wilderness. Forests and mountains were my home." He smiled sadly, his eyes drifting upwards, away from the beautifully planted garden and toward the distant mountains where he lived. It all began to make sense now.

The only thing that didn't make sense was where Penny and Milo were supposed to fit into his life.

"We can't live all the way out there," she said quietly. "Milo loves people, he needs to spend time with other children."

"I know."

"This is one of those sacrifices you would make for your mate." She was beginning to see how it worked. How much power being a shifter's mate wielded. Perhaps too much.

"It is." He smiled sadly as he turned to face her but then his expression cleared. "But you are here, and you have agreed to stay. That's all that matters to me."

"Is that right, though?" Penny's unease would not fade. "You have to give up living on the mountain for us?"

"Would you give something up that you loved for Milo?" It was a rhetorical question, one he knew the answer to and yet he still waited for her to answer.

"Of course. He's the most important thing in the world to me." She put her face close to the glass and watched the child she loved, the person who was most important to her, as he played with Rift. "I don't know if I can be what you want me to be."

"I'm not asking you to change for me," Logan insisted. "I only want you to give us a chance. A chance to figure out how we fit together."

"This is the craziest thing I've ever done." She moved closer to him, her eyes fixed on Milo. "I need you to promise me that you will always put Milo's needs first. Above mine and yours."

He looked at her for a long moment before he nodded. "I promise."

"No matter what."

"No matter what." His fingers flexed as if he was going to reach out and touch her, but he didn't. As much as he talked about mates and them being together forever, Logan seemed stuck, unable to make a move.

Had his first, formative years spent with wolves stunted his emotional growth? If so, what kind of life would they have together? After her disastrous marriage and divorce, she wanted to be loved and cherished. As they stood side by side and looked out of the window, Penny was unsure if Logan was capable of giving her and Milo what they needed.

Perhaps she had made a mistake in agreeing to stay.

12

LOGAN

It was as if he'd closed himself off from his mate. The barriers he'd put up when he'd been taken in by social services when he was found in the wilderness were back in place. Barriers that Valerie had taken years and a whole lot of patience to remove. Barriers he didn't want or need with his mate. So why were they there?

Self-preservation, his wolf told him. This has been a shock. Just like the shock we received when we were taken from our pack.

Their lives were about to change. They would have to give up their home. They would lose the solitude they had craved the last few years. Before Valerie asked him to run the hotel, it was as if he'd regressed into the child he was when he lived with the wolves.

"At any time, if you change your mind, I can leave." Her words struck him like a paw slapped across his face.

"*I* won't change my mind," he assured her. "I never thought I'd find my mate. Now that you are here, I intend to make this work."

"We're both going to need to adjust to all this." She gave a short laugh. "Although, I think I have the most to adjust to since I had no idea any of this was real." She stalled, her voice trailing off as if she were pulling out a memory to examine it. Logan knew the feeling only too well. At first, after he'd been "rescued" by humans from his wolf family, he'd often fall into a daydream where he'd be wild and free with his family. He'd stare into the distance, imaging running and hunting with the other cubs, his brothers and sisters.

"It gets easier," he assured her.

"Does it?" She looked back at her son. "I used to think that. When I met Milo's dad, I thought, this is it, life will be easier now. I was part of a partnership, there were two of us pulling together in the same direction. Then I got pregnant and when Kelvin finally accepted that we were going to have a baby, it was as if we were complete. But somewhere along the way, we began to fall apart, bit by bit until there was nothing left. Life as I knew it, how Milo knew it, ceased to be..." Her voice trailed off and she turned her attention to Logan. "That's how it was for you. When they took you from your wolf family? Life as you knew it ceased to exist."

He nodded solemnly. "My life changed, it spiraled out of control, as a child you have no say in what you want. Other people think they know what is better for you, they think they are doing what is right and if you argue, they think it's because you are too young to grasp what is happening. But when they took me from the wolves, from my family, I knew what was happening and that things would never be the same again."

"I'm so sorry." She placed her hand on his arm and instantly heat flooded from her into him.

"I was lucky that I came here, and Valerie took me in." He smiled softly. "And now we're taking you and Milo in."

"Will Valerie mind?" Penny asked.

"Valerie will be so excited." He looked over his shoulder as if expecting his adoptive mom to come flying in through the door. "I'm surprised she's not here already."

"How does she know about us?" Penny asked. "Oh, is she a clairvoyant?"

"She used to tell us boys that she could read our minds." He chuckled as her eyes widened. "I think if she knows about us, about me finding my mate, it'll be because Ivan picked up the phone and called her."

Penny put her hand over her mouth and stifled a laugh. "I feel kind of stupid."

"Don't. There are people who can read minds. But I think Valerie only told us that so we would behave. Having six boys running around the place could not have been easy."

"Six?" Penny's eyes widened farther. "There were six of you? I have trouble keeping up with one."

"Yes, there are six of us. Ivan and I have been here the longest. Then there are the twins, Aiden and Caleb, they are bear shifters. Valerie said she should have stopped there, but then Rift needed a home, he'd been on the streets for a while. And then there is Dario. He is a horse shifter."

"Valerie must be quite a woman." Penny clasped her hands together, her fingers entwined. "I hope she likes me."

"Are you kidding?" he asked. "She'll love you. You and Milo."

"Milo." She looked back out of the window, but Rift and Milo were gone.

"Come on, I'll show you outside while the weather holds. It looks as if we might have the first snowfall very soon."

"That'll be Milo's fault. He's been wishing for snow since forever." She shivered as they walked toward the door leading from the restaurant area out into the grounds surrounding the hotel.

"You're cold. Do you want to run and get a coat before we

go outside?" Logan placed his hand on the handle but didn't pull the large French doors open.

"No, I'm fine." She looked behind her. "There was a cold spot just there. I'm fine now." Penny didn't look fine; her face was pale, and her eyes startled.

"A cold spot." He stepped back to stand where she'd been standing only a moment before, but he could feel nothing out of the ordinary.

"It was probably my imagination. It's been quite a day." She nodded toward the door. "Go ahead, fresh air might do me good."

Logan pulled the door open and they stepped out onto the paved patio area where guests sat in the summer evenings. Now the tables and chairs were all stacked away in the storage shed next to the hotel. "I think I can hear them."

"Really?" Penny stood still and listened, her breath coming out in small puffs of vapor. "I can't hear a thing."

He tapped the side of his head. "Shifter senses. They are more heightened than a human's."

"Are they?" Fascination covered her face as she stared at him. "What else do shifters do?"

"What do we do?" he frowned.

"Well, you can shift from human to animal and back again. You have enhanced senses, and you know who your mate is as soon as you see them. Is there anything else you can do? Anything else I should be aware of?" She held out her hands to him. "If I am going to survive in this world, then I need a crash course on what to be aware of. Since I am just a human."

"I didn't mean you were *just* a human," he said quickly.

"But that's what I am. That's what Milo is. Compared to most other people in town, we're just ordinary. Aren't we?" she asked.

Tell her she is extraordinary, his wolf said quickly.

"Valerie taught us that no one is ordinary, we all are *extra*-ordinary in our own ways."

Good catch, his wolf replied.

"I like Valerie more and more." They walked in the direction he'd heard the voices and as they rounded a corner, they found Milo and a snow leopard rolling around on the ground wrestling. "Wow." She looked at Logan quickly. "Not as wow as your white wolf, of course."

"Of course," he said in all seriousness, although he was aware of how women liked the snow leopard. More exotic. That's how Rift had been described by a group of women once when Ivan had polled them as to who they would prefer to date—a snow leopard, a white wolf, or a bear shifter. Of course, if Ivan had mentioned dragons, the women would have most likely picked him.

Because they think he has treasure, Logan's wolf licked his paws in disgust at having come second best to Rift.

But Rift isn't the one with a mate, is he? Logan reminded his wolf.

Very good point. Remind me to rub his nose in that one the next time I see him. His wolf was mildly pacified as he went off to nap in the corner of Logan's mind.

"Six boys," Penny murmured to herself as she watched Rift and Milo having fun.

"There were times when we would roll around on the grass play-fighting," Logan admitted. "Thankfully, we were older and had outgrown fighting by the time we shifted. And if ever it happened, we would take it out onto the mountains." He turned and looked in the direction of the highest peaks. "Luckily, Ivan never joined in those fights or else he would have incinerated us all."

"So, he really is a fire-breathing dragon?" she asked. "I mean I know he said he was, but I figured maybe...I don't know, that he was smaller or didn't actually breathe fire."

"Oh, no. He breathes fire. Most of the stuff they show on TV and in books is what a dragon is like. A shifter anyway. Except for eating virgins. As far as I know, he's never eaten anyone." Logan chuckled at the look on his mate's face. Without realizing it, he'd relaxed and could talk to her as a normal person. As normal as it got around here at least.

The warlock is watching us, his wolf suddenly said, and Logan's attention snapped to the yew tree in the center of a wide grass lawn. The tree had stood there for as long as anyone in town could remember, its roots went deep into the earth although it barely grew anymore. It was just there, a part of Wishing Moon Bay, just like the ocean and the mountains surrounding them.

Are you sure he's watching us? Logan asked. *He looks as if he's looking at the tree. Many people are fascinated by it. Maybe he is a druid after all.*

Whatever he is, I don't like him, and I don't trust him, his wolf grumbled.

"Okay, Milo, we should go and get you cleaned up." Penny stepped in as Milo jumped on top of the snow leopard and rolled him over and over. There were grass stains on the child's jeans and his face had a smear of mud down one cheek. But his eyes were bright, and his cheeks flushed a healthy red.

"Oh, can't we play a little longer?" Milo asked as he obeyed his mom and rolled off the feline.

"I think Rift has had enough. You play rough." As she took her son's hand, the air around the snow leopard shimmered and the human form of Logan's brother jumped to his feet.

"I haven't wrestled like that for years." He dusted down his clothes and clapped his hands. "Maybe we can have a rematch tomorrow?"

"Yes, please." Milo's excitement was evident as he grinned from ear to ear.

"You might be wrestling in the snow if those clouds get any heavier." Logan nodded toward the heavy clouds hanging over the mountains to the north. As the day had grown older, the clouds had grown heavier and he was convinced there would be snow on the ground in the morning.

"You might be right," Rift agreed as he came to stand next to Logan. "There is snow in the air."

"Yes!" Milo jumped in the air and punched his arm high. "I love the snow."

"You have never seen the snow," Penny reminded him.

"I have on TV. It always looks awesome and we can build a snowman and have snowball fights," he said wistfully.

"And get cold hands and wet feet." Penny's concern was real.

"We should get you kitted out ready for the snow. You need warm boots and gloves. A thick hat with flaps that come down over your ears." Rift lifted his eyes toward the top of the house. "Valerie keeps everything. Just in case she had another boy to care for, she kept all our old clothes. We could go have a look, see if there is anything that might fit you."

"Are you sure that's okay?" Penny asked. "I don't want to upset Valerie by rummaging through her things. Mothers often keep special clothes as keepsakes."

"She won't mind. Any of the stuff she wanted to keep is in the trunk in her room." Logan turned toward the house and they all followed. "We can go and take a look now before the guests arrive for dinner."

"We've only just finished lunch," Milo reminded him.

"Lunch finishes late and dinner starts early," Logan explained. "As the restaurant got more popular, we had to extend the opening hours to cope with the number of diners."

"Doesn't Ivan get any time off?" Penny asked as they went

around the side of the building and in through a back door where they all removed their shoes, so they didn't track mud through the hotel.

"Shh, we don't mention time off in front of the dragon," Rift joked.

"He does have a couple of mornings off. But only when he's prepared the food so the kitchen staff can heat it up. He's very possessive of his kitchen."

"Most dragons have a hoard of treasure they watch over and would kill for, Ivan has the kitchen." Rift led them down a narrow corridor to a back staircase.

"This is the staircase the staff used to use when the hotel was a house. The back rooms through there are where Valerie's apartment is. It used to be where the servants lived," Logan explained.

"How old is the hotel?" Penny asked as Rift went upstairs with Milo right behind him.

"Hundreds of years old. The hotel and the library are two of the oldest buildings in town. They've always been here." Logan waited while his mate looked up at the high ceiling with its ornate carvings.

"Are those gargoyles?" She tilted her head to get a better look.

"Yes, most gargoyles are on the outside of a building looking out, but these are inside."

"Don't they scare people?" she shuddered as she climbed the stairs after the others.

"Why would they scare people?" he asked. "Gargoyles are supposed to protect us from evil."

"Good to know." Although, Penny did not sound convinced as she kept staring up at the wooden carvings who stared right back.

13

PENNY

"How old is this stuff?" Milo reached the top of the stairs leading into the attic room and turned a full circle.

"Some of it is as old as the house." Logan wiped the dust off the top of a wooden picture frame. "It's accumulated over the years. We used to come up here when we were kids and sort through some of it, but mostly it's just sat up here gathering dust."

"There's so much history right here." Penny had no real past. Her mom had never spoken about her side of the family or their father's. Often, Penny would lie awake at night and wonder who her father was and what their life would be like if he were still alive. After her mom's death, Penny realized she would never know the answer to so many questions. Her mom had taken that knowledge to her grave.

Penny and Helena had sorted through their mom's possessions after she passed, but nothing there gave any answers either. There were a few scattered photos of Penny, Helena, and their mom on vacation here and there. But there were no photos of their mom and dad, none of her mom as a child. It was as if she'd left her life behind. But why? Penny would never get her answers.

"Can we come up here and look through it all?" Milo asked.

"I'd have to ask Valerie," Logan replied as he shifted a few boxes around and opened the lid of a large box containing boys' clothes. "But I'm sure she wouldn't mind."

"Most of it is probably junk." Rift pulled out an old wooden car with a piece of string attached to the front. "The bears used to fight over this, do you remember?"

"The bears?" Milo asked eagerly.

"Valerie adopted six boys altogether," Penny explained. "Two were twins, they are bear shifters."

"Cool." Milo wasn't interested in the hats and gloves that Logan pulled out of the box. Instead, he threaded his small body through the contents of the attic, heading for the stuff way over on the other side of the room.

"We should probably sort through all this and get rid of some of it." Rift lifted up a stuffed fox. "I hope this isn't a relative of someone in town."

Logan chuckled. "Ah, here we are. Boots. Hardly worn. Milo, do you want to come and try these on?"

"In a second," Milo replied as he ducked under something large and emerged on the other side.

"Milo, come back this way," Penny told him.

"Just a second." Milo's voice took on a dreamlike quality, as if he weren't paying any attention.

"Milo," Penny snapped. "We don't know what's back there."

"There's something..." He disappeared from view and panic bloomed in her chest. "Milo."

The sound of something rattling was followed by Milo's voice ringing out, "Coming."

Penny moved a couple of boxes out of the way and held

out her hands to her son. "You come when I call you. That's the deal, all right?"

"Sorry. I wanted to get this." He held up a chain with a small round pendant on the end.

"What is it?" Penny held out her hand and Milo dropped it into her palm.

"I don't know. I just knew it was there." Milo shrugged and then sat down on the dusty floor and tugged off his shoes.

"Try these on." Logan had one eye on Penny as he helped Milo pull on the boots and tie the laces. "There's a lot of junk up here, I expect it's just an old trinket."

"I expect so." Penny stared at it, her fingers tracing the crescent moon that was embedded within the circle. Unfamiliar symbols and runes decorated the outer rim of the pendant. "It looks familiar."

"Probably mass-produced," Rift said as he dusted off a top hat and put it on. "What do you think?"

"You look like the Mad Hatter from *Alice in Wonderland*," Milo remarked. "I like it. Maybe there's a pocket watch up here somewhere." He wriggled around while Logan tied the laces.

"Stand up, let's see if you can walk in them." Logan held out his hand and Milo slipped his small hand into his.

"They fit." Milo jumped up and down as if to prove they were okay.

"Walk a few steps in them," Penny had lost count of the times Milo would say something fit just because he wanted to get out of the store, only to get home and complain the item was too big or too small.

"They fit." He walked around the small space that wasn't cluttered with boxes and stored items.

"Try on these." Logan held out a warm hat with flaps that

covered Milo's ears and some gloves. "They were mine when I was about your age."

"A bit big, but they will keep me warm." Milo held up his hands and wriggled his fingers.

"We could look for something smaller." Logan was on his knees rummaging through the box once more.

"No, I like them. I like that they were yours." Milo smiled up at the big shifter with his most disarming smile and Logan smiled back.

"Then you can have them." He patted Milo lightly on the head. "They'll keep you warm when the snow comes."

"What shall I do with this?" Penny held up the pendant. Now that she had it in her hand, she didn't want to let it go. She certainly didn't want to put it back where it came from so it could be forgotten again.

"We can take it downstairs and ask Valerie about it when she gets home. I'm sure she wouldn't mind you keeping it." Logan held out his hand and she hesitated before she gave it to him. "She might be able to tell you why it seems so familiar."

"I expect Rift is right, it's some mass-produced trinket that you can find in a gift store." She held out her hand to Milo. If that were true, why did her son say it called to him? She shivered as she glanced over to the place where Milo had found the pendant.

"Ivan will be able to tell you if it's made of a precious metal or whether it's junk." Rift had taken off the top hat and put it back where he'd found it.

"Are you sure Valerie won't mind us removing it from the attic?" Penny had no wish to annoy the woman who was a mother to these men. If she was going to have a good life with Logan, she wanted them all to like her.

"No, she won't mind at all," Logan assured her.

"She often let us keep things we found up here," Rift explained.

"But you are her family, I am a stranger."

Rift snorted. "You are the daughter she has always wanted. If you had any idea how many times she told us to get out there and find a mate so that she didn't have to put up with six men on her own..."

"She loves us really," Logan said gruffly.

"Six boys," Penny muttered again. "Valerie must be a saint."

"She is anything but," Rift laughed as they descended the stairs.

Logan closed the attic door and locked it, placing the key on a small ledge to the left of the door before following them down the next flight of stairs. "Valerie takes no nonsense from anyone."

"But she will adore you and Milo," Rift added quickly. "She loves children."

"I can't wait to meet her." Penny glanced down at her son. "She might be able to give me some tips on taming young boys."

"Oh, she's good at taming the wild ones." Rift aimed his comment at Logan. "She had to housetrain some of my brothers."

Logan gave a low growl as they reached the bottom of the stairs. "Are you trying to start something?"

"Are you going to fight?" Milo asked excitedly. "I'd love to see a snow leopard and a white wolf fight."

"We're not allowed to fight each other here in the hotel or on the grounds," Rift told Milo. "Valerie made us promise and you should always keep a promise to your mom."

"Ah, pity," Milo grinned and put his hand on his stomach. "I'm hungry."

"You've only just had lunch," Penny reminded him.

"I'm a growing boy and I worked up an appetite playing with Rift." He cocked his head to one side and aimed a disarming smile at his mom. "Maybe just a small, sweet treat?"

"Let's see what's in the kitchen." Logan led them back to the kitchen which was clean and completely deserted.

Pity, Penny would like to have asked Ivan about the pendant. Logan still had it in his hand, and she itched to ask for it back. There was something about it, as if there was a connection between her and the talisman.

Talisman. Where had that come from? But the more she thought about it, the more she was convinced that's what it was.

"Ice cream, Penny?" Logan's voice cut through her thoughts.

"Yes. Please." She brought her focus back to the room and the ice-cold sweet dessert Logan made with ice cream and leftover brownies, plus a good squirt of chocolate sauce. But no matter how hard she tried to focus, she kept thinking of the talisman.

"Yummy." They stood in the kitchen and ate ice cream out of bowls, and slowly the hold the talisman had over her lessened. Was it some kind of magical trinket that was hidden in the attic for a reason?

"Okay, buddy," she said to Milo when he'd finished his dessert. "We should go up to our room and sort through our stuff." She switched her attention to Logan. "Is it all right if we keep the room, or do you want us to move?"

"Stay put for now," Logan said. "We don't need the room at present, but if things change, I'll help you move into Valerie's apartment." He put his hand up to stop her protests. "She won't mind, honestly."

"There's always Dario's place," Rift suggested. "I'm sure he won't mind if Penny and Milo use his house."

"Oh, no. I don't want to move into someone else's house unless they give the okay. We can stay in the room for tonight and tomorrow I can start making some inquiries as to finding something more permanent."

Logan took the bowls and went to the sink. "I'll ask around. See what we can come up with."

"I can do it on my own," she insisted.

"Or you could let Logan work on his people skills and find you a nice place to stay." Rift patted his brother on the back. "His people skills really do need some work."

"So, I'm a little rough around the edges." Logan washed up the dishes and left them to dry on the drainer.

"I like rough around the edges." Penny's words made her mate blush, she liked that he was rough around the edges and, she suspected, soft on the inside. He'd had a hard start in life, she couldn't imagine what it must be like to be torn away from your family and the people you love. Or animals you love.

"You two are made for each other," Rift sighed before he opened the door leading outside. "I will see you all later. I need to go for a run. Unless you want to join me, Logan?"

Logan stared out of the door, a look of longing on his face. "I can't. I have to check in with Sophie and then make sure everything is ready for the new guests arriving. They aren't due until seven this evening."

"There's no rest for the wicked." With that, Rift slipped out of the door and closed it behind him.

"We should go and let you get on with your work. Unless there is anything else you need me to do?"

"No, go get some rest."

"What time do you want me to start my shift?" Penny asked.

"Your shift?" Logan looked confused.

"Yes. I need to start sometime, so I figured why not this evening?"

"Okay." He didn't look too sure.

"And then tomorrow, I'll start asking around town for some other work. And I have to figure out about school for Milo." Milo made a face at the mention of school. "You do have schools here?"

"Yes, a normal high school, although there are extracurricular activities, depending on what you are."

"What you are?" Her eyes widened. "Oh."

"I don't need to go to school," Milo told his mom. "I can learn to run the hotel with Logan."

"If we're going to stay in Wishing Moon Bay, you need to go to school and I need to find a job to earn enough money for us to rent a place and eat. Okay?" She looked at them both sternly and they both nodded in agreement, even though neither of them was happy with the idea. "Good, I'm glad we have that settled. Now, let's leave Logan to his work and we'll go sort through our things."

With that, she took Milo upstairs, only to groan at the sight of all their belongings strewn across the room. Maybe she needed a nap first. But she didn't want to wake up to this mess and so she started work.

14

LOGAN

Logan didn't like the idea of his mate getting a job in town. He wanted to care for her and provide for her.

She needs to feel in control of her future, his wolf told him. Which means she needs to be independent. At least until you prove to her you're not just going to disappear into the mountains.

Why would she think I'd do that in the first place? Logan asked as he went to the drainer and picked up the dry bowls. He quickly put them away and wiped down the surfaces so that Ivan wouldn't know they'd been in his kitchen. *The guy is very territorial when it comes to his workspace.*

He's very territorial period, his wolf replied.

After double-checking that everything was in its place, Logan went out into the reception area where Sophie was working on the computer. "How is it all going?"

"Smoothly," she replied, her smile bright as she came around the reception desk and stood next to him with a clipboard in her hand. "These are the guests due in the next couple of days. And these are new bookings I've made for next month."

Logan ran his hand through his hair and took a small step to the right. Sophie had a habit of getting really close, which he often found disturbing, not in a good way.

She likes you, his wolf told him bluntly.

But we have a mate, Logan replied, taking another small step away. Sophie closed the space, her arm brushing against his.

What the heart wants, the heart wants, his wolf replied *unhelpfully.*

"That's a great job," Logan complimented Sophie on her work and then walked around her, heading for the stairs. "I'll just go check that everything is ready for the guests checking in tonight."

"Do you need a hand?" Sophie dashed back around the reception desk and then joined him at the bottom of the stairs. "I could do with stretching my legs. No one will miss me for ten minutes if you need help."

"No, I have everything absolutely under control," he assured her. "I'll just go." He pointed up the stairs. "And you stay." He pointed at the desk.

"I don't mind pitching in with anything that needs doing. I know you are trying to run the hotel with Valerie gone, but it's tough when you don't know the business as well as she does," Sophie purred.

"I lived here for years," he told her. "I might be rusty, but I know how to run the business."

"It's such a busy time of year. With the hotel full and the restaurant booked up, you must be shorthanded."

"Which is why Penny is going to help out. She's taking a shift tonight."

"Penny. The woman with the child who gatecrashed the town?" Sophie asked unkindly.

"I wouldn't say she gatecrashed the town, but yes, Penny." He took a deep breath. "She's my mate."

Sophie took a couple of steps back as if he'd struck her. "Your mate?"

"Yes." He smiled, knowing he was crushing her hopes if she truly was in love with him. But the sooner those hopes were crushed into the ground, the better. Sophie needed to know there was no future for them.

Are you sure she's got a crush on me? Logan asked his wolf.

Can't you tell by her reaction? his wolf answered. Right now if she had a Logan doll, she would be sticking pins in it.

"She just shows up in town, just like that, and she's your mate?" Sophie wasn't exactly happy about this news. His wolf was right, how had he missed it?

Because, lately, you go around with your head stuck in the mountains, without really taking notice of other people. His wolf's words cut deep.

"Yes. I never expected to find her. I always thought I'd live alone." He smiled at Sophie, wanting her to understand that even if Penny hadn't come to Wishing Moon Bay, he would never have made a life with her. The last thing he wanted to do was hurt her, but if he read her expression correctly, that's exactly what he'd done.

"Lucky you. Lucky her." Sophie's mouth turned down as she went back to the reception desk and started work.

"I'll go check the rooms." He pointed up the stairs, but she didn't even look up at him.

People person, his wolf said, mildly amused at the mess Logan had inadvertently made of things.

I don't do it on purpose, Logan told his wolf. It just happens. Sometimes I wonder if I'll ever truly get people, even after all these years I still can't find a way to make sense of people's emotions.

Fear settled in his chest as he went into room seven and checked that everything was ready for the new guests. The housekeeping staff had been into the room that morning and cleaned the room and put fresh bedding on the bed. There were mints on the pillows and complimentary coffee and tea on a dresser alongside a kettle and some cups. The room smelled fresh and clean and there wasn't a speck of dust on any of the surfaces. Going through to the adjoining bathroom, he found the same high level of cleanliness. Squeezing the towels, he was satisfied that they were fluffy with a fresh fragrance.

His wolf found the whole routine mildly amusing. *You really have learned a lot from Valerie.*

I never realized how much until I had to take over. But since we grew up here, following her around while she did her chores, it just kind of rubbed off.

But not her people skills, his wolf pointed out.

No one is perfect. Logan moved along to room eleven and did the same checks, and found the same results, the rooms were perfect.

Locking the doors, he went back down the hallway, hovering outside of room eight where his mate was rummaging through her luggage. As he stood outside her room, he was tempted to knock on the door, just so he could see her face. He took a step closer, his knuckles hovering over the door, but then he heard Milo laugh and she giggled along with her son, leaving Logan feeling as if he were on the outside looking in on a world he might never fully be a part of.

Of course, we'll be a part of it, his wolf replied. It's just going to take time.

What if I alienate Penny in the same way I seem to alienate other people?

Your brothers love you for who you are. Valerie loves you for who you are. There is no way fate would have gone to all the trouble of getting your mate here to Wishing Moon Bay if you two were not meant to be together. She'll understand because she has been an outsider herself. She gets you. Or she will get you. One day.

Thanks, I think. Logan went downstairs and headed straight for the kitchen where Ivan was already working on preparing his evening menu. "Ivan, can I ask you about something?"

"I knew you'd come to me for advice about your mate." He looked up from where he was gutting the fish he'd bought this morning from the market.

"I don't need advice about my mate," Logan retorted. "I wanted to ask you about this." He fished the pendant out of his pocket and dangled it on the chain in front of the dragon shifter.

"What is it?" Ivan went to the sink and washed his hands before he reached out to hold the chain.

"I was hoping you might tell me. Milo found it in the attic. He said he was drawn to it. We were trying to figure out if it's just a piece of junk or if it's something else. I couldn't decipher the symbols on it. They're nothing I've ever seen before." He let go of the chain as Ivan took hold of it.

"It's not junk." He weighed the pendant in his hand. "It's a precious metal but not one I've seen before." He leaned forward and sniffed the metal, licking his lips as if he were tasting it. "It's familiar. I recognize the smell."

"What about the runes, or symbols, whatever they are? Penny said she thought she'd seen it before, which made me think it was a common piece. You know, like the kind you find in cheap gift stores." Logan watched Ivan as he placed the pendant on the counter and then reached in a drawer for a flashlight.

"It's not junk. Definitely not mass-produced. That's not to say that there might not be cheap replicas out there." By out there the dragon shifter meant outside of Wishing Moon Bay. Often real pieces of jewelry from town were found and reproduced.

"Is it safe?"

Ivan looked up sharply. "Do you have any reason to believe it's *not* safe?"

"I don't know, after Penny held it, she had this strange look on her face. It was as if she really wanted it back. Really wanted it." Logan pressed his lips together into a thin line as he recalled the look in her eyes. "Then it passed."

"If Valerie was here, she might be able to tell you. Otherwise, I can take it home tonight and have a better look. Valerie gave me some books on symbols and runes to study, but I haven't had time to get around to them yet." He picked the pendant up and shined the light on it from different angles. "I think they are protection runes."

"Protection runes. What about the moon? Is that symbolic or just decorative?"

"If this is a talisman then it's all symbolic, each part of the pendant would have been put there for a reason." He handed it back to Logan, switched off the flashlight and put it back in the drawer. "If Milo was drawn to it and gave it to Penny, who thinks it's familiar, I would give it back to her." He took his phone from his pocket. "Hold it up, I'll take photos and see if I can match the symbols this evening. I could do with the practice. But if that fails, I'll contact Valerie and see if she has seen it before."

"You're certain it's nothing bad?" Logan was dubious about handing the pendent or talisman over to Penny without fully understanding what it was and what power it might hold.

"I can't answer that. Not for sure, but if Penny was drawn here to Wishing Moon Bay and Milo was drawn to the talisman, then there might be a reason for it." Ivan went back to gutting his fish. "Did Penny have any idea about any of this?"

"You mean the town and magic and shifters?" Logan shook his head. "Not that I know of. I'll ask her."

Ivan lifted his head and stared at the door. "You can ask her now, she's on her way down."

"Already?" Logan checked the time. "She's eager to work."

"She doesn't want you to think she's using you." Ivan smiled at his brother. "She's a good woman. You're a lucky man." He pointed his sharp knife at the talisman. "Which is why you should give her that."

"What do you mean?"

Ivan placed the knife down on the counter and looked squarely at Logan. "We don't know why she came here. A wrench in her engine? Do you think that was there just so that you could find your mate? Are you *that* special, Logan?"

Logan shook his head, not wanting to believe what his brother was insinuating. "You think there is something bigger happening here?"

"It could be." Ivan picked up his knife and went back to work. "If there is, I'd start with that warlock. You know, the one who keeps complaining."

"You think he did something to cause Penny to come here?" That didn't make sense to Logan, but that didn't mean it wasn't true. Wishing Moon Bay wasn't exactly known for making complete sense. How could it, when such strange and wondrous creatures lived here?

"I don't know. It could be. All I know is you need to start asking the right questions." Ivan went back to his fish, leaving Logan to go and meet Penny as she reached reception.

"Hi, Sophie." Penny was dressed in smart black pants and a white shirt as she greeted the receptionist.

Sophie raised her eyes from the computer screen but didn't answer. At least not until she saw Logan approaching. "Hello."

"Penny, do you want to come through to the dining room and I'll show you what to do?" Logan ushered his mate toward the restaurant, the talisman weighing heavy in his pocket. Should he give it to her or keep hold of it until Ivan had deciphered the symbols? If they had hidden meaning, they might protect Penny, and possibly Milo, from whatever might have drawn them to town.

"Are you okay?" Penny asked as the door closed behind them. They were alone in the deserted dining room, the restaurant didn't open for another half an hour. Just enough time to give his mate instructions as to how things worked in here. "Logan, did something happen?"

"I asked Ivan about the talisman."

"Oh." Her forehead creased as she studied his face. "What did he say?"

"He said it's made of a metal he's never seen before. Definitely not a piece of junk." He took the piece of jewelry from his pocket and held it out to Penny. "He is unsure what the symbols mean. He took a photo of it and said he'd try to figure them out tonight."

"He has no idea?"

"Not really. He can't tell if they are good or bad. He wondered if they were for protection and if they are, maybe you should have it." He offered her the pendant.

"Does he think I need protection?" she asked, and uncertainty flickered across her face as she stared at the talisman.

"He doesn't know." Logan licked his lips nervously. "He said it depends on why you are here."

"Here? In town?" she croaked.

"Yes, do you have any idea?"

"No. Other than the fact that I met you. Isn't that enough? Couldn't the road be visible to me because I was supposed to meet you?" Penny placed her hand on his chest and his heart beat so fast it drummed in his ears.

"What if it's not?"

"You think Milo and I are in danger?" She looked from side to side as if expecting someone to jump out at her.

"I don't know. But if anyone tries to harm you, they will have to come through me. And my brothers. Rift is with Milo now, he would never let anything happen to your son. And I'm here for you."

A small smile crept across her face. "Now that's something a girl doesn't hear every day." She forced herself to keep smiling. "In here, I have you and your brothers. Out there, I have no one to protect me. I think I'll take my chances with you."

He let out a pent-up breath. "I was worried you might leave."

"So was I," she admitted. "But I think I am safer here with my mate. Don't you?"

"Absolutely."

She stood on tiptoes and kissed his lips as if sealing her fate. Logan slipped his arm around her waist and pulled her close. He never wanted to let her go. Ever. He would lay down his life to defend her and Milo, against anyone and anything that might try to hurt her. As for the talisman, he slipped it back into his pocket. Maybe the white wolf shifter was the only talisman she needed.

15

PENNY

She'd kissed him. It had felt like the right thing to do and as their lips pressed together and his tongue explored her mouth, she knew it was the right thing. The connection between them seemed to grow stronger with each moment they spent together, with each touch, with each and every word they spoke.

Yes, there was a small nagging voice in her head that told her she didn't belong here. But the voice grew quieter until it was only a whisper.

"Am I the only one working?" Ivan stood in the doorway, his hands on his hips and a small smile on his face.

Logan pressed his lips to hers once more before they broke apart. "I was just explaining to Penny how the restaurant works."

"Most people convey that information with words," Ivan said drily.

"What do you need, Ivan?" Penny caught hold of Logan's hand and squeezed it lightly before she crossed the room to the dragon shifter.

"What I need is the tables laid and the wine glasses

brought out." He backed out as Penny and Logan followed. "Melanie, one of the servers, usually does it, but I haven't seen her. Did she call in sick?"

"Not as far as I know." Logan went to the reception desk and spoke to Sophie. "Has Mel called in sick this evening?"

Sophie's gaze flickered to Penny before she looked Logan squarely in the eye and said, "Yes. I told you earlier."

Logan's head jerked back. "No, you didn't give me the message."

"I did before you went upstairs and checked the rooms." Her forehead creased. "You don't remember?"

"No." He shook his head and opened his mouth to speak but then closed it again. "Thanks, Sophie."

"You're welcome." Her brow furrowed deeper as she looked at Ivan and shook her head.

"Did you forget?" Penny asked quietly as they went into the kitchen.

"She didn't tell me," Logan insisted.

"Are you sure you weren't too busy dreaming of kissing your mate to take in the information?" Ivan asked as he indicated the napkins on the counter. "These should have been in the restaurant ten minutes ago."

"We'll take them through." Logan opened the swinging door that led directly from the kitchen to the dining room. His expression was unreadable.

Penny picked up a box containing pristine white napkins and carried them through. "Do you want me to set them out on the tables?"

"Yes, please." Logan followed her through the doors, he started laying out the knives and forks into their correct place settings, working quickly while she followed him with the box of napkins.

"Did Sophie tell you? It's been a strange couple of days. Maybe you forgot." Although Logan didn't seem the kind of guy who would forget something that quickly, even if his mind was fixed on other things.

Logan looked up and shook his head. "No, I wouldn't forget something like that."

"Not even if you were preoccupied with thinking of your mate?" she teased but he wasn't in the mood for teasing.

"No, not even then." He set out the next table ready for diners and moved onto the next, his speed and accuracy incredible. Another unique shifter ability and one she would never match. How would she ever find a job in town if she were up against all these supernatural beings?

"What about the talisman?"

Logan stopped dead, his hand on his pocket where he'd put the talisman. "What do you mean?"

"You don't know what the talisman is for, right?"

"Yes." He went back to work but at a slower pace as he listened to her theory.

"What if the talisman is to blame?" She shrugged. "I thought I'd seen it before."

"Yes."

"Well, my mom was a bit of a mystery. Helena and I never knew who my dad was, and my mom never spoke about him or her life before Helena was born. Maybe she couldn't remember it."

"You think a similar talisman stole those memories? And this talisman stole my memory of Sophie telling me that Melanie was not coming to work this evening?" He shook his head firmly. "She didn't tell me."

"You would *think* that she didn't tell you but maybe she did, and you just don't remember." Her theory was not popular with Logan.

"No. That's not what happened." He glanced out of the main door toward where Sophie was working at her desk.

"That would mean that she lied. Why would Sophie lie?"

"Because I told her I had found my mate." A knife clattered against a fork as he dropped it down onto the table. With an exasperated sigh, he picked up the knife and put it in its place.

"Why would that news make Sophie lie?" Penny already had a good idea. It seemed that the emotional reactions of supernatural people were pretty much the same as for normal humans. "Oh! She likes you."

Logan finished the last place setting and straightened up. "So it seems."

"You didn't know?"

"No." He raked a hand through his hair and color tinged his cheeks. "Reading people and their emotions doesn't always come naturally to me. And I thought since she knew that I was a shifter she'd know I could never have romantic feelings for her. She knows about fated mates."

Penny gave a short laugh. "People don't think like that. Not where love is concerned. That's the beauty of it, we act irrationally."

"Shifters don't."

"Sophie isn't a shifter then, I guess." Penny gave the receptionist a sidelong glance. "What is she?"

"A witch. Some of her ancestors helped found the town, I believe. She's from old magic."

"Not the kind of person you would want to get on the wrong side of." Penny groaned inwardly. The last thing she needed was to get on the wrong side of anyone, let alone a powerful family with magic at their disposal.

"They would not approve of her lying." Logan waited for Penny to finish and they went to the kitchen together.

"Who is lying?" Ivan looked up from the stove where he was frying the fish before placing it on a baking sheet and smothering it in a light sauce. The fish was placed in the oven to warm.

"Sophie. She didn't tell me about Melanie not coming in this evening."

"Oh, you have drawn the wrath of a witch. Good luck with that." Ivan laughed. "She'll turn you into a frog or something."

"Why? I have never led her on in any way," Logan protested.

"Women do not always think clearly where their hearts are concerned." Ivan pointed his spatula at Penny. "Back me up on this."

"I am not getting involved in this debate." Penny held up her hands. "If you want, I can go talk to Sophie. See if I can clear the air."

"No!" Ivan and Logan chorused.

"She might turn you into a frog instead," Ivan told her.

"You're not serious?" Penny didn't know whether the two men were making fun or not as they kept their expressions deadly serious. This was not funny. "I have to think of Milo."

"Witches can't turn people into frogs. It's one of those things that they show on TV or it's written in a book. It's not real."

"I'm not sure if I believe you," Penny admitted. "Or if you're just telling me that so I don't worry."

"It's not a real thing," Ivan reassured her. "If it was then half of the town would be frogs by now."

"Okay. As long as you promise me it's made up." She aimed the question at Logan. "You said you couldn't lie."

Ivan's shoulders shook as he went back to preparing the evening meal.

"I can't lie. And I wasn't lying when I said witches can't turn you into a frog. Their magic is earth-based, it's meant for good. I'm sure Sophie wouldn't hurt you and she certainly wouldn't hurt Milo." He came to her and placed his hand on her arm. "We shouldn't have teased you."

She closed her eyes as she shook her head. "It's okay, I overreacted. This is all so new to me that I no longer know what to believe."

"Your world has been turned upside down." He brushed a stray strand of hair back from her face and tucked it behind her ear. "I promise from now on I won't tell you anything about this town and the people that live here that isn't true. I won't exaggerate or make it sound worse than it is."

"Thank you." She sniffed loudly. "I really do think if I went and spoke to Sophie, it might help to clear things up."

"Give her a couple of days to cool down. Witches are hot-headed, they like getting things their own way."

"Don't we all," Penny replied.

"The rest of my kitchen staff are arriving." Ivan lifted his head as if he were listening to something in the distance, which he probably was.

"We'll go through and finish setting up the tables. The first guests will be arriving shortly." He led the way back through the doors directly into the dining area. Together they made sure the chairs were arranged around the tables and the candles were all lit. As the sun set in the distance, Logan dimmed the lights and switched on strings of fairy lights that hung across the gazebo outside. It gave the restaurant an otherworldly feel. They were in another world, she reminded herself as the door opened and the first of the diners came in.

Logan turned to look, his shoulders sagging when he saw the warlock with the cold shower issue. "I've got this." Penny grabbed a menu and met the warlock at the door. "Good evening. A table for one?"

The guy studied her closely for a moment before he nodded. "A table for one. By the window."

"This way, please." She headed for a table next to the window, looking up briefly to check that it was okay to seat the guy there. Logan nodded on his way to meet the next diners. The restaurant had only just opened, and they began to fill up quickly. Another couple of servers arrived and helped organize the diners, while the warlock perused the menu.

"I'll have the soup, please. Followed by the steak. Which I would like medium-rare." He handed the menu back to Penny. "And I'll have a glass of champagne, I think."

She nodded and backed away. There was something about the guy that she didn't like. Something cold. She shivered and went to the kitchen to place his order then headed to the bar for a glass of champagne.

"Champagne?" Logan asked in surprise. He was at the bar waiting for a drink order.

"Yes, for your friend the warlock." She glanced at the guy who was staring out of the window. "Is that unusual?"

"He's been staying here for three nights and he hasn't ordered champagne before. I think he's only ordered water and never leaves a tip. The other servers avoid him if they can. He's cheap." Logan thanked the bartender for his drinks. "Keep a close eye on him."

"You think he's up to something?" Typical that the warlock should act up on her first shift at the hotel.

"Maybe, maybe not. People act out of character for all kinds of reasons. It could be that he's celebrating. We don't know why he's staying here, I think he's from out of town. Which means he might be here on business and the business ended well." Logan took his drinks and left her to mull over his words. Maybe the warlock had received good news and was celebrating.

"There you go, one glass of champagne." The bartender placed the glass on a small tray. "I'm Terry, by the way. You must be Penny, Logan's mate."

"I am." She picked up the tray carefully. "News certainly gets around, doesn't it?"

"It does. We're a tight-knit community and when someone new comes into town, we all hear about it. When that someone new turns out to be the fated mate of one of the townsfolk, people talk even more." Terry winked. "What can I get you?" he asked a couple who were waiting to be seated.

Nerves kicked in as she carried the tray across the dining room. Was she the talk of the town? Penny looked around at the people in the room, were they looking at her, talking about her? She switched her attention back to the warlock. At least that was one guy who was not taking any interest in her. Or was he?

As she moved across the room, she realized he was watching her reflection in the glass. With each step she took, his eyes followed. A shiver crept down her spine. Were all the people in Wishing Moon Bay creepy?

No, she knew the answer already. But Sophie's bizarre reaction to Penny being Logan's mate and now the warlock watching her reflection were downright odd.

"Here's your champagne." She set the glass down on the table and tucked the tray under her arm as she backed away. "I'll just go check on your order."

Turning on her heel, she hurried back to the kitchen, her heart thumping in her chest as an avalanche of questions beat a steady tempo in her head.

"Are you all right?" Logan asked as she nearly walked right past him.

"Yes, I'm fine." She flashed him a smile. "I'm trying to make a good impression on my boss."

"You already did," he replied smoothly.

"And I know you're telling me the truth because you promised." Penny kept on walking, not wanting to stop because she'd decided to keep the actions of the creepy warlock to herself. This was a new world, a strange world and for all she knew he was watching her because she was an anomaly, something that didn't necessarily belong in his world of magic. She would have to get used to people looking at her and talking about her until the next anomaly came along, and they always did. As long as she could keep Milo safe and no one was mean to him, she would wait it out. And if someone was mean to her son...she would put them straight.

"Soup." Ivan pointed to a bowl of steaming soup and she grabbed it and headed back out into the dining room. The smell of rosemary wafted up from the bowl, which was filled with a creamy orange soup which she guessed was some kind of squash. Her stomach rumbled and she wished she'd eaten before she came down to start her shift, but she'd been too nervous. She wanted this to go right, she certainly didn't want to cause more problems for Logan when he'd been so kind to her. Yes, she knew that was because they were mates but even so, he'd gone out of his way to help her and Milo.

"Here's your soup. Can I get you anything else?" She scanned the table to check there was a basket of fresh bread rolls. There was. Everything looked fine.

"No, this is perfect." He picked up his champagne glass and raised it to her. "Everything is just perfect." He sipped his bubbly and smiled as she nodded and turned away. Heading back toward the restaurant door where Logan was greeting more diners, she could not resist a glance in the window to check out the warlock's reflection. Was he still watching her?

Penny stopped dead in her tracks and spun around on her heel. In two strides, she was back at the warlock's table. He squeaked as she leaned forward and grabbed the bowl of soup. "Sorry, this wasn't your order." She looked him straight in the eye with a glare saved for when Milo had been naughty, which was so rare she couldn't recall the last time she'd had to use it. The warlock jerked backward as if she'd struck him. "I'll go get your proper order."

"Wait!" He held up his hand. "That was my soup."

Penny kept walking toward the kitchen, aware that everyone was staring after the new girl in town. This time, for good reason, she had drawn far too much attention to herself.

16

LOGAN

"What are you doing?" Logan was by her side before she made it back through the doors leading to the kitchen.

"I gave the wrong order to the warlock." She grabbed a napkin off the counter as she reached the kitchen and draped it over the bowl of soup.

Ivan looked up from the pot he was stirring on the stove. "What's wrong?"

"Nothing." She headed toward the door leading outside, dodging past a couple of stunned kitchen staff.

"Penny." Logan was at her elbow as she burst out of the kitchen door and into the cold evening air. "What are you doing?"

"I'd like to know the same thing." Ivan was in the doorway, a wooden spoon still in hand.

"There was a problem with the soup." She didn't turn around as she opened the nearest trash can.

"There was no problem with the soup when it left my kitchen," Ivan protested.

"It was my fault." She lifted the bowl of soup but before she had a chance to dump it in the trash can, Logan caught hold of her arm.

"Let me see."

"No," she ground out.

"Penny. Whatever it is, I need to see." Logan gently took the covered soup bowl from her hand.

Reaching forward, Ivan plucked the napkin off and sucked in a breath. "How did that get in there?"

Penny pressed her lips together. She didn't want to tell them. Was she covering for someone?

No, his wolf replied. She's trying to keep the situation calm. She's trying to keep Ivan calm.

"The warlock." He grabbed hold of Ivan as the dragon shifter's eyes burned a deep orange. "No, this is what he wants. He must know what you are, it's no secret and he wants you to shift and cause trouble. You know how warlocks feel about dragons."

"I'm going to tear his head off and spit it out so he can watch me feast on his bones." Ivan grabbed hold of Logan's wrist and twisted it in an attempt to get him to let go.

"No. Valerie entrusted us to run the hotel and I'm not going to let you destroy everything. Calm down." Logan grabbed hold of Ivan's shoulder with his free hand. "I'll deal with this."

"It's *my* reputation he tried to ruin," Ivan spat but his eyes had returned to their normal brown, the danger of him shifting uncontrollably had passed.

"Penny took the soup before he had a chance to shout about it." Logan let go of Ivan. "We'll take him a fresh bowl of soup and I won't take my eyes off him while he eats it. I swear."

"I'll do it," Penny said. "I'll take him his soup and watch

him eat it. You are needed to keep the restaurant running. I have the least experience." Her hand fluttered in the air and she looked visibly shaken. "With any of this."

Logan's hands tightened into fists as he fought to control his temper. "I'll keep close, if he tries anything, I'll rip his head from his shoulders with my bare hands."

"No, you won't." Penny grabbed hold of his arm and he relaxed his hands. "I need you alive and in one piece and certainly not in jail." Her expression clouded. "You do have a jail here, don't you?"

"Yeah, a magical jail that's impossible even for warlocks to escape from. And that is exactly where that guy belongs." Ivan went back inside and grabbed a bowl. Plonking it down on the counter, he poured in some of the soup and added a sprig of rosemary. "There. If he tries anything, he'll be wishing he'd never come to town."

"That's not exactly what I thought anyone would ever wish for when they came to Wishing Moon Bay, but that guy might be the first." Penny, her face stony, picked up the bowl and left the kitchen, with Logan close behind her.

He hovered around the doorway as his mate took the soup bowl to the warlock and set it down.

"Do you know how long I've been waiting to be served?" the warlock asked.

"Yes." Penny smiled sweetly. "If you'd like to make a complaint, I can take you to the chef. I'm sure he would like to deal with you *personally*." She locked eyes with the warlock, and he shrank back. "Enjoy your soup."

The guy picked up his spoon but before he took a mouthful, he cast a questioning look at Penny. "Thank you."

"You're welcome." She took a small step back but continued to stare at him.

"I'll call you if I need you."

"I'll be right here making sure you enjoy your meal." She smiled sweetly as she watched him.

"You're enough to give a man indigestion," he complained.

"I want to make sure you don't add anything to your soup that might ruin the flavor."

Logan moved away from the door and began seating new diners and taking payments from those who had already eaten and were waiting to leave. Infusing himself with the same sweet tone Penny used on the warlock, he channeled his inner people person as he apologized for the delay. He didn't go as far as offering free drinks, but no one seemed to complain too loudly about being kept waiting, the promise of Ivan's menu was enough to keep them happy.

As he worked, he watched Penny to make sure the warlock didn't try anything else. She watched as he ate each mouthful of his soup and then removed the empty bowl, returning with his perfectly cooked steak. Standing on guard, she watched him cut and eat each morsel before swilling it down with the last of his champagne.

Maybe he'd bought the champagne to congratulate himself prematurely on his success with the soup. He might have thought you would at least give him dinner on the house. Or maybe he's here to ruin the reputation of the hotel and restaurant. So many questions.

Perhaps we should ask him later tonight. His wolf sharpened his claws. *I am good at making people talk.*

We can't touch him, Logan told his wolf firmly. *If anything happens to him and Penny thinks we were behind it, we might scare her off. We need to watch him very carefully until we figure out exactly what he's up to.*

I suppose you are right. His wolf grumbled to himself, not sounding very convinced as he took himself off to a corner of Logan's mind.

The evening wore on, the warlock finished his meal and left the restaurant. Despite Sophie's feelings toward Logan, he went to reception and got her to ensure that the check was added to his bill. Logan also instructed Sophie to call him if, when the guy checked out of his room, he quibbled over any of the charges. Warlock or no warlock, the guy was not going to wriggle out of anything.

"I'll add a note," Sophie said. "Just in case I am not here when he checks out."

"Thanks, Sophie." He smiled as he would normally smile and then left her scowling behind his back. There was nothing he could do to placate her, and he figured she would get over it.

I still don't know why she thought we would be together, his wolf said. She knows we are a shifter. She knows we would only ever settle down with our mate.

Perhaps she was going to slip us a love potion or something. His hand went to the talisman in his pocket. What if the talisman did make people forget? Would he forget his mate if he kept hold of it?

Will Penny forget us if we give it to her? His wolf gave a low growl. What if someone gives Penny a potion that makes her forget us?

Logan shook off his doubts. That way of thinking would only lead to madness. And he did not need that kind of a complication right now.

"I don't think I'll ever eat steak again." Penny met him as he returned to the restaurant dining room which was full of happy diners eating the delicious meals cooked by Ivan.

"You watched him chew every bite. I doubt he'll ever eat steak again without thinking of you." Logan grinned. "Maybe you can watch me eat."

"Don't you think about me all the time anyway?" she asked with a disarming smile.

"I do. I especially think about your lips." His eyes lingered on them and he leaned forward, wanting more than anything to taste her once more.

"Down, boy." She placed her hand on his chest. "If you don't stop drooling, you might put people off their food and then it'll be your head Ivan chews off."

"You have a point." He turned and looked toward the door leading from the reception area. "Rift is coming down with Milo. Do you want to take a break and sit down to eat with them?"

Penny glanced toward the door. "I'd love to." She patted his arm. "I'd also love to have shifter senses."

"You sound like Milo." Logan headed for the door to meet his brother and Milo. "Take an hour off and spend time with your son."

"I wish you could join us."

"Maybe tomorrow. For lunch? I could ask Ivan to pack us a picnic."

"Or I could make us a picnic. If Ivan doesn't mind me using his kitchen."

"Who wants to use the kitchen?" Rift asked as he entered the restaurant with Milo holding his hand.

"I do." Penny held out her arms to Milo and he pulled away from Rift and ran to her. "Did you have fun?"

"Yes, we watched TV and played with some of my action figures." Milo held his mom close. He'd obviously missed her but looked happy. Rift was getting to know Milo well which caused a twinge of jealousy in Logan. Would he ever find time to bond with the boy he hoped to raise as his own?

"Thanks, Rift. I appreciate you watching Milo." They headed toward one of the tables which had just become free.

"I enjoy it. I'd forgotten how much fun being a kid is." Rift held out a chair for Penny to sit down. She still held Milo who sat on her lap while Logan fetched menus.

"I'll come and take your order when you're ready." Logan handed out the menus. "What can I get you to drink?"

"You're busy enough," Penny told him. "I'll fetch the drinks and take our order to the kitchen. You go deal with your customers."

Logan hesitated. If he insisted on serving them himself, he'd at least get to come back and talk to them and check if they were all right. The warlock's earlier behavior had freaked him out just a little. He hated not knowing what the guy's intention was. Perhaps he was purely trying to get a free meal and cause trouble for Logan because of the issue with the cold shower. Or perhaps it was more sinister.

He shivered. Something didn't feel right. His hand unconsciously went to the talisman in his pocket. Was this the source of all the problems?

"If you're sure." He backed away, suddenly feeling the need to talk to Ivan.

"Of course." Penny's smile lightened his mood, she was such a beautiful woman with a beautiful heart. She deserved to be happy.

We all deserve to be happy. But his wolf agreed there was something in the air and he didn't just mean the snow.

"Logan, how are things looking out there?" Ivan asked as he entered the kitchen. "We're running at full capacity here. I'm going to need extra staff if things don't slow down."

"I'll talk to Valerie in the next couple of days. I can't really hire anyone new without her say so. And if Melanie is back at work tomorrow, we should cope. Especially if Penny doesn't have to watch over the warlock again."

"You had to mention his name!" Ivan's eyes flashed bright but only for a moment, he was too focused on getting the next meals plated and out of his kitchen.

Logan watched his brother work, he truly was a master at his trade. Being a chef was not something the dragon shifters were well known for. Usually, they caught their food and ate it raw or burnt and crispy after dousing it with dragon fire. But Ivan had a flair for cooking, it was his passion. As he delicately placed the garnish on his dish and nodded to the server to take it out to the restaurant, Logan asked, "Does something feel wrong to you?"

Ivan wiped his hands on a towel and studied Logan for a long moment. "Why do you ask?"

He rubbed his hand over his chin and glanced toward reception. "I don't know, I can't put my finger on it exactly."

"Maybe I can help."

"So you do think something is wrong?"

Ivan came around the counter and placed his hand on his brother's shoulder. "Here's what I think is happening."

Logan swallowed down the lump in his throat as panic flared in his heart. Something was coming, he could feel it in his bones.

"After so long, you have just met your mate, and she has a son. It's going to knock you off balance. It's only natural."

"Off balance." His finger closed around the talisman in his pocket. "I don't think that's what I can sense. It's something more."

Ivan let go of Ivan and went back to work. "Try to relax."

"That's your advice?" The hairs on the back of Logan's neck stood on end. His mate was about to enter the kitchen and he didn't want her to overhear their conversation.

"That's my advice for now." Ivan let his calm expression slip for a moment. "It might be different when I've deciphered those symbols. I'm guessing this has got something to do with the talisman burning a hole in your pocket."

"Maybe. But I think it's more than that. Something is coming." And he didn't just mean his mate. But as she entered the kitchen, he tried to take Ivan's advice and relax.

Not easy when Penny was close by and all he wanted to do was claim her as his mate. Mark her with his scent so no other man would dare touch her.

17

PENNY

The winter sun rose in the sky as Penny lay curled up under the covers with Milo sleeping peacefully beside her. She really needed to get up and get dressed before going downstairs to fetch them breakfast. But she couldn't move. It wasn't just that every time she stuck her foot out of bed, the cold air chilled her toes. It was more than that.

She turned away from the window and its muted light and stared up at the ceiling. The chill in her bones had nothing to do with the cool air and everything to do with her decision to stay here. She'd gotten caught up in a dream where a man who was a stranger to her told her he loved her and they were meant to be together forever and she'd bought into it because he'd offered her what she wanted. What she thought she needed.

But Wishing Moon Bay wasn't her home and after last night, Penny feared they might not be safe here. There was so much they didn't understand about this new town and the people in it.

"It's me." Logan's voice accompanied a knock on the door.

Finally pushing her foot out of bed and all the way to the

floor, she slid out of bed and shivered as she pulled on a robe. Tying a knot in the belt, she padded to the door on cold feet and opened it. "I was going to come down."

"I was coming up to check on the new guests and figured I might as well bring you breakfast." He held up the tray filled with eggs and bacon and some delicious oatmeal flavored with cinnamon as proof.

"Come in." She stood back and he entered the room, his eyes lingering on the bed where Milo stirred himself from his dreams.

"I didn't realize Milo would still be asleep." He walked silently to the small table and set the tray down without making a sound.

"Rift tired him out yesterday. All that fresh air and wrestling." A small smile crossed her lips. Now that Logan was here, her fears for their future evaporated. The wolf shifter had sworn to protect her, and she believed him with all her heart.

"I'll go." He pointed at the door and moved silently toward it.

"Logan." Milo sat upright in bed and sniffed the air. "You brought breakfast."

"I did." He hovered halfway between the door and the bed, unsure as to whether he should leave.

"Do you have time to sit down and eat with us? Or maybe just have a cup of coffee?" Penny placed her hand on his elbow and ushered him toward the table where the aroma of the food drifted up, making her mouth water.

"I have a couple of chores to do and then I thought I could show you around town. We never got to see much that first day."

"No, the dolphin and the shifting and the...everything." She waved her hands around her head. "Kind of killed the tour."

"I figured I should show you around before the whole town is covered in snow." Logan went to the window and pulled the drapes open wide.

Penny lifted her hand and shaded her eyes as if she were a vampire who couldn't bear sunlight. "Those are heavy snow clouds." When her eyes were accustomed to the light, she dodged around him and went to the window, placing her hands on the sill. "Is that snow in the mountains?"

"Yes, it snowed there last night. The peaks will remain white for the rest of the winter. They always do after the first heavy snowfall of winter."

"And you would be up there?" She briefly looked at him over her shoulder.

He nodded. "I have a lot of cold-weather gear in my cabin. There's always a good supply of wood for the fire which I've built up over the summer." He put his hand in his pocket and took out his phone. "Do you want to see some photos?"

"Yes, please." Milo shuffled down the bed but kept the covers wrapped around him.

"Why don't you put some socks and slippers on and your robe? You can perch on the end of the bed and eat while you look at Logan's cabin." She nodded toward the chairs around the table and Logan sat down.

While Milo put on some warm clothes and moved down to the end of the bed, Penny poured the coffee and dished up the food. "Do you want some?"

"No, thanks. I've already eaten two portions this morning. Ivan always makes too much." He accepted the coffee, though, and sat back in the seat, looking too big for it.

"When can we go to the beach?" Milo asked. "I'd like to see the dolphin again."

"They are not too common around here," Logan told him.

"Especially not at this time of the year. You were lucky to see that one yesterday."

"Or unlucky," Penny said drily. "If that guy hadn't emerged from the water and shifted, we would never have known your secret."

"I would have told you. Although, I probably would have waited a little longer."

"It freaked Mom out," Milo told the wolf shifter.

"It wasn't the kind of thing you expect to see," Penny grumbled.

"What other kinds of animals are there?" Milo asked. "Do shifters turn into anything they want? Like a massive spider?"

"Mostly mammals. And mostly carnivores. Wolves, bears, and big cats are the most common."

"What about dragons?" Milo spread out his arms as if they were wings and pretended to swoop down on a piece of bacon which he picked up with his fingers and popped into his mouth.

"Dragons are rare, they mostly live on an island a few hundred miles across the ocean."

"They do?" Penny covered her mouth as she coughed.

"Yes, they don't like mixing with the rest of us. They see us as lower beings in their grand order of things."

"What about Ivan?"

"What about Ivan?" Logan asked.

"He's not like that," Milo said.

"He doesn't think like them. Probably because he wasn't raised by dragons, he was raised by Valerie." Logan drank his coffee and eyed up some of the eggs.

"Help yourself."

"No, honestly, I'm fine." Logan switched his attention to the weather outside. "We'll need to wrap up warm."

"It's certainly chilly." She shivered and wished he'd put his warm arms around her. Failing that, she'd love to dive back under the bedcovers. "I was going to ask Ivan if I could make a picnic for us, but I think we should take a raincheck on that. Maybe in the summer when the weather is warmer. The weather does get warmer, doesn't it?"

"Yes, in the summer months, it's hot here and there's nothing better than taking a swim in the ocean." He glanced toward Milo. "You might even get to swim with dolphins."

"Amazing."

Penny was making plans about their future in Wishing Moon Bay. Even though deep down she still sensed there was a threat, a danger, lurking just beyond her vision, there was nothing to say that threat might follow them if they left town. Or maybe the threat was waiting outside of town, waiting for her to leave.

"Are you all right?" Logan placed his warm hand over hers. She'd been tapping her fork against her plate.

"Sorry. I was miles away." She dug into her eggs and bacon while Milo sampled the oatmeal. "Is it good?"

"Yummy." Milo spooned the creamy mixture into his mouth, the color returning to his cheeks as he slowly woke up.

"I should go get on with the rest of my chores while you finish eating. I'll meet you downstairs in the reception area when you're ready." Logan placed his coffee cup down on the table and got up.

"Do you want me to text you or something, so you know we're waiting?" She moved her thumbs as if she were typing out a text message on an invisible phone.

"No, I'll know when you are there." He grinned as he opened the door and stepped outside into the corridor.

"Of course you will." Penny picked up the second bowl of oatmeal and tried it. "This is good."

"Can we live in the hotel forever?" Milo asked.

"No, we have to find somewhere of our own to live." She tilted her head to one side. "Why?"

"Ivan is a better cook than you." Milo looked up as she gasped in shock. "I love your cooking, but Ivan is better."

"I know he is. And maybe we can eat here some of the time. But we need our own space, and I don't want to live in a hotel room for the rest of my life, do you?"

"What about the apartment where Logan lives? Can't we live there with him since you are mates?"

She nearly choked on her oatmeal and took a drink of coffee to clear her throat. "Firstly, the apartment belongs to Valerie who owns the hotel. She'll be moving back here, I expect, once she's better."

"Where will Logan live then? With us?" Milo's questions were innocent enough, but she wondered where he'd gotten this from.

"Secondly, we have to get to know Logan and everyone else in town. Slowly."

"But Rift said that you two were fated mates and that you were meant to be together. He thinks that's why the car broke down and why we found the road leading to town." Milo placed his empty bowl on the table. "I like Rift. He would be my uncle if you married Logan."

"I think Rift likes to talk too much. Some things are not meant for your ears. Not until you are older."

"Oh, he wasn't talking to me." Milo gave her one of his mischievous grins. "He was talking to Valerie on the phone while he thought I was asleep."

"You were eavesdropping while pretending to be asleep." Penny got up from her chair and came around the table. "Do you know what happens to little boys who listen to conversations they are not meant to hear?"

Milo giggled and scooted back on the bed. "They get tickled?"

"They get tickled." She pounced on the bed and tickled her son's tummy and under his arms until he giggled so hard, she thought he might be sick. It was her favorite sound. Children should laugh and play, and not get bogged down with the worries of the grownups around them. She'd have to tell Rift to be more careful when he was talking about shifters and mates and all the other crazy things that might happen in Wishing Moon Bay. "Come on, buddy. Let's get dressed. Why don't you wear the warm clothes we got from the attic? I washed them and dried them for you last night. They smell pretty good now."

"Okay." Milo hugged her before he jumped off the bed and ran to the bathroom.

"Make sure you brush your teeth."

"I will." He closed the door behind him, and Penny went to the window to look out at their new hometown. Their room looked across to the bay where the heavy gray sky seemed to sink into the ocean which was equally as gray. The snow was there, ominous and threatening.

Yet when it fell, it would cover everything in pristine whiteness. She'd have to ask Logan if there was a sled Milo could borrow. They could hike over to the lower slopes of the mountains and sled down them. Perhaps his wolf would pull the sled to the top. The wolf they'd seen was so white he'd be camouflaged in the snow. She reached out her hand and touched the cold glass, turning her head from side to side. She was wrong, it wasn't the snow clouds that were ominous and threatening, it was something else entirely.

The sense that she should pack up all their belongings and leave town settled on her shoulders once more. But she wasn't about to give up the promise of her new life. She wasn't going to be chased out of town. She'd been running when she arrived here, she was not going to run again.

18

LOGAN

Logan whistled a happy tune as he went back downstairs, and as he crossed the reception area, Sophie came out from behind her desk with a gift bag in her hand. "Logan."

"Yes." The tune died on his lips as he stopped in his tracks and faced the receptionist. "How are you doing today?"

Sophie looked up at him through her eyelashes which she batted against her cheeks. Her makeup was perfect, as always, her lashes thick and luxurious, but they didn't hide the dark pools of her eyes. Logan shivered as she smiled brightly and handed him the small bag. "I wanted to say sorry for...overreacting."

"Overreacting," he repeated, unsure of what answer to give. "That's okay." He accepted the gift. "You didn't have to get me anything. There's nothing to be sorry for."

"Oh, I think there is." There were those eyelashes again. Sophie smiled demurely. "I made a mistake. You have been so kind to me since I started working here and I repaid you by having a hissy fit because you found your mate. I should be happy for you. Supportive even. Instead, I was rude." She pointed at the gift bag. "I hope you enjoy it, I know you like scotch whiskey."

"I do." He raised the bag an inch or two and smiled. Awkwardly. Because the whole thing was just that...awkward. Sophie was acting kind of creepy.

That's the effect you have on most people, his wolf reminded him with a wolfish snigger.

"Anyway, think of it as an apology gift." She inclined her head slightly. "I am sorry."

"Apology accepted." He backed away toward the kitchen and Sophie went back to her desk.

"Oh, one more thing."

"Yes." Logan was about to turn around and get out of there as fast as possible, but her words stalled his exit.

"Room one."

"What's wrong with that guy now?" Logan sighed, his plan to take Penny and Milo down to the beach fading away.

"Nothing. As in, I think he's gone."

"Gone." Logan's voice rose as he strode back to the desk. "Has he paid his bill?"

"No, but his car was gone when I came into work this morning and the key was here. I went and knocked on the door but there was no answer, and no one has seen him at breakfast this morning."

"He could just have gone out early this morning." Logan ducked his head and looked out of the window at the sky and its threat of snow.

"He might have." She took the key down from the hook behind her and slid it across the desk. "Don't you think you should go and have a look?"

He reached for the key and closed his fingers around it. There was no harm in looking. If Jeremy Barnes came back,

Logan would simply say that he'd gone in to check the shower. "I'll go now."

"I would. After last night in the restaurant...and then you asked me to make sure he doesn't haggle for a discount on the bill... Well...it makes me think he was hoping the issue with his soup might have meant you waived his bill. You know how some people are." Sophie smiled sympathetically. "Do you want me to come with you?"

"No." He shook his head and turned away. "I can manage on my own."

"As you *wish*." She emphasized the word as he headed up the first flight of stairs to the room occupied by the warlock.

Or unoccupied, his wolf remarked as Logan opened the door to reveal an empty room.

"Son of a..." Logan left the word hanging as he stepped inside the room. There was no sign that the warlock had ever been here. The room was completely bare. After a quick look around, he went back out and locked the door behind him.

"Was I right?" Sophie watched him as he came down the stairs, those dark eyes mesmerizing as he reached the solid wooden desk.

"You were." He placed the key on the desk and sighed. "Do we have his credit card details on file?"

"We do, I'll hit him with the charge right now." She tapped on the computer as Logan cursed under his breath. "You look as if you need a drink." She nodded toward the gift bag in his hand.

"It's way too early in the day for alcohol," Logan told her.

"Are you sure? You do look as if you need to calm down. Why not just take a sip?"

"I can't. I am taking Penny and Milo to the beach as soon as I'm finished here. Ivan and Rift are going to manage things for a few hours."

"One sip won't hurt. I'd love to know what you think of

the scotch I chose." She leaned over the desk, her eyes fixed on his, but Logan was immune to her charms and pulled away.

"Could you check those credit card details for me, please?" He tapped the palm of his hand on the desk and she straightened up, her forehead creased.

"Sure, I'll get right on it." She straightened up but as he walked away, Logan could swear he heard her foot stamp on the floor.

Perhaps she's not as over us as she said, his wolf rolled his eyes in wonder.

"Logan. I thought you were going out for the morning with Penny." Rift was in the kitchen talking with Ivan as he approached.

"I was. I am." He sighed and held up the small gift bag from Sophie. "Sophie gave me this." He set it down at the back of the counter.

"A make-up gift?" Ivan asked all wide-eyed and innocent while Rift chuckled.

"She did apologize for the way she behaved." He raked a hand through his hair and decided to leave it at that. Hopefully, if he just continued as normal, she would get over him and move on.

"It's good that you two have cleared the air." Ivan nodded toward a small basket on the counter. "I made you guys a picnic."

"The weather is freezing, you can't picnic outside," Rift said. "Penny and Milo will catch cold."

"I was thinking you could go sit in one of the caves in the cliff face. The tide is low enough for you to reach them with ease and you could light a fire. There are usually stacks of driftwood in the caves." Ivan waved a knife at the basket. "There are hot drinks in there, too."

"You would make someone a proper housewife," Rift joked as he lifted the lid on the basket and peeked inside.

"Don't ever make fun of a dragon with a knife in his hand," Logan warned as Ivan prowled toward the snow leopard.

"I wasn't making fun." Rift let the lid of the basket fall back into place and raised his hands as he backed away from Ivan. "I mean it, a woman would be lucky to have you as their mate."

Ivan's shoulders sagged as he went back to chopping up onions. "I don't know if I'll ever get the chance to find out. I doubt more than one of us is lucky enough to have their mate just drive into town. We're going to have to face it, the rest of us are likely to be single for the rest of our lives."

"Ouch!" Rift clutched at his heart. "You don't need a sharp knife to wound me."

"Come on, guys, I need you to focus. The real news is that the warlock has up and left the hotel." This part of Logan's news was met with surprise.

"He's gone?" Ivan paused chopping the onions, which never made him cry.

"Yes, I went up and checked, the room is empty. Sophie is trying to charge his credit card for the bill. But the chances are it won't go through."

"Wow, he came here and caused trouble, and now he's gone." Ivan waved his knife at Logan. "You didn't have anything to do with his disappearance, did you? You know the two of you never hit it off, all those issues with the shower."

"Me, it was you who wanted to rip his head off last night when he put a mouse in the soup. Only Penny's quick thinking stopped him from making a scene. Remember?" Logan nodded at Ivan. "Did you wait for him to leave the hotel and then swoop down and carry him off into the mountains? You could have just dumped him somewhere and left him to freeze."

"Now you put ideas in my head." Ivan tutted. "But no, it wasn't me. Even if I do wish I'd done that."

"You need to get more inventive with your dragon. He could so get rid of anyone we don't like. Or even just for a time out." Rift nodded. "Are you sure you didn't take care of the warlock? You could just be lying to us. It wouldn't take you long to fly to the mountains and back."

"No, it wasn't me." Ivan wiped his hands and then put his hand in his pocket and pulled out a piece of paper. "Because I was at home last night studying the symbols on that talisman Milo found. I figured it might be important."

"And is it?" Logan unfolded the piece of paper and smoothed it out on the counter. Rift peered over his shoulder as Logan tried to decipher his brother's handwriting.

"I couldn't decipher all the symbols and there are runes carved into the metal that are older than the dragons. But from what I can tell, it is a protection talisman. It disperses magic. So if anyone tried to cast a spell on you or tries anything of a magical persuasion, that will render the spell harmless. Not a bad thing when you're a normal human surrounded by supernatural beings." Ivan was deadly serious as he spoke about the talisman.

"You think it was meant for Penny?" Rift asked.

"That's a question I can't answer," Ivan replied. "Milo found the talisman and he gave it to Penny. But then Penny gave it to you."

"So the talisman could have been meant for any of us." Logan put his hand in his pocket and took out the metal pendant. "I don't see how it was meant for me. I've lived here most of my life and I've survived without protection."

"Things change, people change, and threats change," Rift

said evasively. "Perhaps you are supposed to wear it now so that you can protect your mate and her child."

"I can take a stroll down to the library when you get back this afternoon. I might find some books that contain drawings of the runes." Ivan glanced at the clock and got back to chopping his onions. "You should hold onto it for now. Unless something compels you to give it to Milo or Penny."

"Yeah, Logan, never ignore a good compulsion." Rift picked up the picnic basket and handed it over. "Now, go and enjoy a couple of hours with that adorable new family of yours and let us worry about everything here."

"Okay. As long as you're sure. I have my cell phone with me in case you need to call. Please, don't break anything." He aimed the last sentence at Rift as he backed toward the door leading into the reception. He could sense Penny and Milo coming down the stairs and he didn't want them lingering for too long around Sophie. Despite her apology, he didn't feel ready to trust her with his mate.

"It'll all be okay. Honestly." Rift pushed him toward the door. "Now go."

Logan went. He reached the reception area just as Penny and Milo got to the bottom of the stairs. "Hi, Ivan made us a picnic. He suggested we go to the beach and make a fire in one of the caves to keep us warm." Not that Logan would feel the cold. His hot shifter blood was on fire with his mate so close.

"Yes!" Milo jumped in the air.

"I guess that's your answer." Penny stroked Milo's head. "Ivan is so kind to us."

"Or he didn't want you messing up his kitchen," Milo said.

"Let's stick with him being kind." Logan took a sidelong glance at Sophie, but she was busy working on her computer. "This way."

They left the hotel, Penny and Milo by his side as they crossed the parking lot to his truck. When they were safely inside, he took a quick look around, his eyes scanning the immediate area for danger. There was nothing there, yet as he looked up toward the clouds and their promise of snow, he had the uneasy feeling the clouds were not the only thing brooding in Wishing Moon Bay.

19

PENNY

"Have I ever been on a winter picnic?" Milo asked as they parked at the beach and climbed out of the truck.

"No, and neither have I." She wrapped his scarf around his neck a couple of times and tied it in a knot. "People usually picnic in the summer, not in the winter."

"It's not too cold." Logan was dressed in a waterproof jacket, but he didn't wear a hat or gloves.

"You are a hot-blooded shifter, you don't feel the cold the same as we do." She pulled Milo's hat down firmly on his head. "Keep it on."

"I will." He put his arms out by his sides and twirled around and around like a spinning top. "Can I go down to the beach?"

"Yes, but not too far and stay away from the ocean. It's freezing out there."

"I wanted to go look for dolphins and mermaids." Milo ran down the steps and raced across the sand.

"I was going to tell him there are no such things as

mermaids." She shot Logan a questioning look, but he smiled in reply. "That's what I thought."

"We don't see them in town too often. Mainly in the summer, for most of the year, they keep to themselves."

"How do they?" She screwed up her face. "Do they flop up the road like a fish out of water?"

"No, they kind of shift, their tails change into legs and they walk like a human." Logan chuckled as he saw her expression. "I guess it all sounds strange."

"There's just so much about the town that's different than the world I'm used to." She turned around and looked at the houses and buildings. "Yet from here it looks like any other coastal town. The same kind of stores you would find anywhere."

"We're not so dissimilar. And once you get used to us, we're not that strange." His voice held a note of hope as he turned away from his world and watched her world as he played on the sand. "Our children play on the beach and swim in the ocean, they hike in the mountains and camp out under the stars. Shifters don't shift until they reach puberty so it's not as if Milo is going to be the odd one out at school. The kids there will seem normal to him."

Penny reached out a gloved hand for the handrail that ran down the side of the steps leading to the beach. "Will Milo fit in?" She reached the sand and waited for Logan. "Are there other children here without any kind of magical abilities? I don't want him to get bullied."

"He'll fit in. The kids here are very accepting. They are all different. Even shifters. Different animals, there's always this rivalry between the felines and the wolves but the kids seem to find a way to get past that and just get along with each other. When I first started school...and I know it was a long time ago...but the other kids helped me. Sure, some of them teased me because my speech was behind, and I couldn't read. Sometimes I even forgot to put my pants on."

"Now you're making it up."

"No, I'm not. Clothes were new to me." He blushed a little as he laughed nervously. "My wolf told me I should stop talking now. You don't need to hear about my youth."

"I like hearing about you. I suppose it makes me hopeful that we can fit in here, too." She glanced down at the picnic basket. "So, where are we going for our winter picnic?"

"This way. We follow the coast around, it takes us away from the houses." He pointed to the high cliffs to their left. "There are lots of caves in the cliff face. Some are inhabited, but the ones that flood in the winter when the storms make the waves crash against these rocks aren't. There's usually driftwood in them. People gather it and leave it high up in the caves so that it doesn't get wet or swept out to sea. We use what dry wood we need from the cave and replace it with wood we collect on the way, so it dries out for the next visitor." He led her closer toward the tide.

"I like that. It's like paying it forward and paying it back." Penny wrapped her scarf tighter around her neck as she followed Logan.

"Milo, are you going to help us gather wood?" Logan called.

"Sure." Milo had been following a gull of some kind along the shoreline. She didn't ask if it was a shifter, she preferred to think it was just a friendly bird.

"Our job is to collect the wood and then we carry it to the cave and leave it to dry out. We replace the wood we're going to use. That way there's always wood for the next person who comes along." Logan hooked the picnic basket over his arm and strolled along the shore picking up long lengths of wood.

"What else do you find along the beach?" Milo asked as he

picked up the wood and cradled it in his arms only to drop it when he found a new piece of wood.

"All kinds of things. Shells, starfish. Pebbles that look like gold." Logan picked up a pebble and held it out to Milo. "See, it's like gold. But it's worthless. Unless you throw it back into the ocean when the moon is full and make a wish."

"Is that why the town is called Wishing Moon Bay, because you can make a wish and they come true?" Milo weighed the pebble in his hand.

"Yes, that's where the town got its name, hundreds of years ago." He picked up another pebble and handed it to Penny.

She turned the pebble over in her hand. "It really does look like gold." The pebble had a smooth surface, as if someone had spent hours and hours polishing it. As she held it up, the light glinted off small glittery flecks, reminding Penny of the gold star they used to put on the top of the Christmas tree.

"Come on, Mommy, we need more wood." Milo ran on ahead and grabbed hold of what looked like a huge tree branch which was bigger than he was. Gripping it with both hands, he hauled it along behind him leaving a trail in the sand.

"It's good to see him having fun." Penny fell into step with Logan. As she walked, she picked up wood for the fire, the golden pebble safely nestled in her deep pocket. "Life hasn't been fun for us for a while."

"His dad?"

"Yeah. When he left, it tore us away from everything we knew. Life suddenly became uncertain and he had bad dreams where I was taken away from him." She leaned down and picked up a log, underneath the log was a perfect conch shell. Penny picked it up and examined it closely.

"The same shells," Logan said.

"The same shells." She breathed in the salty air and the cold prickled her throat. "It is beautiful here."

"If you think it's beautiful now, wait until you see it in the summer." He turned toward the cliffs. "Come on, there's a good cave just around the next bluff. It's fairly sheltered, and I doubt anyone else will be there at this time of day."

"Or this time of year." She grinned and rolled her eyes. "I can't believe we are actually having a picnic on the beach in the winter."

"In Australia, they have Christmas lunch on the beach," Milo told them as he walked along the beach like he was drunk, swerving from side to side so that his trailing branch made a wavy line in the sand.

"It's a lot warmer in Australia," Penny replied as they cut straight up the beach. Sure enough, there was the cave.

"I like this. Can we live here?" Milo pulled his log into the dimly lit cave.

"No, the cave fills up with water when it's stormy." Penny dumped the wood on the ground. "You're right, it sure is more sheltered in here."

"The bluff keeps most of the wind out." He dropped his wood to the ground next to hers. Then he leaned down and pulled out two short logs and set the picnic basket down on it. "Can I teach Milo how to light a fire?"

"Yes!" Milo yelled, dropped his branch, and ran back to Logan. "You can."

"As long as you are sensible," Penny warned him.

"We'll talk about how to light the fire safely and how you should only light a fire when there is an adult around."

"What about when I am an adult?" Milo asked cheekily.

"Hey, if you're not going to take this seriously, then I might tell Logan you aren't ready to learn to light a fire."

"You always say it's good to ask questions, that's how I

learn." Milo grinned up at her and her heart melted. He was so damn happy, she could cry.

"It's good to ask sensible questions. And that was not a good question." She grabbed hold of him and hugged him. "And you know it."

He giggled and pulled away. "Okay, sensible questions only."

"I'm going to ask Logan if you've been sensible and since he can't lie to me, he can't cover for you." Her words were met with a shocked expression.

"Logan can't lie to you?" Milo gasped and looked at Logan as if he were the unluckiest man alive.

"No, I can't. Your mom is my mate, and a shifter can't lie to their mate." Logan shrugged at Milo who looked at him with unfathomable pity. "Shall we go find some kindling?"

"What's kindling?" Milo asked as he followed Logan into the cave.

"It's smaller pieces of wood that light more easily. We put them down first and light them. When they are burning hot, we add bigger bits of wood and slowly build up the fire." Logan took a flashlight out of his pocket and switched it on before handing it to Milo. "Can you shine it up there for me? See, that's where the dry wood is. We'll take what we need and then before we go, we can stack our wood up there to dry."

"Cool." Milo held the light above his head so that the beam fell on the wood. Logan climbed the rocks and pulled down some smaller kindling and some bigger wood that would burn longer.

Penny watched them work together while pulling apart their pile of wood and finding some pieces that were dry enough to sit on. She dragged them farther into the cave where a ring of stones filled with charred wood marked a makeshift firepit that had been used recently. Placing her wood around the circle of stones, she then scooped out the charred wood so that they could use the same stones to contain their fire.

Logan carried the larger pieces of wood while Milo carried the kindling as if it were treasure.

"I can't let it get wet," Milo told her as she stared at the ring of stones.

"I'll help you." Penny helped her son carry the wood and then knelt by his side as he watched Logan carefully place the kindling inside the ring of rocks. As she stared at Milo's face, Penny hoped her son would not forget his first experience of lighting a fire under the careful eye of Logan.

How could he forget the day he had a picnic on the beach in the winter? But children forgot so much of their young lives.

While Logan patiently taught Milo the knack of getting a fire started and keeping it alight, Penny opened up the picnic basket, took out the thick blanket which was rolled up tightly, and spread it on the dry sand before unpacking the food.

Logan might be her mate, but she could kiss Ivan for taking time out of his already busy schedule to make such a wonderful selection of food for them, including a flask of hot coffee and another that contained the same wonderful soup he'd served last night in the restaurant. Thankfully, there was no added rodent.

"The fire should keep going now." Logan sat back and stared at the flames for a few moments. "We did a good job." He held up his hand and Milo high-fived him, his hand so big against that of her son. Yet they were gentle hands despite their size. Hands that could soothe away sorrow, hands that could ignite a fire of a different kind with a soft touch or stroke of fingertips across bare skin. "Here, Milo, you can keep hold of this." Logan gave Milo a flint and steel. "Keep it safe and I'll teach you how to use it properly and safely. Okay?"

"But never on your own," Penny warned. She didn't exactly approve of the gift but wasn't going to spoil the moment by insisting Logan take it back.

"I'll be sensible," Milo promised.

"Okay, now that we're all warmed up, shall we eat?" Penny sat down on one of the logs and poured out coffee and soup.

"Are you sure we can't live here?" Milo sat close to the fire, but not too close, with his cup of soup in his hands.

"I'm sure." Penny sipped her coffee and ate a sandwich. "Maybe later today we should go and take a look in town to see if there are any ads for houses or apartments to rent." Did people advertise rentals the same way here as in her world? Would anyone rent to a non-supernatural human? "I can be back in time for my shift."

"You don't have to work a shift if you don't want to." Logan raised his cup of coffee to her. "Okay, I get it, yes, you do."

"I do. I need to provide for us. I don't expect you to understand."

"But I do understand," he replied. "Because it's exactly the same as I feel. As a shifter, I'm driven to provide for my mate and my family."

"And maybe one day I'll be okay with that. But not yet."

"Then I'll back off and give you some room. Just know that I'm here for you no matter what."

"I know." She smiled at him as the light from the fire danced across his face. When he smiled back, small tendrils of desire unfurled in her stomach. Despite her better judgment, she might be ready to trust again.

20

LOGAN

*A*fter they'd eaten, Milo helped Logan to safely put out the fire and place the unused wood back where they had found it. Penny cleared the leftovers from the picnic away and stowed them carefully in the basket before she joined them at the cave entrance.

"Here's your flashlight." Penny handed it back to Logan and he put it in his pocket before reaching for the picnic basket. "I can manage."

"I don't mind carrying it."

"Neither do I. And since you carried it here, it's only fair that I carry it back to the car." She tightened her grip, her expression firm as she stared him down.

"Okay." Logan had already learned there was little point in arguing with Penny when her mind was made up.

"So, where do you suggest we look for an apartment to rent?" Penny was happy and relaxed as they strolled back along the beach. Happy and carefree, the picnic basket swung in her hand as the wind tugged at her hair.

Milo, refueled from the picnic and warmed by the fire, ran down to the tide line. With his head down, he picked up anything interesting and examined it before either throwing it back down on the sand or stowing it in his pocket. The boy reminded him of the countless hours Logan and his brothers spent down here as boys, trawling along the beach looking for anything interesting or valuable. Ivan had a nose for anything of value, while Logan was drawn to anything with an odd shape or texture.

"There's a small real estate agent in town, you could ask there. Sometimes there are ads pinned up in the grocery store. People advertising rooms for rent." He hated the idea of her not living under the same roof as him.

We must let her go, his wolf told him. If we hold on too tight, she might pull free and leave town completely.

She knows what she means to us. Surely, she wouldn't leave now. His fear of losing his mate spiked but he was certain she wouldn't leave unless something happened. She'd told Milo they would at least stay for a week or so. But Logan had gotten used to the idea of her staying forever.

Don't let us be the reason she leaves, his wolf replied.

"I'd ideally like somewhere furnished." Penny watched Milo as he picked up a stone and then ran toward the ocean and threw it in. "We don't have any furniture. I sold it before we moved."

"If you need anything, we can raid the attic. There's other furniture in the garage, too. Valerie is a hoarder."

"I might need to take you up on that offer. As long as it's all right with Valerie." She put her hand up to stop him from protesting. "I know, I know, she'd happily share anything with us. But I'd still like to ask rather than upset her by taking advantage."

"Then we can ask her." They rounded the side of the cliffs and the town came into full view. "I know you want to do this alone. But will you promise me that before you agree to rent anywhere, you'll check with me?"

"Check with you?" Penny arched an eyebrow at him.

"Yes. This is a town like any other town. There are certain neighborhoods where you and Milo wouldn't want to live."

"Really? There are bad parts of town?" Penny chuckled. "Are these bad parts of town bad neighborhoods because of crime or because there are…oh, I don't know, a poltergeist living there?"

"Poltergeists do not strictly *live* anywhere." His serious expression was mirrored in Penny, but he could not keep a straight face. "There are no poltergeists in Wishing Moon Bay. I promise you."

"Okay, so what makes a bad neighborhood a bad neighborhood in your town?"

"Well, some witches and warlocks like to smoke…certain leaves that cause them to hallucinate. Usually, they are innocent enough and there's no harm done. But occasionally things get a little crazy. You want to avoid those neighborhoods unless there is a protection spell on your door."

"A protection spell. That's a real thing?"

"It's made up of runes and symbols. I'll show you." He ran along the beach, grabbed a long thin stick, and tested it for strength. Then he stuck the end in the ground and carved four symbols that represented the four elements. "These are the basis of most spells. You call on the four elements and then add in…directions."

"Directions. Okay."

Logan quickly added the symbols needed to ward off anyone who might try to cause you harm through magic. "It nullifies the spell. Some spells anyway. If the magic is strong… Luckily witches and warlocks are very peace-loving people. They worship nature."

"How do you know all this?" Penny asked as she took out her phone and took a picture of the sand talisman.

"Valerie made us learn about the different people who live

in town. She believes that if you can understand others and understand how they think then there is less chance for misunderstandings."

"Misunderstandings. I expect that gets interesting in a town like this."

"That doesn't put you off staying?"

"No, not really." She lifted her phone and took another photo, this time of the town and the snow clouds above it. "If anything it makes me want to stay. I want to learn all there is to know about Wishing Moon Bay and its people. I've always wanted to set down roots and feel as if I belong." She shifted her attention to him. "Maybe this is the place for me to do that. The place where Milo can call home."

"I hope so, Penny. I want you both to be happy here and I want to share in that happiness."

"You're very sweet. And I'd like you to share in it, too." She linked arms with him as they made their way along the beach toward where his truck was parked. "And Milo is already very happy." Turning around, she walked back up the beach while watching Milo run toward them. "It's the happiest I've seen him for months. He loves it here."

"You'll let me help you?" Logan stopped walking. Milo went off to the right as he spotted something in the sand and leaned down to pick it up. After a quick examination, he curled his fingers around his new possession and scampered toward them.

"I would appreciate your help. Even though I could probably manage on my own." She held out her arms to her son. "What have you got there?"

"A shell." He kept it hidden in his fist. "It's a present for you. A birthday present."

"Oh, honey, that's so sweet." Penny's eyes misted with tears.

"Do you like it?"

Penny leaned down and scooped Milo up into her arms. "I'll love the shell because you found it and thought of me."

"I'll go find more shells." Milo kissed her on the cheek and wriggled out of her arms before running back to the tide line.

"He's a great kid." Logan wanted to be Milo's dad more than anything. He wanted to take the boy to the store and help him choose a gift for his mom. To help him at school, even with his homework, a chore Logan had detested when he was in school. As a boy, he preferred to be outside in the fresh air, racing along the beach with Rift and his other brothers. Time sitting inside figuring out numbers and words was time wasted.

We know better now, his wolf reminded him.

Living at the hotel with Valerie taught him that numbers were needed to figure out a guest's bill, that words were important when dealing with those same guests. Okay, so he hadn't quite mastered the art of using the right words with guests or people and his attitude sometimes came across as abrasive. But maybe that would change now that he had his mate in his life. Finally, he had something to work for. A family of his own.

"When is your birthday?" Logan asked.

"The day after tomorrow." Color rose in her cheeks. "Please don't think you have to buy me a gift or anything."

"It's your birthday..." Logan nodded as she shot him a warning look. "A cake? Ivan could make a birthday cake. You have to have candles."

"Okay, a cake. And only if Ivan has the time."

"A cake it is then." Logan smiled to himself. He told Penny he wouldn't buy her a gift, but he could give the cash to Milo and he could buy it. There was a store in town that sold beautiful silver jewelry. They could pick out something special.

"Five more minutes!" Penny called to Milo as he walked with his head down looking for anything his mom might like.

"In the summer we can come down to the beach and I'll show you the best places to swim. There are secret coves along the beach that we can swim to." Excitement bubbled up inside of him at the thought of sharing all his favorite places with his mate and Milo.

"Milo is not a strong swimmer."

"I'll look after him," he assured her. "Milo can ride on my back. As long as he keeps his arms wrapped around my neck, I'll keep him safe."

"I'd love it if he spent more time outdoors. He has high energy levels." She inhaled the salty air. "I always did like the idea of living by the ocean."

"Don't forget the mountains. As much as I love the beach, the mountains are my home." He shot her a sideways glance. "At least they used to be my home."

"Tell me about this cabin of yours. Maybe we can go there when Milo isn't in school. You can teach him all about nature."

"I built my cabin by hand." He pointed to the exact spot where his home was nestled between the trees. "You can't see it from here, but it's right there. There's a clump of beech trees just below the pines surrounding the cabin, I harvest the nuts when they fall, and they help me get through the winter. The tall pine trees give me pitch which I use for a variety of things and burn the wood on the fire. The smell of pine fills the cabin." He grinned at her. "I'd like to show you it all."

"I'd like to see it. When the weather is warmer. I don't think I'd like to be marooned on the mountain in the snow." She tilted her chin, her attention fixed on the snow clouds above.

"There's more snow heading for the mountains. It'll likely snow again tonight and settle farther down, but it won't snow over the town until late this evening."

"You say that with such certainty."

"When you've lived somewhere most of your life, you become attuned to the seasons and the weather. I've sat on my porch and watched the sky for so many years that I can time when a rain shower will reach me down to a couple of minutes."

"That's amazing." She jumped as her phone rang. Pushing her hand into her pocket, she withdrew it, her face pale when she saw the caller. "It's Helena."

"Oh." Logan's mind raced as she pressed *answer* and put the phone to her ear. What if Helena persuaded Penny to leave town now?

"Hello?" Penny smiled as she answered the call. "How are you?"

"How are *you*? I was just calling to check in on you both. How is your new adventure going?"

Logan took a couple of steps away, not wanting to eavesdrop on her conversation.

"Good. Everyone has been so kind and friendly." She glanced in Logan's direction. Pink tinged the bridge of her nose and spread down over her cheeks. "I *really* like it here, Helena."

Logan's breath caught in his throat as relief threaded through his veins. His mate was happy here with him.

That doesn't mean she'll stay forever, his wolf warned him. Anything could happen to make Penny change her mind.

"You want to come here?" Penny's voice rose and Logan strode back toward her. "Why?"

Logan's fear that Helena might persuade Penny to leave town if she found out about shifters and the other supernatural inhabitants of Wishing Moon Bay left him breathless.

"No, why wouldn't I want you to come?" Penny shook her head. "You don't need to check up on me." She paused. "My birthday. Of course I want to celebrate with you."

He wanted to reach for the phone and tell Helena her sister and nephew were happy and safe. But maybe if Helena came here, she would like it, too, and give Penny the confidence to stay.

"Okay, I'll send you directions but the town itself is hard to find. I'll meet you outside of town." She put her fingers to her temple as if she had a headache. "I'll see you tomorrow." Penny ended the call and cursed under her breath. "Helena's coming to see us. I'm not sure if she's checking up on us or if she's decided that she needs to change her life, too. Or maybe it is just because it's my birthday. Although, when you've seen as many as I have, it's not a big thing to celebrate."

"I think it's a very big thing to celebrate. I love that you were born." He cocked his head and grinned and she giggled.

"Because I am your mate. I get it." She inhaled deeply, her good mood evaporating. "I'm just not sure what'll happen if she finds out about…everything. My mom was superstitious and believed in the supernatural. Helena always thought she was a little crazy."

"It's okay." Logan pulled her into a hug. It was the most natural thing since she was his mate. Penny froze but then slowly thawed, her arms sliding around his waist as she leaned on his shoulder. "Maybe this is how it's meant to be."

"Will she find the town?"

"She might, but you should go and meet her." Logan inhaled deeply, wanting to assure his mate everything would be fine. "Just in case."

"Maybe she'll want to stay, too," Penny suggested hopefully.

But Logan was scared Helena might steal his mate away.

He'd have to make sure everyone was on their best behavior so that didn't happen.

We're just going to have to win Helena over, his wolf said. *Which means you need to be on your best, most polite behavior.*

Easy, Logan replied.

Sure. His wolf settled down for a sleep, not convinced this would be easy at all.

21

PENNY

"Okay, Milo, it's time to go." Penny put her hands to her mouth as she called to her son, but the breeze caught her voice and swept it away.

"I'll get him. You go on to the truck." Logan put his hand in his pocket and pulled out his keys.

"Are you sure?" Despite tensing her jaw, her teeth chattered, not from the cold but from her worry over Helena coming to town. A gloomy mood hung over her like the heavy snow clouds as she walked up the beach and wearily climbed the steps.

When she called Helena with the news they were staying in Wishing Moon Bay for a while, a weight had lifted off her shoulders. Now the weight was back, crushing her as if she were buried under an avalanche of snow, unable to breathe. If Helena found out about Wishing Moon Bay and the people who lived here, she might try to make her leave.

Especially if Helena thought there was any threat toward Penny or Milo from a town filled with people with supernatural powers. And maybe she would be right. Were they safe here or was this all a dream? What if Penny was holding on to a promise of happiness with Logan because she wanted to be loved and cherished again? The breakdown of her marriage had left her broken-hearted.

This might simply be a rebound relationship. She couldn't risk Milo's happiness on a selfish whim.

Yet Logan was her mate. She could feel the connection between them. Why was life so confusing? Why couldn't she find a signpost to happiness, just as she'd found the signpost to Wishing Moon Bay?

Unlocking the truck, she climbed into the passenger seat and stared out across the beach. Logan was with Milo, they were looking at something on the ground. Perhaps a pretty shell or another golden pebble. If she came down to the beach tonight and made a wish under the moon, would it come true? All she wanted was a happy life, one where she and Milo were safe, where they felt secure, where they felt wanted. Kelvin had taken that from her. He'd left her vulnerable, uncertain of the future. As a parent, that uncertainty preyed on her mind constantly.

After examining whatever they'd found, Logan grabbed hold of Milo and swung him onto his broad shoulders. She imagined the squeals of delight from Milo as the wolf shifter ran up the beach toward the truck. A smile crept across her lips. No matter what happened, she trusted in Logan to keep them safe and keep them here in town. Kelvin had tried to ruin her life, but he had no power over her. Not anymore.

She had to shake off her fear of making the same mistake of marrying a man who would betray her. She had to be brave enough to go after what she wanted. And she wanted Logan.

Penny rolled down the window as Logan ran up the steps from the beach with Milo on his shoulders. She welcomed the chilly breeze because it carried her son's laughter with it. High-pitched and breathy, it was the best sound in the world.

Thank you, Logan. He was the father Milo deserved. The husband she deserved. Before she came here, a second husband was unthinkable. But Wishing Moon Bay had taught her the unthinkable could be real.

"How full are your pockets?" Penny patted her son's pockets as he climbed awkwardly into the truck. Logan gave him a boost and he sat down heavily, his cheeks flushed and his nose running from the cold breeze.

"Very." He wriggled to get comfortable, the knees of his jeans patched with wet sand.

"Here." Penny dug in her pocket and pulled out a clean tissue.

Milo sniffed loudly and then wiped his nose. Sand stuck to his face and flecked his hair. Before they went into town, they'd need to go back to the hotel so he could take a shower and change into clean clothes. Tomorrow she'd have to do their laundry.

Leaning across the seat, she dropped a kiss on top of his head while Logan got in the truck and started the engine. "Did you have fun?"

"The best fun." Milo flopped back in his seat. "Logan carried me over the beach, did you see?"

"I did."

"He said when his bear brothers arrive, they would let me ride on their backs."

"Is that so?" A sidelong glance confirmed Milo's words.

"They'll look after Milo," Logan promised.

"I'm sure they will." She put her arm around her son. "It's just going to take a while before I hear, *I'm going to ride on the back of a bear*, without panicking."

Logan chuckled. "I get you."

"But I trust you and I trust your judgment."

"You are my family now and so you are part of their family, too." Logan drove back toward the hotel. "I'd be more worried about them spoiling Milo rotten than any physical harm they might cause."

"I don't mind being spoiled rotten," Milo said brightly.

"I don't suppose you do."

"They'll spoil you, too," Logan told her.

"Well, in that case, spoil away." It would be so nice to be part of a family again.

Perhaps the very reason the boys Valerie had taken in and raised as her own were willing to accept her and Milo was that they had built a bond and grown to love each other even though they were not related. They didn't even shift into the same animal, except for the twins. But their bond was strong, she could hear it in their voices when they spoke about each other.

"I'm lucky that I'm the first one of us to find our mate. And you are lucky because that means they will make a big fuss." Logan seemed more relaxed as he parked the truck outside of the hotel.

Penny helped Milo out of the truck, noting the sand under his fingernails. "You need a soak in the bath."

Milo giggled and put his hands on his pockets to stop the items he'd found on the beach from falling out. "I can pretend to be a merman."

"As long as you don't splash around too much." She reached for his hand and walked around the truck to meet Logan. "What's wrong?"

"They're here."

"Who is here?"

"Valerie and the bears."

"Oh." She flattened her hair and wished she'd applied makeup this morning. She screwed up her face and then sighed. "I am really hoping you're right about them loving us because I'm your mate."

"They will. I promise."

"Good, because we're not exactly going to make a good first impression. We're dirty and windswept."

"You are perfect." Logan grabbed the picnic basket from the truck and turned around. "If you want, we can go around the back. I'll drop this into the kitchen, and you can head up to your room if you'd rather wash up first. But Valerie will love seeing Milo with his hands dirty. She believes kids should be allowed to get messy and have fun."

"Then she'll love me." Milo held up his dirty hands. "I am messy, and I sure did have fun."

"Okay, either way, I'm okay. If Valerie is free when we go in, we can say hello, if she's busy then we'll go up to the room and change before heading off into town." She grinned at Logan. "We are letting fate decide. Just like you say fate decided that I am your mate."

"I'm okay with that." Logan crossed the parking lot and led them around to the back door leading into the kitchen. After placing the picnic basket under the counter, he closed the door and took them around to a second door. "This way, Ivan will be upset if we trail mud through his kitchen." Taking a key from his pocket, he unlocked it and they went inside. "This is one of the storerooms. We keep the cleaning equipment in here along with new bathrobes and soap, plus toilet paper."

"We might need all that soap to get Milo clean," Penny joked despite her nerves at meeting Valerie.

Milo chuckled and stared at the big stack of toilet paper that sat next to a large box labeled soap. "Can I come in here and explore one day?"

"You can come and help me do inventory," Logan offered as he unlocked the door on the other side of the storeroom. It opened out into the corridor next to the stairs leading to the attic.

"What's *inventory*?" Milo asked.

"You get to count all this stuff." Penny patted a box labeled toothbrushes. "How cool is that?"

Milo's eyes narrowed. "That sounds like homework to me."

"It's fun." Logan didn't sound too convinced.

"I'll think about it," Milo replied.

"Valerie is in the reception area with Sophie." Logan's shifter senses sure were useful.

"Then let's go and meet her." Penny nodded, perhaps it was best to get this over with.

Logan took them along the corridor and through a door into the reception area where an elderly woman with a walking stick was leaning on the counter talking to Sophie. They both looked up as Logan and his mate walked in.

"I should get going," Sophie announced. "It's my afternoon off and I have plans."

"Thanks, Sophie." Valerie hobbled toward them, leaning heavily on her stick. "There you are, Logan."

"How are you?" Logan hugged her close and kissed her cheek.

"I was just catching up with things." Her eyes met with Penny's as she patted her son's back. "Are you going to introduce me?"

"Yes." Logan took hold of Valerie's hand as he let her go. "This is Penny and her son, Milo. This is Valerie."

"Hi." Penny held onto Milo's hand as her nerves kicked in. Her first meeting with Kelvin's parents hadn't gone smoothly, she suspected they never quite agreed with their son's choice in a wife. Certainly, they had taken his side when it came to the divorce and had broken all ties with Penny. "It's good to meet you."

"Can I have a hug?" Valerie's eyes misted with tears as she held out her arm, while she rested heavily on Logan.

Penny nodded. As she wrapped her arms around Valerie,

it was like hugging her mom. The same warmth, the same calm comfort. "It's good to finally meet you, Valerie. I've heard so much about you."

"Oh, dear. I dread to think what Logan's been telling you."

"Only good things," she assured. "I can't imagine how you raised six boys and still stayed sane."

"Oh, my boys kept me sane. They filled my life with love and mischief. There were times when I wondered what I'd done but I would not change a thing." She half-turned to look at Logan. "Neither would I have changed any of my boys. They all deserved love and they all earned that love from the day they came to me."

"Children do have a way of capturing your heart, don't they?"

"They sure do." Valerie eased away from Penny, a smile on her face as she looked down at Milo. "I can see you know from experience just how special children are. It warms my heart that Logan will be a father to your son. It's the one thing I could never provide for my boys."

"We did just fine without a father," Logan reassured her.

"I know you did. But I always felt guilty there was no man to take you camping and out into the mountains to teach you about the wonderful world around you. Not that I believe only men are capable of teaching those things. But with the hotel to run, I never had the time. Or the energy." Valerie leaned heavily on Logan. "But you found those strengths in each other. You pulled together and helped each other even though you were all so different."

"Except us." Two men came from behind Penny. She clutched Milo's hand tighter as she turned around to face the newcomers.

"Wow. You look exactly the same." Milo pulled his hand out of Penny's as he drew closer to get a better look.

"We're identical twins. Although I maintain I'm the handsome one."

"You certainly are not the modest one," the other twin answered.

"How are we supposed to tell you apart?" Milo asked.

"I told you, I'm the handsome one." The first brother winked at Milo who looked confused as he continued to stare.

"I could always punch you in the eye, then it would be easy. Aiden would be the one with the black eye." Logan made his hand into a fist and ground it into the palm of his left hand.

"Ah, Logan." Aiden cocked his head to one side. "You always did think you were funny." He lifted his hand and beckoned to the wolf shifter. "Just try it!"

"As I said, children have a way of capturing the heart, while grown men have a way of making me angry." Valerie wagged her finger at the wolf shifter and his bear brothers. "No fighting. At least until after dinner."

"It's easy to tell them apart," Rift came into the reception area. "Aiden has more gray hair around his temples, but Caleb has more wrinkles on his forehead."

"Hey," Caleb covered his brow with his hand. "That's not a wrinkle, it's a scar. A scar given to me by a certain dragon when he first shifted."

"Oh, I see it!" Milo's eyes widened as Caleb uncovered his face.

"My gray hairs are from having to put up with my twin," Aiden said. He turned his head from side to side. "Can you see the subtle difference?"

"I can," Penny confirmed.

"The more time you spend with us, the easier it is to tell us apart." Caleb grinned at Logan. "This means we need to spend a lot of time with your mate and Milo. Don't worry, we'll tell her all about you."

"Stop teasing your brother," Valerie warned. "I'd tell you they aren't always like this, but I'd be lying."

"Just boys being boys." Relieved that Valerie liked her and that Logan's brothers all seemed welcoming, she made her excuses and went to their room. Despite Valerie's arrival, she still planned to go into town and begin her search for somewhere for them to live. First, Milo needed a good soak in the bathtub while she sat on the bed and figured out how she was going to handle Helena's visit.

It had to go well. Their future literally depended on it.

22

LOGAN

"We are going to town." Penny met Logan and Valerie in the reception area. Logan was on duty, having taken over from Rift. Sophie was working the evening shift and Logan hoped she was in a better mood when she came back into work. Hopefully, the arrival of Valerie, who had hired Sophie around six months ago, would ease the tension between them. He wasn't sure how things had escalated so fast. Until Penny arrived in town, Logan had no idea Sophie had feelings for him.

Even if Penny wasn't here, Sophie knew he was a shifter and that there was no future in a relationship with him. Since she was an employee, Logan would never have risked dating her short-term, for him that would be unprofessional and might cause trouble for Valerie.

"I've written down a couple of places you could check out if you're looking for an apartment to rent." Logan handed his mate a piece of paper.

"You're looking to rent in town?" Valerie asked. "Aren't you going to live with Logan?"

Penny glanced down at Milo. "Moving to Wishing Moon

Bay wasn't in our plans at all. We need to take things slowly. I said I'd stay for a week to see if we like it here. But part of my decision also depends on finding somewhere to live and school for Milo."

"Of course, I understand, sorry. I'm just excited for you both. For all three of you." Valerie held out her arms and hugged Penny. "I'm so incredibly happy for you all. I know you're going to be happy here in town."

"I hope so. Everyone's been so kind to us. But I need a little independence. I'd like to find a job and rent an apartment for a few months. Just to see how things go."

"That's sensible and understandable. Don't mind me, I just want the best for my boys. I always have. Just as you want this best for your young man." Valerie leaned down so her head was level with Milo's, even though pain deepened the wrinkles around her eyes. "You're welcome to come and play on the hotel grounds anytime, Milo. And when you are settled, we can go up in the attic and take a look at the toys up there."

"We went up into the attic yesterday," Milo told her. "We didn't bring down any toys, but we did find a pendant. It had these symbols on it."

Logan put his hand in his pocket and took out the talisman. "Ivan looked up the symbols in the books he borrowed. He said he thought it was for protection."

"Let me see." Valerie squinted as she stared at the pendant. "I don't recall seeing this before. It must have been here when I bought the place. I was so busy I never had a chance to go through everything up in the attic. And then I stored your old things up there and I forgot about the stuff left by Rad."

"Do you know what the symbols mean?" Logan asked.

"I'd have to take a proper look at it. My eyes aren't what they used to be, so I'd need to look at it under a magnifying glass." She held the pendant closer to her eyes. "But I think

Ivan is right. He's been studying runes and symbols for some months now. If he thinks it's a talisman for protection, he's probably right."

Penny placed her hands on Milo's shoulders. "Milo was drawn to it."

"It called to me," Milo added. "Or whispered. Yes, it was like someone whispering in my ear."

"In that case, you should wear it." Valerie slipped it over Milo's head.

"Really?" Milo held the talisman between his fingers and thumb and tilted it up so he could look at it.

"Really. One lesson you should learn is to never ignore a hunch. If something whispers in your ear, you should listen." She held her fingers to her ear and wriggled them.

"Oh, that way lies trouble," Penny covered Milo's ears. "Next thing I know Milo will be telling me a voice is telling him not to do his homework or that he's allowed to eat candy for dinner."

"I would not." Milo pulled his mom's hands away from his ears, but his smile said differently.

"Ah, but the spirits wouldn't be happy if you put words in their mouths," Valerie warned Milo. "They'll know if you're making things up and they might be displeased. And displeased spirits are mischievous spirits."

"What would they do?"

"That is a secret and I do not tell secrets." Valerie winked at Penny. "You have a lovely child, Penny."

"He is my favorite child," Penny admitted.

"I'm your only child," Milo corrected her.

"And that is why you are my favorite." She grabbed hold of his hand. "Right, we should go. Maybe that lucky talisman will help us find an apartment we can afford."

"I like living in the hotel," Milo insisted.

"We'll see you later. Rift said he'd watch Milo again this

evening, so I'll be back for my shift at five." She waved as they disappeared out the door.

Logan stood still for a long moment, his senses locked onto his mate until she started her car engine and drove away.

"I'll go grab us some coffee," Logan offered. "I can watch the desk while we sit in the dining room."

"That sounds like a plan." Valerie ran her hand over the reception desk, just as she had every time she walked past it for as long as Logan could recall.

Logan went to the kitchen and made a fresh pot of coffee then added some cookies to the tray before carrying it through to the dining room where Valerie was seated at her favorite table overlooking the gardens.

"I like her." Valerie turned away from the view outside as Logan placed the tray down on the table.

"I like her, too." His smile broadened. "It's more than like. But I don't want to frighten her away."

"I don't think there's a chance of that. The way she looks at you..." Valerie reached out and touched his hand. "She can see you have a good heart. A heart big enough to care for her and her son. And her son is the most precious person in her whole world."

"She hasn't had an easy time these last few months. Penny likes the idea of stability. She'd committed to staying here for at least a week..." He looked out the window, the light outside was dimming, the heavy snow clouds blocking out the afternoon sun.

"What's wrong?"

"Penny's sister is coming to visit." He ran his hand through his hair as his temper flared. "Penny was supposed to go and stay with Helena, but she wound up here. I'm just worried Helena might persuade Penny to leave."

"Why would she do that?" Valerie asked. "She'll see that

Penny and Milo are safe and happy here. She'll see how much you and the rest of the family care for them both."

Logan nodded. "I'm sure you're right. I'm just concerned, that's all. I'm scared she'll leave my life as quickly as she came into it."

"That is not going to happen." Valerie's lips were a thin line as she sipped her coffee.

"We can't be sure about that." Logan stared out the window. If he had his way, he'd simply take Penny and Milo to his cabin in the mountains and hide them away. But that wasn't possible. "Penny's been hurt. Her ex-husband left her wounded and alone. I'm scared she won't believe in me and how much I love them."

"You don't think Penny, or anyone for that matter, can see how much you care for them?" Valerie asked.

"Sometimes it's easier to do what's expected and Helena expected Penny and Milo to go live with her. What if she persuades Penny that she's been reckless with Milo's future?" He leaned forward, his elbows resting on the table.

She shook her head. "Or she might see that this is where they belong."

Logan leaned back in his chair, the air leaving his lungs as he processed her words. "I hope you're right."

"You deserve to be happy, Logan. And so do Penny and Milo." Valerie drank her coffee and stared into the distance. "Fate wouldn't be so cruel to you."

"Are you so sure?"

"You just need to make them all see you are there for them."

"That I can do. I'm not going anywhere."

"Unless Penny and Milo leave Wishing Moon Bay. You know that's a possibility." The rings around Valerie's eyes darkened. His mom was supposed to be making things easier, instead, she was worrying about Logan, just as she'd always worried about him.

"You should go get some rest." He stood up, leaned forward, and kissed her cheek. "Thanks for coming."

"Are you kidding? I came as soon as I heard." She leaned back in her chair and smiled. "At last, one of my boys has a mate. You have no idea how happy that makes me."

"I think I do." He held out his hand to her. "Come on, you need to rest."

"If Rift wants company tonight, tell him to bring Milo to the apartment. We can watch TV together or play a game. Maybe tomorrow you should go into the attic and find some toys and games he might like." Valerie walked stiffly, leaning heavily on her walking stick.

"Okay. But you need to take care of yourself. Don't overdo it. I know how much you loved running around after us when we were kids, but..."

"Don't tell me I'm too old." Valerie waved her walking stick at him.

"I wouldn't dream of it!" Logan chuckled as he watched her go and then took the tray of dirty cups to the kitchen. Ivan had gone home, the hotel was quiet, as if it were waiting.

His wolf shuddered. *Waiting for what?*

I don't know. As a child, Logan had always thought of the hotel as a living thing. Maybe it was haunted. Although, he never believed in ghosts. Valerie had taught them all that dead meant dead. Unless you were a vampire. But vampires were held together by magic and ingesting the essence of life —blood.

The bell on the reception desk pinged and Logan headed back out of the kitchen, greeted the new guests, and checked them in.

"Could you give us a hand with the luggage?" the elderly

guest, a Mrs. Madilyn, asked. "We're not as young as we used to be." She stared up at the ceiling and turned in a circle. "It's changed a lot since we were here last. The hotel was darker when Rad owned it. The décor was like something out of a gothic movie. This is much nicer."

"My mom renovated the hotel after Rad died."

"Died?" Mrs. Madilyn asked.

"That's what everyone assumed. He just disappeared. There are countless stories about what happened to him, but no one knows the truth. Except for Rad, I guess." The hairs on the back of his neck stood on end as he came around the desk and followed the guest out to her car where her husband, a thin man in his sixties, was wrangling a suitcase out of the trunk. "My mom, Valerie, she bought the hotel. It was all legal and above board."

"Oh, I'm not trying to imply that anything underhanded occurred," Mrs. Madilyn told him quickly. "I was only commenting on the decor."

"I'll take your bags up for you." He helped the elderly gentleman drag the bags out of the car and then headed back into the hotel loaded up like a pack mule with all the luggage. As he climbed the stairs, he shivered, it was as if he was being watched but when he pushed his shifter senses outward, he couldn't sense anyone close by, the other guests in the hotel were in their rooms.

Something is stirring, his wolf told him. But neither of them had a clue as to what that something was.

23

PENNY

Her head throbbed as she opened her eyes, her tongue too big for her mouth as she tried to speak.

"Mommy." Milo's quiet voice next to her sent chills through her body. Something was wrong, something was very wrong, but her brain was full of cotton balls, and putting two cohesive thoughts together was impossible. "Mommy, are you awake?"

Awake? She forced her eyes open but there was no light, only darkness surrounding them.

"Where are we?" Penny put her hand to her head as she sat up, but a wave of nausea hit her, and she slumped back down to the floor.

Floor. She was lying on the floor. *Inside.* The air was cool but smelled stale, as if the room they were in had been shut up for a while.

"Mommy. You need to wake up." The urgency in Milo's voice gripped hold of her and forced her to focus.

"I'm awake, honey. But my head hurts, and I feel sick. I just need a moment." She breathed in through her nose and let it out slowly through her mouth. Her head started to clear but she still couldn't recall how she'd ended up here.

Wherever *here* was.

The last thing she remembered was saying goodbye to Logan and Valerie and driving into town. They'd checked in at the two real estate agents who had given them a couple of brochures on properties to rent. Then they'd spotted the diner and gone in for ice cream and waffles.

Penny put her hand to her head and attempted to sit up once more. The room spun around her, at least it would have spun, if she could make out any features. It was all so dark.

"We need to get out of here." Milo pulled on her sleeve, and she reached out and covered his hand with hers. His skin was so cold and as awareness came back to her, she felt his small body shivering against hers.

"We will." She put her right hand behind her back and pushed herself to sit up straighter. There was a hard wall behind her. Reaching out, she ran her fingertips down the unmistakable log wall. They were in a cabin. Or a shed or a barn. Certainly not the hotel.

How did they get here?

"The lady said she'd be back. I don't like the lady." His small voice conveyed his terror.

"What lady?" Penny asked. Why couldn't she remember anything past going into the diner?

"The old lady. She came into the diner and sat down at the table next to us."

"I don't remember. Did you know the lady?" Penny's mind brushed up against a wall in her head. It was as if someone had put up a barrier to stop her from remembering.

"No, I don't think so. She spoke to you. She said Logan had told her we were looking for somewhere to live. She said knew somewhere." There was nothing familiar in Milo's words.

"Did we go with her?" Penny couldn't remember seeing an old lady. She certainly couldn't remember going to see a house or apartment. Penny looked up at the ceiling. "Is that what happened? Did we go with her and she brought us here?"

"No, we were waiting for our order and she went to the bathroom, and then she left." Milo took a shuddering breath. "We ate waffles and ice cream. They were good."

"Then what?" Penny's stomach convulsed

"Then we went to the car. You started acting strange. The old lady came and said she would drive us home. But she brought us here instead."

"Do you know where here is?" Penny asked.

Milo shook his head, his hair brushing her arm as he moved. "She kept looking at me, telling me I'd go to sleep soon, and everything would be all right. But I didn't feel sleepy. But you were asleep, so I pretended. I lay down next to you on the back seat. I couldn't see out of the windows." He hiccupped as he took a breath and she held him close, rubbing his small body. It was so cold, he was so cold.

"You did the right thing." Penny put her fingers to her pounding temple. "She must have drugged me."

"What are we going to do?" Milo's small fingers clutched at her clothes. "She's going to come back."

"Sit there. Don't move." Penny eased her son back against the log wall and then pushed herself to a kneeling position. Her head pounded in her skull and she needed to rest for a moment to stop her stomach from lurching into her throat. As her nausea subsided, she reached out in front of her, trying to feel her way in the dark. They needed light and warmth. After that, she'd figure out how to get out of there.

Shuffling forward, her hands grasped at open air, so she kept moving. Her senses told her the room they were in wasn't vast, so sooner or later she'd touch something. She shuddered, her skull prickling as if her hair stood on end. What if they weren't alone in there?

She stopped moving and sat back on her ankles. Closing her eyes, she kept still until the pounding in her head quieted. She listened, straining against the silence as she slowly turned her head from side to side. Was that someone breathing? Perhaps it was Milo.

"Are you okay, Milo?" she whispered into the darkness behind her.

"Yes." His voice was small, scared, and she wanted to unleash her rage on whoever had done this to them.

"Just stay right there." She shuffled forward, her eyes were gradually getting used to the dark and she could make out the vague outline of objects. Was that a bed? Her hand touched a mattress, that seemed to be covered in a sheet, but no other bedding. Sliding her hand farther upward, she smoothed her palm over the wide empty expanse. "Okay, Milo, do you think you can come over here? Follow my voice."

"Okay." He scrambled toward her, his shoes scraping against the wooden floor.

"That's it, keep coming." She held out her hand to him and he curled his cold fingers around hers. She closed her hand, holding him tightly as she helped him up onto the bed. "Okay. Stay there. I'll check out the rest of the room."

"Don't go too far," he pleaded.

"I won't." Penny sat on the side of the bed and spread her hands out over the rest of the mattress just to check that there was nothing else or no one else on it. Completely empty. She let out a long breath and moved to the head of the bed. Most people had a nightstand next to the bed and on that nightstand, they had a light. Or a clock.

Shuffling forward, she reached out her hands and touched the hard-wooden nightstand. Carefully moving forward a little more, she felt the surface of the nightstand, searching for a light. A smooth domed shape that could be a lamp sat on the surface. She used her fingers to explore the contours of the lamp, searching for a switch. There. She flicked it on, but nothing happened. Perhaps it wasn't plugged in. She felt around the edge of the base, found the cord and traced it back to a plug in the wall. Penny flicked the switches, trying every combination before admitting defeat. Either the lamp didn't work or there was no power coming into the cabin. Which made sense. The musty smell indicated that the cabin had been shut up for a while, it made sense for the power to be turned off. All she had to do was find the main switch and switch it on.

"I think there's a window there." Milo pointed in the darkness and she could just about make out the outline of his hand.

"Stay there, I'll go take a look." She climbed over the bed and stood on the other side, her head pounding as she straightened up. Taking a couple of small steps forward, careful not to trip over anything, she made it to the log wall and lifted the blind across the window.

"What can you see?" Milo asked.

"Nothing really. We're not on the ground floor. All I can see is trees." She squinted into the darkness. "And snow. There's snow on the roof outside." No wonder it was so cold.

"It wasn't snowing when we were in town." Milo slid across the bed and came to stand by her side. "Can I see?"

Her jaw tightened as she fought the throbbing in her head. Leaning down, she hooked her hands under his arms and lifted him just as she'd done a thousand times or more. "See?"

"I don't remember it snowing on the way here," he whispered.

"Maybe the snow was already here." She leaned her head

against the cool glass, trying to think clearly. "Do you remember if we drove up a hill?"

Milo was quiet for a moment. "We might have. I remember rolling back on the seat."

"Then we could be in the mountains."

"I always wanted to visit the mountains."

"Okay, we have to find a way out of here." Penny eyed the snowy roof. Climbing out of the window would be the last resort. If either of them slipped on the roof, they could injure themselves and then freeze to death before anyone found them.

Would that be better than the fate that awaited them if they were here when their captor came back?

Something bumped outside of the room and she jumped, clinging tightly to her son. What if their captor had never left?

"What was that?" Milo cupped his hands to her ear and whispered.

"I don't know." Penny worked her way to the side of the window, feeling around for some way to draw the blinds back. She found it and rolled the blind up slowly, thankfully it didn't squeak or creak and alert their kidnapper.

Although if they had been kidnapped by a shifter, they would already know their prisoners were awake and moving around. Being a mortal in a supernatural world wasn't fun at all. As the blind slowly lifted up, the scant light from outside illuminated the room enough for them to make out the rest of the furniture. What little there was of it. Either no one used the cabin, or this was the guest room. "Let's check out the dresser for some warm clothes."

She held her son in her arms as she tiptoed toward the dresser, which was pushed back against the same wall as the window. Penny placed her foot on a floorboard that creaked as she transferred her weight forward. She snatched her foot back and nearly overbalanced. Swaying slightly as her heart hammered in her chest, she held her breath and listened for any movement from outside the room. Everything seemed quiet. Perhaps they were alone. But she wasn't going to take that chance. Stepping forward once more, she placed her foot a little to the left, avoiding the creaking floorboards. Two more steps and she stood in front of the dresser.

"Can you sit on my hip and hold on tight?" Milo nodded and wrapped his arms around her neck as she adjusted his weight. Just like when he was a baby, he rested on her hip, with one arm around his waist to help support him. With her free hand, she touched the top of the dresser to check if there was anything useful there. It was empty.

Penny curled her fingers around the handle of the top drawer and pulled it, the dresser rocked forward before the drawer slid open a couple of inches. She put her hand inside, gingerly checking if there was anything inside. Empty, confirming her thoughts that this was a guest room or that the whole cabin was unused.

She didn't push the drawer closed, instead, she checked the next two drawers, all she found was a towel, which she handed to Milo. "What am I supposed to do with it?" he hissed.

"You can wrap it around your shoulders, it will keep you warmer." She helped him drape it around his shoulders and then pull it tight and tuck it under his legs, so it didn't slip off. "Now we're going to go to the door and see if we can get out."

"Okay." Milo took one last look at the window before he switched his attention to the door leading out of the room. She could feel his small heart beating rapidly and his grip tightened around her neck, nearly cutting off her breath.

"It's okay. I've got you." Penny rubbed her hand up and down his back.

"What if she's here?" Milo asked.

"I don't know," Penny answered honestly. "But I don't think she wants to hurt us. If she did, she would have done it by now. She needs us for something."

"Why?" Milo asked the same question Penny had been asking herself over and over again since they looked out of the window. What did this old woman want with them? They were new in town. They weren't magical. She lifted her chin. Perhaps that was why she wanted them. Maybe she needed normal humans who didn't possess magic. But why?

"I'd rather not ask her." Penny reached for the door handle. "If we never see her to find out, that is fine with me." Was it? If she didn't find out what the old woman wanted or why she'd brought them here, how would she ever feel safe?

Logan had promised to protect them but how did you protect someone from the unknown?

24

LOGAN

He checked his watch once more and then glanced at the clock in the kitchen just to double-check his watch wasn't wrong. "She should be back by now."

"Relax," Ivan told him as he made a sauce for the evening meal. "She might have found the perfect home for her and Milo and can't bear to leave. That would be a good thing, wouldn't it?"

"I guess. Although, I'd rather Penny and Milo stayed here at the hotel or moved in with me."

"The cabin is fine for a bachelor wolf but it's too far out for a child to go to school every day. Unless you had a dragon, who could fly back and forth each morning and afternoon." Ivan waggled his eyebrows at Logan.

"I don't mean them sharing the cabin with me. I could rent a house with them in town. Or maybe on the edge of town." He sighed and left the kitchen. "I'm going to check if they haven't managed to sneak past me. They might already be in their room."

"Do you think it's even possible for your mate to sneak

past you?" Ivan asked as he stirred the sauce with a wooden spoon.

"No." Logan left the kitchen all the same. He needed to be doing something. Standing still, waiting for them to arrive back at the hotel was almost impossible when his concern was starting to grow. If Penny was going to be on time for the start of her shift, she should have been back at least ten minutes ago. "Have you seen them?"

Rift also shared his concern, he'd gone out into the parking lot to check that her car wasn't there. "No sign. I went along to the garage in case her car has broken down again. Frank hasn't seen them since they picked up the car."

"So, where is she?" Logan raked a hand through his hair and ran upstairs to her room. He hadn't gone inside out of respect for Penny's privacy, but he put his ear to the door and listened. There was no one in there.

We knew that before you listened, his wolf told him. We would sense her if she was in the hotel.

His wolf was right. Of course, he was right.

Plus, if Rift says her car isn't in the parking lot, I think we can be certain Penny and Milo never made it back to the hotel.

His heart was like a lead shot in his chest. *What if something had happened to her?*

Worse, his wolf replied. What if she chose to leave Wishing Moon Bay because she doesn't want to be with us?

At least she would be safe. Logan didn't want to think about his mate leaving but that was easier than the thought of them being hurt. Or worse. They had stumbled across a town filled with supernatural beings and had no idea how to handle some of the odd inhabitants.

Are you thinking a rogue vampire might have sucked their blood? His wolf snarled and snapped at the air.

No. Although now that his wolf had put the idea into his

head, Logan had trouble getting rid of it. *But other people in town might want to cause her harm.*

Like who? His wolf's eyes widened. What about the warlock who disappeared? He might have gone after Penny and Milo as an act of revenge. His wolf shuddered and bared his teeth. I can track them down.

Let's not jump to any conclusions. Logan tried to calm his wolf. It made no sense for the warlock to disappear and then go after Penny and Milo.

Did you check if Sophie managed to charge his card? His wolf paced up and down in Logan's mind.

I'll go check myself. Logan ran back downstairs, Sophie was due back on duty in half an hour. He didn't want to wait that long. He needed answers now.

Logan tapped on the keyboard and the computer came to life. Clicking the screen with the mouse, he entered the guest registry and found the warlock. "There you are, Jeremy Barnes."

He clicked on billing. The encrypted credit card details were all there but there was nothing to say Jeremy had been charged for his stay at Wishing Moon Hotel. If it had failed, the bill should have been logged as needing a follow-up. There was nothing. Sophie was usually very thorough with these things, particularly since he'd spoken to her about it himself.

Perhaps she was in the middle of doing it when Valerie returned and then she forgot. His wolf always tried to see the best in people. However, Sophie's whole attitude had been off over the last couple of days.

Logan ran his finger under the card details and then checked through the receipts. If Sophie had charged the card, there would be a receipt. There wasn't. Logan checked the bill and then clicked to charge it to the card they had on file.

The computer buffered before he got a *success!* notification. Weird.

So this means the warlock wasn't committing fraud? his wolf asked.

I don't know what it means. Maybe he was just hoping he'd get his stay for free if he complained enough. I don't think he was upset enough to take it out on Penny and Milo. They had nothing to do with what happened.

It was Penny who took the soup away before he had a chance to scream mouse. His wolf gnashed his teeth together. *If we find out he's touched one hair on their heads...*

"Logan." Sophie walked in through the main door and Logan jumped, looking guilty.

"Hi there." He smiled, smoothing over his features as he tore off the receipt for the warlock's bill. "I was just checking through the receipts and noticed you hadn't charged our missing warlock's account."

She frowned. "I didn't? I'm sure I did." She tilted her head to one side. "At least I was sure I was going to. I must have forgotten. There's been so much going on these last few days. I'm really sorry." Her expression faltered. "You're not going to fire me, are you?"

"No, of course not." Logan shook his head a little too enthusiastically.

"Great. I was worried after the other day. I wanted to apologize if I offended you or Penny. I realize you make such a great couple and since you are a shifter, you have no choice in who you love." She ducked her head and batted her eyelashes. "You can't help who you fall for. At least not if you aren't a shifter. I envy you in some ways. It must be incredible to know without a doubt who your mate is. The pull of a true mate must be strong. Unbreakable even."

"It is." He nodded and looked around. "I don't suppose you've seen Penny or Milo, have you?"

"No, not since... I think it was around an hour ago, I thought I saw Penny's car heading toward the tunnel." Sophie pointed away from the bay, in the direction someone would go if they were leaving town.

"You saw them leaving?" Logan choked on the words.

Sophie came around the desk and put her arm around his shoulders. "I'm sure they weren't leaving just because they were driving that way. They could have been going anywhere..." Her voice trailed off. "Penny looked so happy with you. And it's obvious you all dote on Milo. Did something happen?"

"Her sister is coming to town tomorrow. Maybe she went to meet her earlier. Penny might have gotten another message from her." He raked his hand through his hair, at this rate he wouldn't have any hair left by the time he found his mate. *If* he found her.

"Wouldn't she have had the decency to tell you?" Sophie's barbed comment was said with a dose of sweetness.

There is something about her I don't like. His wolf sniffed Sophie and wrinkled his nose. There is something off about her.

This isn't the time to pick a fight. We have enough to deal with and if we have to go out and search for Penny, we're going to need Sophie here to keep an eye on things. Logan smiled warmly at Sophie. "I'm sure Penny just lost track of time. Maybe they're down at the bay watching the moon come up. I told them about the wishing moon this morning and they each have a pebble. You know what it's like with kids, they have no concept of time."

"I know, but Penny made out like she was so conscientious about pulling her weight and working a shift. She must know you can't just pick and choose these things. People are relying on her." Sophie clamped her mouth shut. "I'm sorry, there I go again. I just want the best for you, Logan, and even though she's your mate, I just worry you could do so much better. I suppose if Penny was a shifter, too, then she'd understand you more. But she's from out of town, all this is new to her and she just doesn't get it."

"Thanks, Sophie. I'll go find Rift and we'll go out and look for her, I'm sure she's down by the beach." He ground his back teeth together as he went to find Rift. Sophie had begun to sow seeds of doubt in his mind. Not about his mate, but about Sophie. What was the receptionist trying to do?

She's jealous, she probably sees this as her opportunity to drive a wedge between us and our mate. She might think she knows how shifters feel about these things, but she has no idea if she thinks that's going to work.

Okay, we find Rift and round up the twins. Between us, we should be able to trace Penny's steps. He hurried into the kitchen where Rift was talking quietly with Ivan.

"Have you found her?" Rift looked up as Logan entered.

"No. Sophie said she saw Penny's car driving toward the tunnel." Logan rubbed his chin and turned away from his brothers to stare toward the reception desk where Sophie was greeting a couple of guests and handing over their keys. "She insinuated that Penny was leaving."

"She wouldn't do that to you," Ivan said firmly. "If she left, she'd tell you, she knows how much you mean to her."

"And I know how much Milo means to Penny." He turned to face his brothers. Perhaps Sophie had managed to seed those doubts after all.

"Penny would tell you if she was leaving." Rift came to Logan and put his hand on his shoulder. "You know she would."

"Do I?" He shook his head. "Penny knows how much she means to me and that might be the problem. She might have changed her mind about staying and thinks I'd force her to stay."

"So she left before you could do anything about it." Rift

pondered this for a moment. "No, Penny knows you won't ever hurt her, that you would support her in any decision she made. She wouldn't leave the town of her own accord without telling you."

"Of her own accord!" Logan raked his hand through his hair. "You mean someone took her?"

"Maybe. But I don't know who. Her ex-husband would never find the town, would he? I doubt the town would reveal itself to a guy who dumps his wife and kid and leaves them practically destitute." Rift's eyes flashed with anger.

"I don't think he even knows they are here. Unless Helena told him." Logan chewed the inside of his cheek. "Unless it was the warlock."

"The warlock? You mean the guy who put a mouse in his soup?" Ivan's spoon clattered to the floor. "Does the guy have a death wish?"

"No, but he might be out for revenge, and what better way than to take Penny and Milo?" Rift shook his head and sighed. "Okay, let's backtrack a little way." He held out his hand to Logan. "You're just going on Sophie's word that she saw the car leaving town."

"You think she's lying?" Logan whispered.

"I think that we have to look at this from all directions. Firstly, she might be outright lying. Secondly, she said she saw *the car* leaving town. What if someone stole Penny's car? Thirdly, she might just be mistaken."

"Rift, the voice of calm reason." Ivan threw the spoon into the sink and went to the drawer for another one. "My advice is to start the search for yourself. Ask questions, try to find someone who can corroborate what Sophie saw."

"That's a good plan." Rift pointed at the dragon shifter. "Can you look after things here if I go with Logan to search the town? We can grab the twins on the way out. They are good at tracking. I'm sure we can round up a few other people to help. People we trust."

Logan nodded. "I need to go find Valerie and tell her what's happening. I don't want anyone else speaking to her and poisoning her mind against Penny."

"Go. I'll find the twins and we'll make a plan."

"If you haven't found her by the time the restaurant closes, I'll help. We can extend the search further afield."

"Thanks, guys." Logan nodded.

"We will find her," Rift assured him. "If she's in town, we will track her down."

"What if she's not in town?"

Neither of his brothers had an answer for that.

25

PENNY

Penny put her hand on the doorknob and closed her eyes in silent prayer before she turned it. If the door was locked, she'd have to choose whether to try to break it down or try to climb out the window. Slowly, she turned it and pulled the door toward her.

"Damn it!" The door didn't budge. It was locked.

"What are we going to do now?" Milo asked.

"I'm going to put you down and take a look at the door. Is that okay?" He nodded and slid out of her arms to land lightly on the floor. Penny knelt next to him and used her fingers to feel the door, exploring the lock and handle for any weaknesses. "I sure wish we had a light."

She put her ear to the door and listened. Was there someone out there?

"What can you hear?" Milo asked.

"Nothing." She slithered onto the floor and looked under the door, it was just as dark on the other side.

"What was that?" Milo jumped back from the door.

"It sounded like a groan," she whispered. "There is someone else in the house."

"What do we do?" Milo's wide eyes begged for an answer, but she didn't know what that answer was.

"I need a moment to think." She leaned back against the door and slid to the floor.

"The door rattled," Milo hissed.

"I don't think it matters if someone in the house knows we're awake."

"No. The door rattled. That means the key is in the lock. Doesn't it?" Milo's excitement roused her. "I saw it in *Scooby-Doo* once. If you push the key out and then pull it under the door you can unlock it." He cupped his hands around his eyes and looked into the keyhole. "I'm sure it's there."

Penny stood up and grasped the handle with both hands. This would go one of two ways, they would knock out the key and get out of there or they would get a visit from their captor. If the former happened, great, if the latter happened... Penny clenched her fists. She was ready for whoever had hurt them. She was a single parent now, the sole protector of her son, and she sure as hell was going to protect him. "Okay, let's try rattling the door."

"Wait, I can try to poke it out with this." He held out the flint and steel Logan had given him, he'd secured it to a belt loop on his jeans.

"Okay, give it a try." Penny stood back out of the way, giving her son room.

Milo knelt on the floor and lined the steel up with the lock. The thin, round cylinder-shaped piece of metal slid into the keyhole.

"Wait." Penny put her hand on his shoulder and then hurried to the bed and stripped off the sheet. Coming back to the door she threaded the sheet under the door, positioning it so that when the key dropped out of the lock, it would land on the fabric and they could pull it back under the door. "Okay, ready."

Milo pushed the flint into the keyhole once more. He paused, took a breath, then with the flick of his wrist, Milo pushed the steel forward and shunted the key out of the lock, it dropped on the floor with a thud. "Is it on the sheet?"

"Yes." Penny could barely breathe as she inched the sheet back toward her. "I don't think it's going to come under the door, it's too thick." She stopped pulling the sheet and examined the gap under the door. "It's wider on this end. Not by a lot but it might be enough." Shuffling backward, she pulled the sheet along the bottom of the door. "This is it."

"You can do it, Mom." Milo placed his small hand on her shoulder and Penny blinked back the tears that misted her eyes. She had to focus but fear gripped her. Fear of what would happen to them if this didn't work.

"Slowly." She slid the sheet under the door, and the key came with it.

"You did it."

Her hand trembled as she picked up the key and put it in the lock. With a satisfying click, the key turned and unlocked the door. "Come on." She held Milo's hand and stepped into the hallway beyond.

"Someone's in the other room." Milo pulled on her hand as the groan sounded once more, this time unmistakable.

"We should just go." Penny could see the stairs. There were no lights on downstairs, it looked as if whoever had kidnapped them had left. But they could come back at any time. Or they could be asleep in that room, groaning in their sleep. Or maybe they were a shifter and their animal groaned.

"There's a key in the door." Milo yanked his hand out of hers and ran back to the door.

"Hello?" a muffled voice called out. "Is there someone there? Please, help me."

"It might be a trick," Penny warned as Milo turned the key.

"What if we were still locked in the room and someone could let us out but didn't?"

"Why do you always make such good sense?" Penny leaned against the door and tried the handle. The door was locked. "Who's in there?"

"Jeremy Barnes. I was kidnapped." He paused. "I know your voice."

"I'm Penny, the server who stopped you from telling everyone there was a mouse in your soup." She stepped back from the door. "Why did you bring us here?"

"Me?" Jeremy squawked. "I didn't. I've been kidnapped." He paused. "Is this a joke? This is your revenge for the soup incident."

"This is definitely not a joke. My son and I were drugged and brought here." She ran her hand through her hair, her instincts telling her to leave him and run, get as far away from here as possible. Her head told her that the warlock might have answers. Answers they needed. He also might have magic, and they were going to need all the help they could get if their kidnapper returned before they'd gotten away.

"Please, help me."

"Okay, I'm coming in. If you try anything, so help me..."

"I'm tied up. I can't do anything."

"Ready?" she asked Milo. "If anything happens, you run downstairs and get far away."

Milo nodded, his eyes fixed on the lock as she turned the key and then twisted the handle. The door swung open slowly, the room so dark that she couldn't make out any features at first. "Where is he?"

"I'm tied to the bed." A faint movement that looked like a hand waving caught her attention.

"I'm going to the window. Milo, you stay by the door." Penny walked toward the sound with her arm outstretched. "Ouch." Her knee knocked into a cedar chest at the foot of the bed. This room was bigger than the other room and there was something familiar about it. She inhaled deeply, that scent. It reminded her of something, something that made her feel safe. "Logan." She reached out and her fingers brushed against a sweater lying on the box. Closing her fingers around it, she lifted it to her nose and breathed in the scent of pine and spice. "This is Logan's."

"I knew it!" The warlock roared in rage. "That's who brought me here. I knew it was for revenge."

"No, Logan would never hurt us," Penny replied. She knew it, deep down in her soul. Despite the conclusion she might otherwise jump to, she knew Logan would never drug them and bring them here. "He would never put us in danger. But this is his sweater." She went to the window and pulled open the blinds. In the distance, she could see small twinkling lights. "We're in his cabin."

"Why?" Jeremy asked. "Why are we here?" He pulled at the rope securing him to the bed. "And why am I tied up?"

"How did you get here?" Penny asked as she went to the bed and untied his right wrist. She sure hoped she wasn't making a mistake in setting him free.

"I don't know. I left the hotel. I went into town, it was late, I was angry at you for taking the soup..." He ran his hand through his hair.

"Why did you do that?" Penny moved away from the bed, her hands on her hips as she waited for her answer.

"Because that's what I do. I travel a lot. It's expensive." He reached for his left wrist and unknotted the rope.

"You're a conman."

"Yes, I am." He pulled his wrist free and flexed his hands before rubbing his wrists.

"Why?" Penny went to her son and put her hands on his shoulders. Had she made a mistake in freeing Jeremy?

"Because that's about all I'm good for." He swung his legs over the side of the bed and stood up. "I need the bathroom."

"Don't let us stand in your way." She stepped back as Jeremy darted out of the room, he stood in the doorway looking right and then left before disappearing from view. "Come on, let's go downstairs."

"Shouldn't we wait for Jeremy? If he's a warlock, he has magic." Milo hung back. He looked so small, so vulnerable in the dim light.

"I'm still not sure I trust him." She beckoned to Milo. "I don't think there's anyone downstairs. Let's get out of here before the old lady comes back."

Milo followed her, keeping close as they crept toward the stairs. Penny was certain there was no one down there but she wanted to make absolutely sure. Taking one step at a time, she went down to the ground floor, stopping and listening after each step. There was no sound other than the toilet flushing in the bathroom and the sound of the faucet running. If nothing else, Jeremy had good hand hygiene.

They reached the bottom of the stairs as Jeremy opened the bathroom door and came out. "Do you know how hard it is going to the bathroom in the dark?"

Milo giggled but Penny replied, "Keep your voice low."

"There's no one here." Jeremy ran down the stairs and joined them in the downstairs hallway.

"How do you know?" The hairs stood up on the back of her neck. So he did know more than he was telling them.

"Because if there was someone here, they would have stopped you from getting to me. Whoever took us wanted to keep us separated and keep us locked up." He looked around. "Why is it so damn dark?"

"The electricity is off. So there's no power for the lights," Penny explained.

"There must be candles or a flashlight." He put his hands out in front of him. "Let's split up and see what we can find."

"You don't think we should just make a run for it?" Penny held onto Milo with her left hand and thrust her right hand in front of her as she went right, and the warlock went left.

"And go where?" Jeremy opened a door, his voice muffled as he went inside. "We're in a cabin. You think it's your boyfriend's cabin. And where is that?"

"The mountains." She pressed her lips together. "We came here in my car, it might be outside."

"With the keys in it just waiting for us to drive away?" A crash followed by a curse came from the other room. "Damn it. I hate this."

Penny headed for the large rectangle of dim light on the opposite side of the room. Pulling the blind up didn't help her see much in the room, all she could make out was a table and a counter. "We're in the kitchen."

"Great. Check for a flashlight or candles. There must be something we can use." Another crash and something hit the floor. "I don't think there's anything in here, I'll come and help you."

Penny opened the cupboard under the sink and felt inside. Nothing of any use. She stood up and opened a drawer, it rattled, this was where he kept his knives and forks. She worked her way methodically around the kitchen as Jeremy joined them and began opening random cupboards.

"I found some cans of food. Oh, and this sounds like potato chips. We won't starve."

"What time is it?" Penny opened a tall cupboard that reached from the floor to the ceiling.

"Why, am I keeping you from something?"

"Is it late at night, close to morning? If it's close to getting light, we could wait." Her hand touched something cold, hard, and metallic. "I think I've found a flashlight." Her hand closed around the curved handle and she picked it up, hoping they'd get lucky and it had batteries in it. Feeling around the outside of the flashlight, her finger brushed against the switch and she flicked it on.

"Don't shine it in my face!" The warlock covered his face with his arm.

"Do you complain about everything?" Penny's harsh voice was met by a hurt expression as he lowered his arm.

"Oh, I'm sorry. Forgive me for not being in a peppy mood. For your information, I do not enjoy being kidnapped and tied up."

Penny didn't answer as she shone the light around the kitchen. "Okay, let's go take a look outside."

Jeremy didn't answer but he followed her out of the kitchen so she took it as a silent agreement that they should check to see if her car was outside. If it wasn't, she planned to check the other outbuildings to see if there was any other mode of transportation they could use to get out of there.

If they found none, they would have to decide if they would risk leaving on foot or go back inside and prepare to fight.

26

LOGAN

"What can I do to help?" Valerie glanced down at her leg. "If only I was capable of coming out there with you and searching the town."

"I appreciate you wanting to help. The best thing you can do is stay here and call us if Penny and Milo come back. You have everyone's numbers, so you could work as a hub and relay any information to each of us." Logan took his phone out of his pocket and checked for messages. There were none. No missed calls, no unread texts.

"Have you tried calling her?" Valerie asked gently.

"Yes. It just rings and rings and then goes to voicemail. I've sent texts, too, but there's no reply." He sighed and shoved the phone back in his pocket. "I don't understand."

"She wouldn't have left," Valerie said firmly. "I saw the way she looked at you. She is in love with you, Logan. You are offering her everything a woman could want."

"What if her sister put pressure on her to leave? Helena could have called while Penny was in town and said something to make her leave." He raked his hand through his hair before he could stop himself.

"She would have told you."

"Would she?" Logan shook his head. "I put too much pressure on her."

"Don't do this." Valerie took hold of his hand and held it tight. "You need to focus on finding her. Whoever put this idea into your head that Penny took Milo and left is just plain wrong."

Sophie. His wolf huffed. She's the one who said she saw the car heading out of town.

We don't know that she's lying. Logan kissed Valerie on the cheek. "Thanks, Mom."

"Now, go. I'll pass on any information I find." She sat down and picked her phone up from the table in front of her. "While you're all searching, I will start calling around to everyone I know. Someone must have seen something. Even the smallest clue will help."

"I'll see you later." Logan slipped from the room and headed out of Valerie's apartment that was built on the back of the hotel. This was where she'd raised her six boys while running the hotel. At the time, Logan hadn't realized just how much work it must have been. Valerie's endless energy and enthusiasm had carried them all through, no matter what life threw at them.

"We're all ready to go." Rift met him in the reception area. "The others are waiting outside."

"Do you want me to come help, too?" Sophie asked. "Valerie could man the reception desk. I can cast a location spell."

"You could do the spell from here, couldn't you?" Logan asked.

"Sure." Sophie leaned down and picked up one of the folded maps they handed out to tourists who didn't know the area well. "It's going to take a few minutes." She opened the map up and spread it out. "I'll have to go grab some ingredients and I'll need something that belongs to Penny. Something personal."

"I'll go grab something from her room." Logan went around the desk and grabbed the key to Penny's room.

"Okay, I'll get started on the spell." Sophie smothered a smile as she grabbed a bag and placed the contents on the top of the desk.

"I'll be fast." Logan ran to the room and unlocked the door. Penny's things were gone.

He stumbled into the room and sat down on the bed. How had she managed to sneak in and get everything without him noticing? Something didn't add up.

Or are we hanging on to hope when we should admit Penny left town? His wolf raised his head and howled.

No. He refused to believe it. There had to be something here that Sophie could use for her location spell. A strand of hair, a... He sniffed, he could scent Milo. Pulling back the bedcovers, he found the small plush wolf. "Mr. Wolfy."

As a child, Logan had a favorite toy, a soft furry dog he used to take to bed each night. He couldn't sleep without it. Milo wouldn't have left without it. He had been carrying it when he arrived in town, he would have sat with it in the back of the car when they left.

Logan closed his eyes and put the toy to his nose and inhaled deeply. "I'm going to find you, Milo. You and your mom."

Let Sophie do the spell, his wolf said. *Let her tell us if Penny is in town or if she's left. At least that way we'll know where to look.*

We'll let Sophie do the spell. Logan placed Mr. Wolfy on the nightstand and left the room, locking the door behind him.

"They took their stuff." Logan went back downstairs. "But I managed to get a couple of hairs from Milo's pillow."

"Great." Sophie held out a small bowl into which she

ground up herbs and then added pink liquid. "This won't take a second."

Logan watched as she used a mortar and pestle to grind up the hairs, then she added them to the pink mixture. She closed her eyes, an incantation Logan didn't recognize filled the reception area as Sophie began to chant. Her voice rose until it suddenly stopped dead and she swirled the mixture around as she poured it onto the map in a spiral pattern. The liquid seemed to have a life of its own as it coalesced and then moved across the map, heading away from town and out into the world beyond. "What does that mean?"

Sophie looked up at him, her eyes big filled with tears, for him. "I'm so sorry, Logan. Penny's not in Wishing Moon Bay anymore."

His jaw tightened, his fists clenching as he fought the urge to hit something. "Are you sure?"

She nodded. "I've used the spell many times. It's never failed me."

"Thank you." Logan nodded. "I'll go speak to the others."

She reached out and covered his hand with hers. Logan fought the urge to recoil. "Take your time. I can look after things here."

Logan nodded, slid his hand out from under hers, and turned and walked away.

She's lying, his wolf snapped.

I know, but we don't want her to know that we know. He pushed the door open and stepped out of the hotel entrance. Inhaling deeply, he let the cold air fill his lungs.

It's starting to snow. His wolf's concern for his mate and Milo grew as they watched the lazy snowflakes fall to the ground.

"Logan, the twins didn't want to wait any longer, they took off toward the beach." Rift came toward him. "We're going to take the west side of town... What's wrong?"

"We have a problem." Logan's voice was so quiet that only a shifter would hear.

We don't know that the witch has some way to hear us, his wolf said.

"What kind of problem?" Rift matched the volume of his brother's voice.

"I think Sophie is involved with Penny's disappearance."

"What?" Rift hissed.

"Don't turn around," Logan warned.

"What's going on?" Rift's head drifted to the right, but he didn't turn around.

"Sophie did her location spell." Logan wandered toward the road, keeping his back to the hotel.

"Did it work?"

"She told me Penny was outside of Wishing Moon Bay."

"How does that make Sophie involved in all this?" Rift stopped walking. "Talk to me, Logan."

"I gave Sophie some hair and told her it belonged to Milo. She put the hairs in her potion and did the spell. She poured the liquid on the map and it told her he was outside of town." He rubbed his hand across his chin, not wanting to believe the truth. He liked Sophie. Until Penny had come along, he would've said they had a good relationship. Sophie was certainly a good employee. "But the hairs I gave her were mine. And I am right here in Wishing Moon Bay."

"Crap." Rift rocked back on his heels and turned his face to the sky. Snow floated down and rested on his cheeks before instantly melting. "What are we going to do?"

"I have no idea. I'm afraid to confront her because we have no idea where she might be keeping Penny and Milo."

"Logan, have you considered the possibility that she isn't keeping them..."

"Don't!" Logan cut his brother off sharply. "I can't think like that."

"Okay. I'm sorry. I just..."

"I know." He took a big breath. "But wouldn't I know? Wouldn't I feel it in my heart? In my soul? We share a connection. If that connection was ripped away, I'd feel it."

"You would," Rift agreed whether he believed it or not.

"I need you and the others to go on searching. I'm going back into the hotel. I need Sophie to think I believe her. But I can't stop searching for Penny and Milo." He clenched his fists. "It's taking all my self-control not to go in there and make her tell me."

His wolf leaped at the edges of his mind, wanting to be set free so he could get the information they needed from Sophie.

We need to bide our time. If Sophie thinks we suspect her, she might disappear, and we'll never find Penny and Milo.

His wolf gnashed his teeth but calmed down, slinking off to a corner of his mind, where he waited for the moment their mate might need them.

"I'll meet with the others and let them know what's happened. Keep us updated." Rift placed his hand on Logan's shoulder. "We will find them."

"I know we will." He nodded. "We have to." Because anything else was unthinkable.

He stood and watched Rift as he shifted into his snow leopard and ran off down the road toward the beach. While he watched, he took the time to get his breathing and his temper under control. He had to make Sophie believe he'd accepted that Penny had left town.

"How are you doing?" Sophie met him at the door as he entered the hotel.

"Not great." He gave a raw laugh, exposing his underbelly to her.

"I'm so sorry things didn't work out for you. Penny was

so sweet, and she had that cute little kid." Sophie patted the air as if she were patting Milo's head.

"*Has* a cute kid," Logan corrected. "She might be gone from town, but I'll find her."

"You're going after her?" Sophie didn't hide her surprise.

"First thing tomorrow. She's my mate. They need me." He forced a smile onto his face. "Thanks for telling me where she is. I'd have torn the town apart looking for her if you hadn't been able to locate her."

"That's great. I mean, you have to follow your heart." She placed a comforting hand on his arm. "Maybe she'll come back. She might have had business out of town and then she'll decide to come on back to you."

"She might. Thanks, Sophie. I don't know what we'd do without you."

"No problem at all. Glad I could help."

Logan turned away from Sophie and went to the kitchen where Ivan was busy keeping up with orders from the restaurant. "How are things?"

"Busy. It's hectic when we're so shorthanded."

"I can get out there and serve." Logan went to the sink and turned on the hot water.

"What? Why are you here? You should be out there searching for your mate."

"I think Sophie has something to do with Penny's disappearance," he told Ivan, hoping the sound of the running water would smother the sound of his voice.

"What!" Ivan's eyes flashed as he turned to his brother. "Why would you say that?"

"She did a spell to locate Milo and said he was out of town. I gave her my hair." He tapped his head. "Why would she lie?"

Ivan sighed. "So you're playing along with it?"

"Exactly. I want to watch her every move. I believe Penny

and Milo are still in town and that Sophie will lead us to them."

"So, I do get to join in on all the fun."

"You do."

"Great, now get these out to table six, they have been getting impatient."

"Yes, chef." Logan saluted Ivan and headed out of the kitchen and into the restaurant. He needed to keep calm and carry on if he was going to fool Sophie. She was a witch, but he had no idea how strong her powers were.

Or what she wants, his wolf reminded him. I don't think she'd go to all this trouble just because she thinks she's in love with us and wanted to get rid of the competition.

You're right, I think it goes much deeper than that. Much, much deeper.

The evening wore on and Logan was proud of himself for getting through it without verbally biting someone's head off. His temper was frayed, and his nerves were on edge, but this was Valerie's hotel and he had to behave.

The twins and Rift have returned, his wolf snapped in his head.

"I hope you enjoyed your meal." He picked up the plates from table eleven and headed back into the kitchen.

"Logan." Aiden looked worried.

"What did you find?" His heart went cold as he placed the dirty dishes down on the counter and opened the dishwasher.

"We picked up Penny's scent. We were told she and Milo went to the diner for ice cream. We followed the scent out to the parking lot. Her car had been parked there."

"Is there more?"

"There is." Aiden looked at Caleb.

"There was another scent, too."

"Who was it?" Logan's gaze bored through the wall

between the kitchen and reception area. He already knew whose scent it was, this would only confirm his suspicions.

"We didn't know, but Rift identified it," Aiden said.

All eyes turned to Rift. "The warlock."

"The warlock who put a mouse in my soup?" Ivan spat.

"The same." Rift held out his hands. "I have no idea what it means."

"Sophie and the warlock might be working together," Ivan suggested.

"But why? None of this makes any sense. I can understand Sophie having this misguided idea that we might be together if Penny and Milo were out of the way. But how does a warlock fit into this?" Logan wanted to smash his fist into the wall, but Ivan would kill him stone-cold dead if he damaged the kitchen and spoiled his food. "Unless..."

"Unless what?" Rift asked.

Logan turned back to his brothers. "The warlock left without paying his bill and I asked Sophie to charge it to his card. She didn't. I did it this afternoon."

"You think the warlock did it for money?" Ivan folded his arms across his chest. "Money and passion. The root of most crimes." He grabbed a bag of garbage and took it outside while the others fell silent.

If Sophie has an accomplice, she might not lead us to Penny until it's too late, his wolf said.

What if we've got it wrong and the warlock is calling the shots? Logan replied.

But why? That was the question he could not answer. He'd never met the warlock before so why would the man steal Logan's mate?

Ivan came back into the kitchen, his face pale. "I just found this in the garbage dumpster." He held up Milo's backpack, the one he was wearing the first night Logan met them in the street. "I think the rest of their stuff is in there, too."

Logan's relief was unexpected. "She didn't leave me." And short-lived.

"Of course she didn't, you idiot." Ivan passed the backpack to Logan. "I think it's time we had a chat with our receptionist."

But when they entered the reception area, Sophie was gone.

27

PENNY

"No car." Penny shone the flashlight around the immediate area outside of the cabin. "I'm going to look for tracks." She turned around to face Milo and Jeremy. "Why don't you two stay here while I go and check."

"Sure." Jeremy put his hand on Milo's shoulder. "I'll take care of him."

Penny adjusted the angle of the flashlight and shone it at Jeremy's face. "You'd better not be in on this."

"I'm not, honestly. I was brought here at the same time as you. Only you got to travel in the back seat."

"What do you mean?" Sophie asked.

"It was all a little hazy at first but it's coming back to me. I was in the trunk of the car."

"You couldn't have been. We drove up here in my car and you were not in the trunk when we left the hotel."

"No, you stopped off on the way and picked me up. She made me get in the trunk."

"Who made you get in the trunk?" Surely the old woman couldn't have forced this guy into the trunk. Unless she had a gun.

He tapped the side of his head. "There was an old woman at the hotel. She knocked on my door and asked me if I had hot water in my shower. I thought she was making fun of me, that she knew I was inventing all that crap about the hot water not working." His eyes went out of focus and he looked a little crazy as he ran his hand through his hair. "I don't know what happened, but the next thing I remember is climbing into the trunk of a car. There was someone on the back seat, lying down. I didn't get a look at who it was, but I recognize the boy's sneakers." He pointed at Milo's feet. "He was curled up next to you."

"Did she drug you, too?" Penny's hands clenched at her sides, she sure would like to wrap them around the old woman's throat right about now.

He shook his head. "I don't see how. I had breakfast in my room. The receptionist brought it up to me, the morning after I...after *you* took my soup."

"You put a mouse in that soup!" This guy sure didn't like taking responsibility for his actions.

"And is this my punishment?" He held his arms out. "Getting kidnapped and then tied up in a remote cabin in the woods? Maybe it's me who should be asking what your involvement is in all this."

"We're in this together. Whoever brought you here brought us here, too." She sighed. "Look, it's cold, I'm going to search for tracks. Why don't you both go back inside?"

"I don't want to leave you, Mommy." Milo reached for her hand and she took it, holding it in both of hers.

"You need to stay warm."

"So do you." He looked pale in the dim light.

"Okay, stand there. I'll check for tracks and then we'll go look in the shed." She pointed to the silhouette of a large building situated behind the cabin and shuddered, scared at what they might find in there.

"We'll stay right here," the warlock assured her.

Penny stepped into the snow that had drifted up against the porch steps. Maybe she should have checked the house for rain boots before she ventured into the snow. Her boots only just skimmed her ankles, and her feet and the bottom of her jeans would be wet in no time. She couldn't afford to get too cold. The cold killed. She didn't need any special survival skills to know that.

Taking short strides, she shuffled forward in the snow that covered the area immediately next to the cabin. About ten feet away from the cabin, she found what she was looking for, indents in the snow made by a car. More recent snow had covered the tracks, but there was no mistaking the uniform tracks that led away from the cabin. Penny followed them, leaving fresh footprints in the snow. They led away from the cabin, following a trail that curved to the left and then headed downhill. Penny kept walking, the snow thinner beneath the trees.

"How far are you going?" the warlock called out.

"I just want to see how far we are from town," she answered, although that wasn't the only reason, she wanted to look out on the mountainside below.

Her breath came in short puffs as she reached a point where the trees thinned, and she had a clear view out on the town below. She was no expert, but she figured they were five, maybe ten miles away from town. Too far to walk at night in the cold unless they could find warm clothes and food. Even then it was a risk, especially for a young child. She closed her eyes and blinked back tears. Milo was going to make it out of here alive.

Shaking off her fears, she opened her eyes and scanned the mountainside below for any signs of a vehicle coming their way. There was no sign of headlights bumping along the trail, heading back to the cabin. They had time.

Turning her back on the town below, she ran back to the cabin, her feet wet and her legs aching as she climbed the porch steps.

"What did you see?" Milo slid his hand into hers, the talisman grasped tightly in the other.

"The town is too far for us to walk in the dark at night. One wrong move on the trail and one of us could end up injured and with no way to call for help, we would be in real trouble."

"So whoever brought us here took your phone, too?"

"I don't think someone would have gone to the trouble of kidnapping us and locking us up if they were going to leave our phones." She lifted Milo into her arms. "Okay, let's go check out the outbuilding back there. Then we have to make a plan."

"A plan?" Jeremy asked. "If there's no transportation in that shed, what plan do we have other than waiting for our kidnapper to come back and whacking them over the head with a baseball bat if there is a baseball bat in the cabin? Does your guy play?"

"I have no idea, we've only just met." Penny tramped through the snow, which was deeper around the back of the cabin where there were no trees for shelter.

The warlock followed her, grumbling as he walked. "So what's the story? You act like a married couple."

"We aren't. We met when I came to town because my car broke down a couple of days ago." Although it felt like months since her car had kangarooed down the road into Wishing Moon Bay. "He's a shifter, we're mates if you're wondering about the whirlwind attraction."

"Ah, that explains it. Lucky, lucky shifters." They reached the outbuilding, which was a large timber building, it was either a large shed or a small barn.

"Okay, can you open it?" She glanced at the warlock, who looked right back at her. "I kind of have my hands full."

"I'll try." Jeremy approached the door and slid back the bolt. "It's locked."

"Can't you use magic?" Milo asked, his head resting on Penny's shoulder and his arms wrapped tightly around her neck.

"Good point, Milo. Why don't you use magic?" Penny asked. "You could have escaped from the bed and gotten out of the house..." She backed away. "You are in on this, too."

"No, I'm not." The warlock searched around on the ground, kicking up the snow to the side of the barn as he searched for something.

"Then why not just use your magic?" Penny asked.

He stood up, his shoulders slumped forward as he turned to face her. "Because I have none. I'm what's called a *scrub*."

"A scrub?" Her forehead creased as she watched the guy.

"Magic sometimes skips a generation, or, in my case, skipped me. I have no magic, so the only thing I'm good for is scrubbing floors." He rolled his eyes. "That's what my adorable, amazingly talented sister tells me, anyway."

"So you have no magic?" Penny was both relieved and disappointed. A magic-user right now would sure be useful, not only to get the barn door open but also to combat the person who had kidnapped them when they returned. If the three of them were still at the cabin. Penny cast a worried glance over her shoulder. Was that an engine she heard in the distance?

"I have no magic." He kicked at the snow, his foot coming into contact with something hard. "Ouch."

"What are you doing?" Penny moved forward to watch the warlock. Was he still a warlock if he had no magic?

"I might not be able to unlock this with magic, but I've found most locks break if you hit them hard enough."

"I get the feeling this isn't the first time you've broken into a barn."

"Nope." The warlock raised the stone with both hands and brought it crashing down onto the lock. "Third time's the charm," he said after he repeated the process.

"Third time's the charm it is." Penny helped him open the doors and shone the flashlight around the building.

"Well, that was a waste of time unless we want to abseil down the mountain with rope." The barn was practically empty, there was no vehicle, and the shelves around the room were filled with tools and a couple coils of rope.

"Okay, plan B, back to the house, let's see what we can find to defend ourselves." Penny ran out of the barn but stopped dead in her tracks. "I can hear an engine."

"Maybe it's Logan?" Milo whispered hopefully.

"Maybe, but we can't take any risks." She held Milo tightly as she ran for the cabin. "Jeremy, close the doors."

"What if we used the rope?" Milo asked as Jeremy shut the barn doors and ran after them.

"How would the rope help?" Penny's voice wavered as they reached the porch and ran for the door.

"We could make the part that goes around your neck big enough for all three of us." His idea sounded crazy, but so did the idea that a witch was coming for them. A real witch.

"Would that work?" Penny asked Jeremy as they entered the kitchen and closed the door behind them.

"I don't think so." He shook his head and held out his hand to Milo. "Can I see the pendant you're wearing?"

"You'd better not try to take it," Penny told him.

"I wouldn't do that to a child." Jeremy looked appalled at the idea. "I think they're ruins for protection. I want to see if we can use it to protect all of us."

Milo pulled the pendant out from under his clothes. It hung so far down his chest that when their kidnapper had searched them, she hadn't seen it. Or maybe it had protected Milo by keeping itself hidden.

"Logan showed me how to make a ring of protection. I took a photo of it…it's on my damn phone. I should have taken more notice of it. If I would've memorized it, we might stand a chance."

"This might do." Jeremy looked hopeful as he pointed at the talisman. "I can draw it in the snow. Although some of the runes are unfamiliar to me. But if I can replicate it, we can stand in the center and she shouldn't be able to reach us." He cocked his head to one side. "The only problem we have is freezing to death. But one problem at a time, right?"

"One problem at a time." She nodded and let Milo slip to the floor. "Honey, you go with Jeremy and help him carve out the runes in the snow. You'll need the flashlight."

"What are you going to do?" Jeremy was already backing toward the door.

"I'm going to get some warm clothes and blankets and some food and water." She dashed forward, kissing Jeremy on the cheek before ushering them out of the door. "Please take care of my son."

"You are going to join us in the circle, aren't you?" Jeremy asked.

"I am. Now go." She hugged Milo and sent him after Jeremy. With a deep breath, she cleared her mind and focused on her part of the plan.

Taking the stairs two at a time, she ran to Logan's bedroom, stripped the blankets off the bed, and then ran back downstairs. Her eyes had gotten used to the dark, although she couldn't see anything clearly as she opened the kitchen cupboards and rummaged for any food they could eat cold. She also found what she hoped was a couple of bottles of water. Barely stopping to catch her breath, Penny bundled everything up in the blankets and ran outside. Automatically, she paused to shut the door behind her, the engine was getting closer, the sound louder as it strained to get up the steep mountainside.

"If you wreck my car, you're going to pay for it!" Penny yelled, although she was unsure if it was her car approaching or another since the snow distorted the sound.

"It's stopped!" Milo called, the flashlight weaving all over the place as he tried to fix it on his mom.

"She's killed my car." Penny turned and ran for the others. "At least it buys us more time."

"We're going to need it." The warlock had completed half the talisman, the runes and symbols covered a large area of the snow, leaving enough room for them in the center. "Be careful not to smudge any of it. If it's not perfect, it won't work."

"Then you'd better make sure it's perfect," she retorted as she dumped her haul on the ground. "What can I do?"

"Can you draw this shape over here?" He pointed at the snow. "It's a repeating pattern all the way around the edge of the talisman, calling for protection."

"Sure." She used her fingers to make the shapes in the snow, repeating them as she completed the circle. "What's next?"

"Um..." Jeremy raised his eyes and looked in the direction of the trail. "She's coming."

"Then we'd better work fast." She took hold of the warlock's trembling hands. "What's next?"

"One of these." He held up the talisman and Milo shone the light on it. "There."

"Okay." She set to work, as the temperature seemed to drop. Was it the deepening night or something more sinister at work? Penny refused to get distracted. They needed the symbols and runes to ward off whatever approached.

"She's close," his voice wavered, and his hand stilled.

"Keep working," Penny snapped. "Next?"

"This symbol repeats. We're calling on the elements to protect us." He pointed at a symbol that looked like a flame. "Repeat them until you join up with those." He pointed to where the symbols started. "I'll work on the runes."

"It's so cold." Milo's teeth chattered and the flashlight shook in his hand, but he didn't drop it and kept the angle of the beam aimed perfectly so both Penny and Jeremy could work.

"We're not going to finish in time," the warlock ground out.

"Okay, does this thing protect the wearer from magic?" She jabbed her finger at the talisman.

"Yes." His eager eyes fell on it. "Not powerful magic. But most witches don't wield that kind of magic."

"And can you remember all the runes you have left to mark on the ground?"

He stared at the talisman and then nodded. "Yes."

"Then give me the talisman." She held out her hand. "I'll buy us some time."

"It's too dangerous," the warlock whispered.

"Mommy, don't do it," Milo whispered.

"Jeremy is going to keep you safe." She hugged Milo. "I love you."

"I love you, too. But don't go. Please, don't go." He held onto her so tightly and she wanted to stay more than anything, but she had to buy them some time.

"The talisman will keep me safe. And when Jeremy finishes this, you will be safe, too." She took hold of his hands and gently eased him away from her. "This will be over soon and then we can make a new life here."

"Hurry." Jeremy's pale face showed his fear as he nodded toward the trail leading away from the house. "She's so close, I can feel her."

"I thought you didn't have any magic." Penny carefully stepped over the runes and symbols carved into the snow.

"I don't. But I was raised around witches and warlocks. I can sense magic, and this is strong magic, she's drawing on the elements around her."

"Like she's charging a battery?" Penny asked.

"Exactly." Jeremy paused for a moment. "Be careful."

"I will." Penny turned away from her son and the warlock and hurried toward the trees. She needed the element of surprise. But she had no idea if the witch could sense her and would act before Penny had a chance to pounce.

28

LOGAN

"Where did she go?" Logan pushed his senses out, trying to locate Sophie.

"We'll track her." Aiden and Caleb ran out of the door, out into the parking lot, and shifted.

"Rift, you stay here." Ivan took off his white chef's coat and handed it to his brother. "The kitchen is closed, all you have to do is make sure the diners pay for their food and leave happy. Can you do that?" His eyes flashed as he grabbed Logan and propelled him toward the door. "We should be able to track Sophie from the air."

"Thanks." Logan ran after Ivan, who headed into the middle of the road before shifting.

Logan had seen the dragon many times, but he still found the sight of the huge beast with scales that shimmered like an azure sea...*incredible.*

Amazing, his wolf agreed.

The dragon swung his huge head around and dropped his shoulder so that Logan could climb on his back. He hadn't ridden on the dragon's back for years, and as the mythical creature crouched down and then leaped into the air, the memories came rushing back. He truly was an incredible beast.

With several downbeats of his leathery wings, Ivan rose into the cloudy sky. He'd have to keep low if he wanted good visibility and if they planned to use their senses to track Sophie.

"Can you see the bears?" Logan leaned forward as he called out.

The dragon swung his head from left to right before angling his body as they banked to the right.

I guess we have our answer, his wolf said as they pushed their senses out, trying to locate their brothers. Ivan had always had the strongest shifter senses out of all six brothers. Valerie claimed it was because dragons were such ancient beasts and even a young dragon had a depth of wisdom that some shifters and humans never gained.

Rift had teased Ivan over this statement whenever Ivan messed up or got things wrong. When they were younger, Ivan would scowl and get upset, however, as he got older, he'd matured enough to let it go.

I can feel them, his wolf said. *They are on the other side of town, in pursuit of a car traveling toward the mountains.*

Is it Sophie's car? Logan couldn't tell, but his wolf's senses were keener.

Yes, I believe it is. His wolf gnashed his teeth and snapped at the air. How he'd love to get his teeth and claws on the woman who had taken their mate.

We still don't know for sure, Logan reminded him.

We'll know when we catch up with her. But the dragon didn't increase his speed, he kept back, watching and waiting. Despite Logan's need for revenge, they needed Sophie to lead them to Penny and Milo.

The bears had dropped back, the car going too fast for

them, but they kept going, following the trail as Sophie left the town behind and climbed into the mountains.

The snow will slow her down. Sophie's car slid as it hit pockets of deeper snow, her tires spinning as they tried to grip the road. Her speed slowed and Ivan circled around, like a vulture watching his prey.

She's heading toward the cabin. His wolf snarled. *She took our mate to our cabin.*

If she's going back there now, at least it means Penny and Milo are still alive. Logan dared not let his mind wander any further. He didn't want to explore the deep, dark thoughts that threatened to break him.

They clung to hope while they clung to the dragon's back as he stalked the car, waiting to pounce. Logan could sense his brother's pent-up fury, only contained because they needed Sophie alive. At least until Penny and Milo were found.

Ivan is not a murderer, his wolf reminded him. No matter what Sophie has done, she belongs in the hands of the authorities.

I thought you wanted to rip her throat out, Logan replied.

Oh, I do. But wanting that kind of revenge and taking it are two different things.

The car reached thick snow and could go no farther. Sophie got out of the car and started to walk, it was another mile to the cabin over difficult terrain. The trail leading to Logan's cabin was no more than a rough path threading through the trees. In normal conditions a car would make the journey easily, these were not normal conditions. The closer they got to the cabin, the more the snow deepened, and the temperature dropped.

Logan could see his breath as he breathed in and out. With each breath, the dragon emitted a cloud of vapor that instantly turned to water droplets and fell to the ground like rain. If it got much colder, their breath would freeze instantly.

Beneath him, the dragon suddenly wheeled to the right and glided away on silent wings, Logan wanted to yell at him and ask him just what the hell he was doing, but that would give away their surprise and he trusted Ivan. With his life and that of his mate.

Landing silently in the snow, the dragon turned his head to look at Logan. He got the message and slid to the ground so that Ivan could shift. They needed to talk.

"She's going to your cabin. I can't tell if Penny and Milo are there, can you?" Ivan asked as soon as he regained his human form.

Logan shook his head. "I need to be a little closer."

"Me, too. It's like something is blocking me. I suspect it's Sophie, she's also making the temperature drop." Ivan's jaw tightened.

"What is it?" Logan asked.

"She's powerful. Very powerful, and I can sense something else in her." He put his fist to his chest, "It's like…rage. She's consumed with it. Which makes her very dangerous."

"We should split up. I can shift and run from here. Unless she can sense me, she won't be able to see me against the snow. This is my territory, I know it like the back of my paw." Logan raked his hand through his hair. "Can you distract her?" He sighed. "I hate to ask and put you in danger."

"You don't have to ask. For your mate and her child, you know I would do anything." He stepped forward and hugged Logan. "We're brothers. Blood or no blood, that doesn't change what we are. Penny and Milo are my family, and a dragon would die for those he loves."

Logan swallowed a lump in his throat. "Thank you. It's more than I could ever ask of you or any of the others."

"You know we all feel the same way. At least, Dario would if he ever gets back to town." Ivan nodded. "I might have to incinerate Sophie to stop her."

"Let's make sure we exhaust every other plan first. I don't want this on you, Ivan." Logan patted his brother's back. "I love you, man."

"Of course you do. Everyone loves a dragon." Ivan winked and then turned and ran from his brother, shifting in midair to fly into the sky as if he'd never been there.

Except for the big footprints in the snow, his wolf said lightly.

Yeah, those would take some explaining anywhere but here. Logan stared in the direction of his cabin, forcing his shifter senses to penetrate the barrier that seemed to surround it. Ivan was right, Sophie was a powerful witch.

How come we never sensed her before? His wolf snapped at the air, wanting to taste witch blood.

She must have kept her power low, so we couldn't sense it, now she's drawing in all the power she can. It's like she's a bomb about to explode.

Then it's time we took her down. His wolf sprang free as soon as Logan relinquished his hold on the world around him. This was their fight and they planned to take it right to the witch.

And win.

His wolf ran through the snow, his white fur blending in perfectly. Even in daylight, he'd perfected the art of melting into the snowy scenery around him. His white fur was made for snow, even if it gave him a disadvantage when the sun shone, and the leaves were green.

As he neared the cabin, the temperature once again began to drop. He could sense the witch but little else.

Is she blocking it out or is she just so powerful that we can't focus on anything else? Logan didn't have the answer, but despite the power of the witch they were about to confront, he didn't slow his pace.

Life without the mate he'd just found was unthinkable. That wasn't how this was going to turn out. Not if he had any say in it.

She's close to the cabin, his wolf told him. I can get a sense of the others there. Three others. His wolf shook his head. Who is the other person?

And is he a friend or foe?

The warlock, his wolf growled as they neared the scene. *He has Milo.* He moved his head from side to side trying to locate Penny. She was closer to the witch who was almost upon them.

Logan's wolf flattened as he ran at full speed toward the place he called home. He would not let the witch hurt them. As for the warlock, he was going to get what was coming to him.

Logan wove in and out of the trees, the snow flicking up as his paws bit into the cold snow.

"You escaped the cabin," Sophie's voice carried across the distance between Logan and the cabin. "Bravo." Only it didn't sound like Sophie's voice. There was something different about it.

Cracked, like broken glass, his wolf replied.

"Leave now, witch," the warlock's voice boomed.

"Not when I am so close to completing my cunning plan." She cackled into the frosty air.

"What plan?" the warlock asked.

"Why don't you join us, Penny, instead of skulking in the trees? Don't you think I see you?"

Logan was close enough to watch the events unfold but too far away to stop them as the witch pulled Penny out of the trees, her fingers curled as she beckoned to her.

Penny was powerless to stop it. "What do you want?" his mate asked.

"Oh, so much." She cackled again and as Logan got closer, he saw her face was as cracked as her voice. "I have a list."

"What do you want with *us*?" Penny was closer to the witch now, ten feet or less. He needed to act.

"Well, I didn't want anything with *you*. You just showed up and got in the way." Sophie tapped her chin. "And then I thought…this is a sign."

"What kind of sign?" Penny was calm despite the imminent danger she was in.

She has a plan, his wolf said.

We can't be sure, Logan answered, pushing his wolf to get closer, to help his mate.

"Well, since you are not going to make it out of here in one piece, I'll tell you. Not because you deserve to know, but because the misery of your mate will shatter your heart." The witch stepped closer to Penny who seemed to be resisting. "Come to me, my pretty. Oh, I can't wait to wear that young body of yours." She shivered in delight.

"You're crazy." Penny stood still as if frozen. But the temperature was growing warmer, the snow on the tree branches melting as if the sun were shining down on them.

"That might be true." Sophie sighed. "But sometimes only a crazy plan will do."

"Out with it, witch," the warlock called.

They're stalling for time, his wolf said. The warlock is doing something.

"It all started forty years ago, there was a hotel in Wishing Moon Bay where a powerful warlock lived. He hosted the best parties and people came from all over the world to attend them and stay in the hotel. He had a beautiful young fiancée who loved him so much. They promised each other there would never be anyone else. But then the warlock made a mistake and disappeared. His beautiful fiancée could feel him, trapped in the very hotel he loved so much. But she was powerless to free him."

"You're talking about the Wishing Moon Hotel and you are the beautiful fiancée?" Penny asked. "Although, the beautiful part is not so obvious now. Perhaps you should have moisturized a little more."

"Joke all you want. But soon I will have your young face." Sophie touched her wrinkled skin.

"You plan to take over my body?" Penny didn't hide her shock.

"I am." Sophie wagged her finger at Penny. "It's all your fault. If you hadn't come here, I was just going to bring back my beloved and put him in the body of Logan. Valerie would leave him the hotel when she *permanently* retired and then he'd have realized I was the one he was supposed to be with. Delayed fated mating. At least that's what everyone would think."

"You were going to steal Logan's body?" Penny asked in disgust.

"His body, his life. But not for myself. For my beloved Radley." Her expression softened as the snow continued to melt.

"Rad the Bad."

"The one and only. But then you came along, and my plans changed." Sophie sneered. "Logan was locked onto you, his mate, and suddenly he was out of my reach."

"And so you chose…" Penny half-turned to look at the warlock.

Sophie sighed. "I'd have preferred to look at Logan's face every day. But then I had a plan for revenge. What if I take *his* mate? Rad can have the warlock's body since it's wasted on him. So much potential but no power. And I will have yours. We would be lovers."

"And Logan will lose his mate." Penny looked down at the snow, her foot kicking at the slush before she lifted her head and faced Sophie. "You're melting the snow."

Sophie laughed, bent double as she held her hand against her stomach. "You thought you were stalling so the warlock could finish the runes of protection in the snow. But I was making things toasty so there would be no snow."

Penny reacted in a sudden flurry of movement, her arms outstretched as she ran at Sophie. The witch raised her hands to stop Penny in her tracks, but her powers had no effect.

No! Logan yelled at his wolf, who sprang forward, using his shifter speed to reach their mate as she closed her arms around the witch.

"You can't hold me forever," Sophie wriggled in Penny's arms as she fought to get free.

"Run!" she called to the warlock and Jeremy took hold of Milo's hand and made a dash for freedom.

Logan's wolf closed the distance between him and the witch who wanted to take his mate from him. As he reached them, he shifted into his human form, balled his hand into a fist, and slugged Sophie in the jaw.

"I have never hit a woman before," he ground out as Sophie reeled away from him, her eyes rolling back in her skull as she lost consciousness.

"Logan." Penny sobbed as she fell to the ground with Sophie. "You found us."

Above their heads, a shadow fell on them. Four faces turned upward in awe as the dragon landed only feet away.

"Ivan." Logan wanted nothing more than to pull his mate into his arms, but he resisted the temptation. The witch might be down, but she wasn't out. As soon as she regained consciousness, she would be a threat to them all.

"Her power has seeped away." The warlock let go of Milo, turned, and ran away.

"Coward." Ivan ran toward them.

"He's gone for the rope in the shed," Penny said quickly, her arms tightly wrapped around the witch.

"You can let her go, if she tries anything, I'll incinerate her," Ivan said bitterly.

"The twins are here." Logan shifted his attention to the path where two large bears appeared out of the darkness.

"We missed the fun," Aiden said drily, as he shifted into his human form. Caleb remained a bear, his eyes fixed on Sophie, ready to attack if she stirred up more trouble.

"We're going to fly back to town. Can you drive the car back, if it'll start?" Logan glanced over his shoulder as the warlock came back with the rope.

"We'll go now if you are okay here," Aiden eyed the witch nervously.

"We have it under control." Logan nodded his thanks to his brothers.

"Here, here's the rope." The warlock came back as Aiden shifted back into his bear and joined Caleb as they ran back down the mountain.

"Tie her up, bind her hands. I'll take her back to town." Ivan helped Jeremy bind Sophie. "Logan, call Valerie and tell her we're coming. She needs to alert the authorities."

Logan nodded and tapped the phone screen to call Valerie. The night was almost over, the threat to his mate almost gone. But until the witch was dealt with properly, she was still a threat.

They had underestimated Sophie once, they could not afford to again.

29

PENNY

"We're all going to ride on the back of the dragon?" Penny asked.

"Yes!" Milo pumped his fist in the air, his excitement chasing away his fear.

"Yes. We need to hurry." Logan held out his hand. "Can I have the talisman? I'll hold onto Sophie. If she regains consciousness, with the help of the talisman, I should be strong enough to keep her contained until we get to town."

Ivan shifted into his dragon and lowered himself closer to the ground as Logan picked up Sophie and carried her to the dragon. Jeremy had brought rope from the shed and tied up the witch tightly. Possibly a little too tightly, but no one argued for the ropes to be loosened. They were all aware of the danger she posed, even with her arms bound to her side.

"Don't let her speak," the warlock advised as Logan mounted the dragon and positioned Sophie in front of him.

"I won't." Logan bound his arms around the witch and gripped a bony horn along the dragon's back.

"You're up next," Penny said to the warlock. "Then Milo can sit behind you and I'll sit at the back."

The warlock scrambled onto the dragon's back without hesitation. As soon as he was seated in position, he held out his hand to Milo. "Come on, Milo."

Milo scampered onto the dragon's back and settled himself down, his short legs hardly long enough to reach either side. He looked so small up there, but his smile was broad, the danger of the night forgotten as he readied himself for their next adventure.

"Penny." Logan's voice propelled her to move and she climbed onto Ivan's leg, reached for Jeremy's offered hand, and then finally scrambled onto Ivan's back.

The dragon waited for her to wrap her arms around Milo before he crouched down and leaped into the air. The world below them faded into darkness as he headed for the stars, now partly obscured by the steadily falling snow.

Tears blinded her eyes as the cold air hit her and then snowflakes flew in her face. She kept hold of her son, who trembled in her arms, she suspected, and hoped, from the thrill of excitement.

"This is amazing!" His voice was swept away as the dragon swooped down and flew straight and true toward town.

"It is!" Even in these potentially dire circumstances, their journey was incredible. Perhaps when the summer came and the weather warmed, she could ask Ivan to give them another ride, one that they could enjoy fully. One free from peril.

In minutes they had passed over the mountains and were gliding over the tops of buildings, most of which Penny didn't recognize. They were traveling toward the far side of town, past the hotel.

She tilted to the left to check on Logan, the old woman in his arms still unconscious, or pretending to be. Would the witch wake up and cause them harm before she could be taken into custody?

And what kind of custody would she be taken into? How would they contain such a powerful witch?

The dragon slowed, his wings dipping as he came in to land. With barely a thud, his feet struck the ground, and he eased his wings back before tucking them into his sides.

"We need to get off, quickly," Jeremy called to Penny.

She hooked her stiff leg behind her and slid down onto Ivan's leg as he crouched close to the ground. Holding her hands out to Milo, she grabbed her son as he slid off the dragon and then hurried out of the way.

The warlock dismounted and then turned around to help Logan, but before Penny's mate could drag the witch from the back of the dragon, she made her move.

Sophie sat bolt upright, her arms clenched by her sides as a rush of wind swept toward her, leaving the hair on Penny's neck standing on end. A guttural cry emanated from her as she chanted a spell.

Penny backed away, holding Milo in her arms. She was torn between protecting her son or helping Logan who wrapped his arms tighter around the witch. She screamed, curses flying in the air as Logan restrained her.

Then, from behind Penny, a new chant rose like a choir singing and Sophie went limp in Logan's arms. He lifted her and hooked his leg over the side of the dragon, sliding down with the witch in his arms.

"We will take her from here," a woman's voice said quietly. She stood at the front of a small group of people, a mix of men and women. Penny guessed they were witches and warlocks, and it was these powerful people who would take Sophie into custody.

Logan handed Sophie over to a large broad-chested man, dressed in jeans and a thick winter coat. Somehow, she'd imagined witches and warlocks would wear cloaks and old-fashioned clothes, but these people looked as if they had just stepped away from a family dinner, or a night out at a bar.

"Thank you." Logan nodded his head and relinquished his hold on Sophie, a look of sorrow on his face as he glanced down at the old woman. "Goodbye, Sophie."

The chanting faded as they walked off into the night, the snow now falling all around them.

"It's over," the warlock assured Penny.

"Not quite," Logan said. "Ivan is going to take us back to the hotel."

"We get to ride the dragon again?" Milo asked.

"We do." Logan held out his hand to Milo and Penny. "Let's go home."

The warlock stood still, and Penny tugged on Logan's sleeve. "He saved our lives."

"Then he'd better come with us," Logan grumbled but his gruff voice didn't hide his true feelings. "Thank you for saving my mate and her son."

"No problem at all."

"We did save him, too," Milo piped up. "He was tied up in your bedroom."

"What?" Logan snapped.

"You're lucky I never soiled the bed since she left me there for hours," Jeremy answered.

"That is an image I never want to think of again," Logan groaned as he sprang up onto Ivan's back and reached down for Milo.

"We can go clean your cabin tomorrow." Penny helped her son and then climbed on the dragon's back, her legs ached, and she was grateful for the ride back to the hotel. "We need to change your bed anyway, since your bedspread is outside, along with the contents of your food cupboard."

"As long as you're both safe, that's all that matters." He

turned around and kissed her cheek as the warlock climbed on. Then Ivan shifted his weight and sprang into the air, flying low over the rooftops as he carried them back to the hotel.

They landed safely in the hotel parking lot, and the four passengers scrambled off the dragon. Ivan shifted into his human form and stretched his arms above his head. "I should fly more often, I'm a little stiff."

"We can't thank you enough." Penny wrapped her arms around him, and after a moment of surprise, he lowered his arms and hugged her back.

"You are welcome." Ivan's arms tightened around her. "You're family now. We'd all do anything for you."

"I think I'm getting that now." She took a step back and sniffed loudly. "I should get Milo to bed." She leaned down and held out her arms to Milo, who looked as if he might fall asleep on his feet now that the excitement of dragon-riding had passed. "Are you all right?"

"I rode on the back of a dragon." He rested his head on her shoulder. "I'm more than all right."

"Children are good at forgetting the bad stuff and holding onto the good." Logan stroked Milo's cheek. "You were very brave."

"You're all safe!" Valerie burst out of the hotel, Rift supporting his mom as she hobbled toward them.

"We are." Logan hugged his mom and then slipped his hand into Penny's. "Although, we're going to need a new receptionist."

Valerie covered her face with her hand. "I am so sorry. I had no idea about Sophie. No idea at all. She seemed perfect."

"You know what they say, if something seems too perfect, then it probably is," Rift cut in.

"Oh, I don't know about that." Logan lowered his head

and kissed Penny on the lips. She shuddered and nestled closer to him.

"I'd have to agree," she murmured.

"I'll have to start looking for someone new tomorrow," Valerie sighed.

"I would like to apply for that job." Jeremy put his hand up and they all turned to look at him.

"You put a mouse in my soup," Ivan said hotly. "You planned to blackmail the hotel into giving you a free stay."

"Exactly, I know all the sneaky tricks a guest might try. I've checked into plenty of hotels." He held out his hands, pleading with them to give him a chance. "Just give me a trial, please."

"We would not be here now if Jeremy hadn't helped us. He could have cut and run but he stayed with us. He protected Milo." Penny's voice wavered, the realization of what could have happened sweeping over her like an avalanche until she could hardly breathe.

"Hey, it's okay. It's over." Logan cupped her face in his hands. "And I promise you, these kinds of incidents are rare in Wishing Moon Bay."

"Logan's right." Valerie tilted her head back and looked up at the hotel. "I'll have to get someone in to deal with Rad's spirit. If it really is stuck in the hotel, I want it gone."

"I thought you always told us there were no such things as ghosts." Logan tightened his grip on Penny.

"There isn't. But no one ever knew what happened to Rad. He just disappeared." Valerie turned to look at her family. "I just want to make sure you are all safe." Her eyes glistened with tears. "I'm sorry if we put you in danger, Penny, and you, Milo."

"None of this was your fault," Penny assured her. "The only person to blame for Sophie's actions was Sophie. She's been planning this, getting stronger ever since Rad disappeared. I think she's mentally unhinged."

"Let's go inside." Logan ushered Penny toward the hotel. "You're shivering."

"It's cold and I don't have your warm shifter blood." Her teeth chattered as they approached the door. Penny hoped that Sophie's actions hadn't stirred the ghosts of the past. Valerie might think they weren't real, but Sophie was certain she could pull Rad's spirit into Jeremy's body.

"I've put all of your stuff back into your room," Rift told Penny as they assembled in the reception area.

"Sophie cleared your room to make it look as if you'd left town," Logan explained.

"Oh. Did you believe her?" Penny glanced up at her mate. "I wouldn't leave town without telling you." She turned to face him. "I'm not planning on leaving town at all."

"I was just scared," Logan confessed. "The last couple of days have been full-on for you. Finding out that so much that you believed wasn't real is true."

"The one thing I have found to be real is your love and the love of your family. I'll take that over witches and spells and anything else that wants to make trouble. I'm strong enough to conquer it all with you by my side." She kissed his cheek.

"Ah, there you are." An elderly man came downstairs with an elegantly dressed woman by his side.

"Mr. and Mrs. Madilyn, is everything all right?" Logan slipped away from her and she missed the warmth of his body. Even inside the hotel, Penny couldn't shake off the chill in her bones.

"We just wanted to say we love what you've done with the hotel." Mr. Madilyn reached the bottom of the stairs and went to Valerie with his hand outstretched.

"Thank you," Valerie said.

"Mr. and Mrs. Madilyn used to stay here before you bought it." Logan's voice held a hint of wariness.

Mr. Madilyn chuckled. "We had always dreamed of coming back here. And when we got your kind offer of a half-price stay for previous guests, we couldn't resist."

"Even though we said we would never come back," Mrs. Madilyn glanced at her husband.

"I'm sorry, I have no idea what you are talking about." Valerie glanced at Jeremy. "Is this the sort of scam you pull?"

"Scam?" Mrs. Madilyn looked quite offended as she reached into her purse and pulled out an envelope, which she handed to Logan. "See for yourself. You sent a handwritten invitation."

Logan opened the envelope and pulled out an invitation card. "Sophie."

"Sophie?" Mr. Madilyn's voice wavered.

"I think our receptionist sent this to you. Although I have no idea why." Logan handed the invitation to Valerie. "That's Sophie's handwriting. She's tried to forge my signature, but it's not right."

"Sophie is still here?" Mrs. Madilyn hooked her hand under her husband's elbow and steered him back toward the stairs. "We should leave."

"Wait." Ivan dodged behind them and blocked their way. "We've just had an encounter with Sophie. She's now in the hands of the authorities. So why don't you tell us what exactly is going on?"

"Sophie has been arrested?" Mrs. Madilyn's relief was evident.

"You know Sophie?" Penny asked.

"She was the reason I disappeared." Mr. Madilyn turned to face them all. "I am Radley Lomax, aka Rad the Bad."

"Sophie had a fixation with Rad," his wife explained. "We could sense the darkness in her. She was so jealous of our relationship. Then one day I nearly died in an accident. Only it wasn't an accident."

"Sophie tried to kill Camilla, that's when we realized that the only way to escape Sophie was through death."

"I left Radley. We had a blazing argument and I stormed out, taking all my belongings with me." She clasped her husband's hand. "Radley stayed on here. He pretended he was over me while I made a new start outside of Wishing Moon Bay."

"After a few months, I staged my disappearance and left everything behind to go join Camilla." Radley's adoration shone from his face. "I loved her enough to give up everything."

"Rad's reputation of being something of an experimental warlock meant that people were all too willing to believe he had done something to himself." Mrs. Madilyn sighed. "We lived a good life but Wishing Moon Bay was always our home."

"Sophie must have discovered your secret." Logan turned to face the reception desk. "A location spell."

"She must have tracked me down. Although, I have no idea why. I'm too old for games."

"She planned to put your spirit into a younger body." Penny's words were met with horror from the Madilyns.

"That's the darkest, most heinous magic on this Earth," Camilla whispered.

"Luckily, we don't have to worry anymore." Logan steered Penny toward the stairs. "Come on, Milo is already asleep, and you look as if you need something to eat."

"Goodnight, everyone," Penny said with some relief, her arms were aching from holding her son. "And thank you all again."

"Here, why don't you let me take Milo?" Rift offered. "I'll

get him into bed while you go grab something to eat and take a hot shower."

"Use my apartment," Valerie offered. "If Mr. and Mrs. Madilyn have the time, I'd love to ask you all about your time here at the hotel."

"If you're going to ask me about the staircases moving, then I'll tell you straight, it never happened," Radley said.

"I don't know who would believe it did," Valerie said.

They all shot a look in Ivan's direction, but he turned and headed back into the kitchen. "I'll fix you something to eat, Penny."

Logan slipped his arm around Penny's shoulders as Rift carried her son upstairs to bed. She snuggled into her mate's arms, welcoming the warmth of his body and the comfort of his presence.

Logan made her feel safe, made her feel as if she were home.

Made her feel as if she never wanted to leave.

30

LOGAN

"Do you feel better now?" Logan asked as his mate came into the living room, wrapped in a bathrobe with a towel wound around her damp hair.

"So much better." She slid down onto the sofa next to him. "I can actually feel my toes again after being under the hot shower." She lifted her legs and wiggled her toes. "I don't think I've ever been so cold."

"I'm sorry you got caught up in all of this." Logan leaned forward and lifted the cover off the tray Ivan had brought in. "Aiden also found your phone in Sophie's car." He passed the phone to her, happy she was here with him and not a hundred miles outside of Wishing Moon Bay.

"Oh, that smells divine." Penny inhaled deeply.

"Dig in. You should feel better once you've eaten." Logan reached for the tray and placed it on Penny's lap. "He took some food up to Milo, too, but he's sound asleep."

"He's so tired." Penny picked up her fork and dug into the lasagna Ivan had heated up for her. There were thick slices of garlic bread and a chocolate dessert on the tray, too. "I should be with him."

"Rift likes watching over him." Logan paused. "I'm sorry. Really sorry."

"Don't be. None of this is your fault. As I said, Sophie is the only one to blame. How could you know what she was planning?" She tasted the food and her eyes rolled up into her head. "This is amazing."

"I just can't believe she's been hooked on Radley for so long." He raked his hand through his hair, his body tense. "Or what she planned."

"It's a good thing I came to town or she would have had her very wicked way with you." Penny placed her hand on Logan's thigh. "And that pleasure is all mine."

His mouth twitched, her sour mood receding. He would love to be very wicked with his mate.

"She really thought she could take control of Radley and put his spirit in my body." He shook his head. "That's crazy. Even if she would've succeeded, Radley wouldn't love her."

"Maybe she thought by giving him the gift of a new youthful body, he might fall in love with her."

"Youthful, huh?" Logan laughed. "I'm not that young."

"And you're not that old." She narrowed her eyes at him. "I guess it helps that you are smoking hot, too."

"Smoking hot. Are you getting me confused with that dragon shifter?" Logan's cheeks flushed pink as he chuckled.

"No, I know exactly who I am talking about. I'm just glad Sophie didn't get her delusional hands on you." She leaned across and kissed his cheek. "I like that you are all mine."

"And always will be." He leaned back on the sofa as she ate her food. "Do you want a drink? I could make you some coffee, or cocoa, or I have some whiskey."

"I think we deserve a whiskey. Don't you?"

"I think we deserve whatever we want." Logan pushed

himself to his feet, defeating the urge to stay with his mate and not let her out of his sight. The hours she'd been missing were the hardest of his life.

And the longest, his wolf added.

And the longest. The thought of life without Penny and Milo was enough to bring him to his knees. He didn't want to let either of them out of his sight ever again. But he couldn't smother them either.

He pushed out his senses, locating Milo in the room above them, while making sure Penny was still seated on the sofa, eating her meal. Satisfied they were safe, he took two glasses out of the kitchen cabinet and retrieved his stash of whiskey, which he hid at the back of the cupboard where Valerie stored the cans of vegetables.

The whiskey wasn't hidden there because he was ashamed of drinking, but because his brothers would have quite happily drunk the whole bottle between them and left it empty. Logan had learned that from experience.

"Here." He took the two large glasses of whiskey back to the living room.

"Thanks." Penny reached out for the glass. She'd eaten her lasagna and garlic bread and had moved onto her dessert. "I'm going to struggle to keep my eyes open once I've finished this."

"Don't worry, if you fall asleep, I'll carry you up to your room," he promised.

"Now that is an offer I can't refuse." She placed the glass down on her tray and spooned her dessert into her mouth, savoring the taste. "This is so good."

"I can't remember the last time Ivan cooked something that wasn't good. He is a masterful chef."

"He is." Penny placed her spoon on the tray and then lifted the tray and put it on the table before retrieving her whiskey. "Here's to us and to those we love. May they always stay safe and be loved."

"I will drink to that." He touched her glass and they sat in silence, savoring their drinks.

"I can't believe how fast things have changed for us since we came here," Penny eventually said. "When I was driving to Helena's, I felt so alone. So weighed down by everything. Even though I know Helena loves us, it's not where my heart belongs."

"You're not on your own," Logan assured her. "I will always be there for you."

"I hope so because now I know where my heart belongs. With you, Logan." She took a swig of whiskey and then placed the glass on the table. "My home is here in Wishing Moon Bay. I know I said I needed time to think it over, but that's changed. I've changed."

"I love you, Penny. I know it's too soon and too sudden."

She put her finger to his lips. "No, it's not too soon and it's not too sudden. I love you. I don't know where it came from, but I know it without any doubt. You fill my heart with happiness."

"That is a relief." He let out the breath he'd been holding in.

"You have cast your spell over me, and I know Milo will be happy here. And he'll have five uncles who will play with him and probably spoil him a little too much. But I also know he'll have a father who will be there for him and will never leave." She cupped his face in her hands. "And that father is you."

"Does that mean we can live together as a family?" Logan wanted nothing else in the world than to wake up every morning with Penny beside him.

"I think it does." She leaned forward and pressed her lips

to his. "I'd like to kiss your lips last thing at night and first thing in the morning for the rest of my life."

"That can be arranged." He threaded his arm around her waist and pulled her close.

"Do you have a bedroom in the apartment? Somewhere a little more private?" She looked up at him through her lashes as color crept across her cheeks.

"I do." He eased himself away from her. "Are you sure? You must be exhausted." He opened his mouth and then closed it again. "Or am I jumping to the wrong conclusion?"

"You have jumped to the right conclusion, but now that I've eaten, I have just about enough energy to ravish you." She giggled nervously. "That sounded much better in my head."

"It sounds wonderful to my ears." Logan downed his whiskey in one gulp and as the liquor infused his veins with warmth, he leaned down, scooped Penny up in his arms, and carried her out of the living room, along a corridor to his room.

"Was this your room when you were a child?" Penny asked as he carried her to the bed in the center of the room.

"It was but I had to share with Rift. My side of the room was next to the window and Rift had that side of the room. We argued sometimes but we spent so much time outside that we never really fell out." Logan straightened up and cast a glance around the room. "I never imagined this would be the room I'd bring my mate to."

Penny reached for his hand. "You didn't ever dream of bringing your mate back here?"

"Maybe when I was a teenager, not long after I had my first shift and hormones raged inside. But as I grew older, I dreamed of a place of my own, of building a home for my mate and our kids."

"The cabin?" Penny pulled him down onto the bed next to her.

"No, the cabin was the place I ran away to when I figured that I might never find my mate and I had to learn to live with that. I retreated into myself, in some ways I regressed into the lonely boy who missed running with his wolf pack." He brushed her hair back from her face. "That's all behind me now. You are my future, and we'll find a place to live closer to town, somewhere we'll be happy. Where Milo will be happy."

"And where we could raise another child or two." The hope in her expression brought tears to his eyes.

"I would love to make babies with you, Penny." He leaned forward and kissed her lips. He wanted her so much it hurt, his stomach twisted in knots as his longing intensified.

"We could start trying now." She tugged at the buttons of his shirt, undoing each one with trembling fingers.

"Shall I help?" He took hold of his shirt and ripped it off. The buttons flew across the room and the remainder of the shirt followed.

"You have an impatient streak." She pressed her lips to his chest and heat flared across his skin.

"I want to be naked with you." He tugged at the hem of her sweater and she held up her arms so he could drag it over her head. "And the rest."

She wriggled out of her long-sleeved shirt, then covered herself with her hands, before diving under the sheets.

Logan fumbled with the clasp of her bra as she tensed. "Are you okay? If we're going too fast, we can stop."

Penny didn't meet his eyes. "No man has seen me naked except Kelvin for years. After giving birth to Milo, my body was never quite as…pert. As Kelvin often reminded me."

"None of that matters to me." He stroked her cheek with his thumb. "I love you just the way you are. We're both old enough and wise enough to know we have scars and imperfections." His mouth twitched at the corners. "That's what makes you so perfect to me."

"I'm perfect because I'm not perfect." She tilted her head to the side. "You say just the right things."

"Only to you." He chuckled. "To everyone else, the words come out wrong."

Penny eased her hand down, letting the sheet drop away. "You want to try taking my bra off again, or do you want me to do it?"

"I am not going to be beaten by a bra." He reached for the clasp and flicked it open. "I still have it." He winked at her and she laughed as she leaned closer to him.

"I think you most definitely still have it." Penny flicked her tongue over his nipple and the breath hissed between his teeth. Inching closer, she grazed her teeth over the taut bud while he unzipped her jeans and slipped them down over her hips. "I think you need to be naked, too."

Logan slid out of the bed and stood up. In a flash, he unbuckled his belt and slid his pants to the floor. Stepping out of them, he slipped into bed and pulled the covers over them both as Penny shivered. "I'll warm you up."

"I was hoping you might say that." She trailed her fingertips over his chest and pressed her lips to his, their kiss deepening as his arousal increased. He was hard, his body desperate for release, but he wanted to take things slow, he needed Penny to enjoy every moment of this.

However, as Penny trailed her fingers down his body, inching lower as she tempted and teased him, it seemed she had no intention of taking things slow.

"Oh." Her hand curled around his hard length and she squeezed him, stroking her fingers up and down until he couldn't think straight.

Somewhere in the fog of his brain brought on by the

touch of his mate, he galvanized himself into action. Logan cupped her breast in the palm of his hand and lowered his head, nipping her soft flesh before sucking the taut bud into his mouth and swirling his tongue around and around until she whimpered in need.

"Make love to me, Logan." She slid her foot up and down the inside of his leg and his thighs tensed.

Penny drove him wild, awakening the primal beast in him. Pressing the palm of his hand to her shoulder, he pushed her down onto her back before sliding between her thighs. She eased her legs apart, guiding him inside of her.

The feel of her around him, her warm slick heat enveloping him was too much. He fisted the pillow beneath his mate's head, his breath labored as he fought for control. Inhaling deeply, he let the breath out slowly, grounding himself before he exploded inside her. He had to hang on.

Slowly, he regained his control and thrust deeper inside her. Skin against skin they moved, her inner walls gripping him as he filled her. Penny stroked his back, her touch light as she kissed his neck, sending shivers down his spine.

They were joined together, a wolf and his mate. This was so right. So damn right.

He lunged forward, groaning as he filled her completely, burying himself in his mate. As he lay still for a moment, he stroked her hair back from her face before kissing her lips.

Her teeth grazed his bottom lip, before her tongue snaked out and soothed the bruised flesh. Penny opened her mouth and their tongues entwined, tasting, teasing as they enjoyed a moment of calm. But the heat between them grew, a heat that would only be quenched when they reached a climax.

Penny tilted her pelvis, changing the angle of her body and pressed her hand onto his butt. Logan didn't need any more encouragement as he slid out of her, only to lunge deep inside her again and again.

They raced together, their bodies moving in perfect sync as they inched toward a shattering orgasm.

His body jerked forward, and his essence filled her. Penny raked her fingernails down his back as she cried out his name, her body tense as she came. Logan groaned, jerking into her, filling her with his seed, hoping that they might conceive a child their first time together.

A brother or sister for Milo, a celebration of their love. Could they be that blessed?

"Tomorrow night, we should go down to the bay and make a wish," Logan murmured as Penny lay in his arms.

"I think my wishes have already come true," she whispered sleepily. "All I ever wanted was for Milo and me to be happy. And right now, we are." She lifted her head off the pillow. "I should go check on him."

"I'll come with you." He closed his arms around her and pulled her back down onto the bed. "But first, let's just lie here for a couple of minutes longer. I want to know you are real and this isn't a dream."

"This is real," she assured him. "And it's forever."

Logan kissed her skin and inhaled her scent. He no longer felt the pull of the wild. His old life was gone but he could not wait to start a new life with his mate and her child.

EPILOGUE

"Good morning." Logan carried a tray of food into Penny's hotel room and set it down on the small table by the window.

"Déjà vu." She slid out of bed and pulled on a robe as Milo stirred, dragging himself out of his long slumber.

"Do I smell Ivan's pancakes?" Milo opened his eyes and stretched before scrambling out of bed. "I am starving."

"That's because you went to sleep last night before you ate. I don't think I've ever seen you so tired." She held out her arms and he jumped into them. "We had quite an adventure. Are you okay?"

"I will be when I've eaten some of those pancakes." He kissed his mom on the cheek and wriggled out of her arms.

"I wish a plate of pancakes was all I needed to forget what happened last night." She smoothed her hands over her hair. "My head is filled with what-ifs."

"Hey, it's okay. Sophie can't hurt you anymore." Logan reached for her hand and pulled her toward him.

"It was you she was trying to hurt. All she wanted from me was my body." She smiled wryly and he grinned.

"There we go. Once you have eaten pancakes and drunk coffee, you'll feel like your normal self. I guarantee it." He kissed her cheek. "And I can't lie, remember?"

"I do remember. I remember it all, vividly." Penny ran a hand through her hair. "Maybe pancakes, coffee, and a hot shower will do the trick."

"I can watch Milo for an hour if you want to soak in a bath. I thought we could go play in the snow."

"It snowed!" Milo ran to the window and looked out. "The roads are covered in white. It's all over the cars and everything. Can we go out now?"

"Not until we've eaten our breakfast and put on our warmest clothes."

"Your Mom is right." Logan led her to the chair next to the table laden with food. "But first, sit and eat."

"Yes, sir." She gave him a mock salute as Milo continued to stare out of the window. "Are you going to join us for breakfast?"

"I've already eaten, but I'd love a cup of coffee. Jeremy is coming in later so I can assess him. I'm still not sure he's hotel material."

Penny nearly choked on the piece of food in her mouth. "And you are?"

"This isn't about me," he reminded her. "I'm only here temporarily."

"Are you sure? Valerie is going to need help for some time. Even when she says she's strong enough, taking care of the hotel is a hard job with long days on her feet. I've seen the way you run around after the guests." Penny ate thoughtfully. "What if we made this our permanent job?"

"You'll work here with me?" Logan straightened up.

"Possibly. We could give it a trial run and see if we get along okay. We might hate working together."

"Believe me, there is nothing about you I could ever hate."

His mouth twitched up at the corners as he poured the coffee.

"Does that mean we're going to live here in the hotel?" Milo's excitement brimmed over as he finally sat down to eat.

"I don't think there is room for us to live here," Penny told him. "We need more than one room, and the only apartment belongs to Valerie." She glanced up at Logan. "I'd like a house of our own. Somewhere we can escape to, just the three of us, and forget all about work."

"I like that idea. I like it a lot." His eyes darkened as he gazed at her and her heart fluttered in her chest. She was in love with this man. It was a deep love, one she could trust in even though they had only known each other for a few days. It was as if loving Logan was the most natural thing in the world, as natural as breathing.

Maybe the town had cast its spell on her, but she was ready to take a chance with him. Logan placed his hand on her shoulder and squeezed it lightly, the warmth from his touch spread out through her body.

"I like that idea a lot, too." She placed her hand over his.

"My phone." He jumped as his phone rang and he stuck his hand in his pocket and pulled out the device. "Hello." He glanced down at Penny, his eyes wide as he listened to the voice on the other end of the phone.

"What's wrong?" she whispered.

"Thanks, Rift. Tell her Penny and Milo will be right down." Logan ended the call.

"Tell who?" Penny stood up abruptly and covered her mouth with her hands before tugging off her robe and grabbing an armful of clothes. "Milo, you need to get dressed."

"Why?" Milo asked through a mouthful of food.

"Aunt Helena." She glanced at Logan for confirmation.

"She's in the hotel reception area."

"I completely forgot she was coming." Penny grabbed her phone. "Oh my goodness, I didn't realize it was so late."

"I let you both sleep in since you were so tired last night." Logan helped Milo find some clothes as Penny lingered in the bathroom doorway. "How did she get here?"

Logan looked up and shrugged. "We can ask her when you're dressed."

Penny nodded and went into the bathroom and closed the door. As she got ready, she checked her phone. Ten missed messages and three missed calls. When they went to bed last night, she'd switched her phone to silent, so nothing disturbed her sleeping son.

She tapped the screen, ready to compose a reply but then placed it down on the chair situated in the corner of the bathroom. What could she say? *Sorry, I forgot you were coming because a crazy witch kidnapped me and Milo because she wanted to take over my body?*

That conversation would be better face to face or not at all.

Helena was only visiting for a few days. All Penny needed to do was show her sister that they were happy here. There was no reason to tell her about shifters and magic. Not unless she had to.

Dressed in jeans and a warm sweater, Penny emerged from the bathroom to find Milo dressed and still eating. "We need to go down and meet Aunt Helena."

Milo slid from his seat, still chewing his food. "Can I eat some more when we come back to the room?"

"You can." Penny nodded. "If that's okay with you, Logan?"

"Whatever you want." He looked at the tray of food thoughtfully. "Why don't I bring you some fresh coffee and a tray of cookies and pastries?"

Penny glanced around the room, it was a mess. Sophie

had taken all their luggage out of the room so Logan would think they'd left town. Rift had kindly brought it all back last night, but Penny hadn't had a chance to unpack. "Could we sit in the restaurant instead? If it's not too much trouble. I hate to impose."

"Hey." He slid his arm around her shoulders. "I want Helena to like Wishing Moon Bay and like me. I also want her to see how happy you are here." He kissed the top of her head. "Which means I want you to be happy here."

"I am." She reached out her hand to Milo. "Aren't we, buddy?"

"I love Wishing Moon Bay." Milo jumped up and down as he headed for the door.

"Thank you." She grabbed hold of Logan and kissed his lips, a brief chaste kiss, that held the promise of more.

"Are we going to tell her about us?" he asked as she lingered in his arms.

"Of course. I am not ashamed of us even if our relationship did take off like a rocket. Helena will probably try to convince me I'm on the rebound, but I know that's not true." She took his hand and led him to the door. "What we have is very real."

"Okay." He took a deep breath and let go of her hand. "I'll carry the tray downstairs and then take a fresh tray to the restaurant. It's empty so you'll have the place to yourselves."

"You spoil us."

"I like spoiling you." The tray rattled as he picked it up and they all left the room.

"Aunt Helena!" Milo called out as he reached the bottom of the stairs and Penny hurried after him.

"There's my favorite nephew." Helena held her arms out and crouched down as Milo ran to meet her.

"I'm your only nephew!" He launched himself into her arms.

"You'll always be my favorite." She stood up, holding him in her arms. "Have you grown?"

"I have." He hugged her as Penny reached them.

Logan slipped past the family reunion, carrying the tray to the kitchen.

"It's good to see you, Helena. I was worried you might not find the town." She glanced at Rift who was watching them with open curiosity. "Morning, Rift."

"Morning, Penny. How are you doing, Milo?" Rift asked.

"I'm good, Logan is getting us a second breakfast."

"Preferential treatment?" Helena arched an eyebrow at her sister.

"Logan said we can sit in the restaurant, he'll bring us some coffee." She inclined her head toward the restaurant door.

"So, is this Logan the reason you decided to stay in town instead of coming to stay with me?" Helena asked, as forthright as usual.

"He is part of the reason. I also think this is a good place to live. Lots of open space, the beach the mountains."

"The good-looking men." Helena looked up as Logan came in with a tray of coffee.

"Hands and eyes off, he's mine." Penny winked at Logan. "Logan, this is my sister, Helena. Helena, this is Logan."

"I've come to check you out," Helena told Logan who smiled warmly.

"Check away, I have nothing to hide." Logan grinned and set the tray down on a table by the window.

"*Everyone* has *something* to hide," Helena replied.

"Behave," Penny warned as she linked arms with Logan. "I'm happy."

"I can tell." Helena's eyes narrowed as she looked at the couple. Milo, bored with the conversation, was more interested in the pastries on the tray. "It looks good on you."

"So, you haven't come here to tell me I am being rash and acting on the rebound?" Penny asked.

"No." Helena averted her eyes and looked out of the window. Something was wrong and Penny's stomach clenched.

"You found the town all right?" Logan asked as the silence between them grew.

"Not really." Helena laughed. "You need to check your phone more often, Penny."

"Sorry." Penny tapped her phone screen. "I set it on silent."

"Your messages are all from me asking where you are and why can't I find the road leading to Wishing Moon Bay. I drove back and forth along the same stretch of road four times. I was about to give up when this damn horse appeared in the middle of the road. I swerved hard so that I didn't hit it with the car." She took a breath, her eyes wide. "And there it was, the turnout to Wishing Moon Bay. If the horse hadn't appeared then, I'd never have found it."

Logan tensed by Penny's side. "A horse."

"Yes, a bay horse with a long mane and tail. In the middle of the road." She shrugged. "Unless I was hallucinating because when I stopped the car and went to check if it was all right, it was gone. Like it was never there at all."

"Dario," Logan whispered.

"You know the horse?" Helena asked. "Someone really needs to tame it."

Logan chuckled. "You might be right."

Penny met Logan's gaze and he waggled his eyebrows at her. It seemed there was a reason Helena had found Wishing Moon Bay. And that reason might just lead her sister to her own happy ending. One, Penny hoped, that was as magical as her own.

THANKS FOR READING!

I hope you enjoyed my book!

The next book in this series is 'The Horse Shifter's Mate', which you can find on my website: harmonyraines.com/all-books/bond-of-brothers-series

If you'd like to keep up with my new releases, and any offers, you can follow me on Facebook at:

facebook.com/harmonyrainesauthor

Or you can head over to my website and sign up to my newsletter for notifications about releases and exclusive deals.

Feel free to message me on Facebook, or send an email to harmony@harmonyraines.com.

HARMONY.

THE HORSE SHIFTER'S MATE

THE BOND OF BROTHERS - BOOK TWO

Get it here:
US: amazon.com/dp/B08T6DWQVR
UK: amazon.co.uk/dp/B08T6DWQVR

31

HELENA

"A horse?" Penny studied her sister as she ate a delicious pastry in the restaurant at the Wishing Moon Hotel. Outside, the ground was covered in a two-inch layer of snow. If more snow fell today or overnight, Helena might be stranded in the small town of Wishing Moon Bay.

"A horse. Yes. It just appeared like that." She clicked her fingers and Milo, Penny's son, jumped and fixed his attention on his aunt.

"And that's how you found the road leading to town." They had gone over this a couple of times already since Helena had arrived, but Penny kept asking for more details, even though there were none.

"Yes. I told you, I followed the directions you gave me. I drove back and forth along that one stretch of road but couldn't see you or a sign for Wishing Moon Bay. I was just about to give up since you weren't answering your calls or your texts..." Helena's jaw tightened as she fixed her sister with an accusing stare.

"Sorry, we had a long day yesterday and Milo was so tired I didn't want him woken up by my phone. Then I forgot I'd set it to silent." Penny's excuse sounded plausible, but Helena was suspicious she was holding something back.

"Well, I guess it all worked out all right." She took a bite of the croissant she'd carefully cut into pieces. The buttery flakes of pastry melted in her mouth. "These are the best croissants I've ever tasted."

"Ivan baked them. He's the chef here. All his food is incredible." Penny took a bite of her blueberry muffin.

"Is he single?" Helena asked.

"Ivan?" Penny coughed and took a sip of her coffee.

"Yes, I could marry a man who bakes this well and forgive him a lot of faults." She grinned at Penny's shocked face. "I'm joking."

"Sorry." Penny cleared her throat and frowned. "So the horse..."

"He appeared from nowhere, I turned down the road leading to Wishing Moon Bay and when I stopped the car and got out to check if he was all right, he was gone. Not a sign that he was ever there." She rubbed the crumbs off her fingertips. "Maybe he wasn't there at all. Maybe he was a figment of my imagination." Helena rested her chin on her palm and stared out of the window, lost in her own thoughts. Perhaps there was something wrong with her.

"Helena." Penny reached out and clasped her sister's hand. "What's wrong?"

"Nothing." She smiled brightly and picked up another piece of her pastry. "I'm just tired, that's all."

"I know you, that look doesn't say you're just tired." Penny let go of her sister's hand and glanced at Milo. "Perhaps I can ask Logan or Rift to take Milo for a couple of hours and we can go for a walk on the beach."

"The beach!" Milo, whose attention had been firmly fixed on what was on the other side of the restaurant window until now, turned around to look at his mom. "I'd like to come to the beach. Maybe Logan can come, too."

"I'd like some time alone with Helena," Penny explained. "We need to talk. You know, catch up on what's been happening in our lives."

"Oh!" Milo's eyes widened and he looked from his mom to Helena. "Are you going to tell Aunt Helena about Logan?"

"What about Logan?" Helena tilted her head to one side as her sister's cheeks flamed red. "Oh, now I'm interested."

"Logan is the sweetest, most incredible man I've ever met, that's all." Her breasts rose and fell as she inhaled deeply. "I think I'm in love with him." She closed her eyes for a moment. "I know I'm in love with him."

"Love? Isn't that fast? I mean, I know people say love at first sight is real. But it's also possible to get caught up in a dream, a romantic dream, that won't last long." She pressed her lips together as she looked at her sister, who had been hurt so badly by Milo's father. "I don't want to shoot down those dreams, but I also have to protect you. You and Milo."

"We don't need protecting from Logan. I promise." Penny was so certain. Her sister had loved her first husband, Milo's father. But this was different. Helena longed to have the same certainty about a man even if it was for a fleeting moment. Surely it was better to experience love, heady, giddy love, for a short time and have your heart broken than to never experience it.

Helena had never felt that kind of love. Not ever. The sad truth, that she'd never admitted to anyone, not even Penny, was that she had never been in love. Lust, yes. And sure, she'd convinced herself she was in love a couple of times just so she didn't feel like she was a freak of nature. It wasn't as if she didn't know what love was. She loved her dead mom, she loved Penny and Milo. But real, earth-shattering, I'd-die-without-you love, that had evaded Helena her whole life.

"I'd like to get to know him while I'm in town." Helena finished her muffin and eyed up a buttery pastry.

"How long are you staying?" Penny's eyes darted toward the door leading from the restaurant to the kitchen. The same door Logan had used when he left them alone. Could she sense him out there?

Helena tensed. Was he out there listening to their conversation? What if he wasn't who he said he was? What if this was one big conspiracy? She swallowed hard and grabbed her coffee cup, taking a long drink. When she met Penny's gaze, it was filled with concern.

"Sorry."

"You seem a little jumpy." Penny's eyes narrowed. "Are you sure you're okay? You can go take a nap in our hotel room if you need to."

"No, I'm fine. And in answer to your question, I'm staying as long as it takes." She looked down at her empty plate. Would it be greedy to have another one? Or perhaps she could wrap one in a napkin and slip it into her purse to eat later.

"As long as it takes to what?" Penny's suspicions were raised.

"As long as it takes to make sure that what you have with Logan is real and you are doing the right thing." She leveled her gaze at Penny.

"Helena..." Penny leaned back in her chair and shook her head. "You had me for a moment there."

Helena chuckled. "I thought you might throw the rest of those delicious pastries at me."

"The thought did cross my mind, but that would be an insult to Ivan's baking skills, and I do not want to upset my future brother-in-law." Penny waited for Helena's reaction.

Helena wasn't sure how to react. "You aren't joking, are you?"

Penny shook her head. "He's the one, Helena. The man of my dreams and he'll be there for me no matter what. Unlike a certain other person."

"And Ivan is Logan's brother?" Maybe Helena could seek Ivan out and while congratulating him on his amazing culinary skills, find out about the real Logan. If the man had stolen Penny's heart in a matter of days, then she wanted to find out all his secrets and any skeletons he might be hiding in his closet.

"Yes. Adopted brother. There are six brothers altogether. Logan, Ivan, Rift, Caleb, and Aiden. Plus, Dario, who I haven't met yet. Valerie, who owns the hotel, adopted them all when they were young."

"Six boys, she must either be crazy or superwoman." Helena could understand the need to adopt a child, her biological clock wasn't just ticking, it was starting to wind down. If she didn't meet the right man and settle down in the next couple of years, she would never fulfill her dream of being a mother. Penny might have been emotionally scarred by her jerk of a husband but at least they had a child together. Milo was an incredible boy. Who deserved an incredible father.

"She's quite a woman," Penny agreed. "They all love her very much."

"And what about Milo?" Helena switched her attention to her nephew. "Do you like Logan and all the people here?"

"Logan is fun. Not as fun as Rift, but fun."

"Maybe Logan doesn't need to hear that," Penny told Milo quietly.

"He knows, Rift told him." Milo slipped off his seat and ran up and down the window, staring at the snow outside.

"Of course he did," Penny rolled her eyes.

"Do the brothers get along?" Helena asked.

"Yes, they love each other and are there for each other

whatever they need." Penny reached across the table and took Helena's hand. "Like us."

Helena's tight smile didn't reach her eyes. "I'm happy for you, Penny. You and Milo."

"But..." Penny didn't let go of Helena's hand as she studied her closely. "What's wrong?"

"Nothing." Helena slipped her hand toward her, but Penny didn't let go.

"You've been acting weird since you arrived. And I don't think it has anything to do with being tired." She studied her sister closely and Helena's cheeks flushed pink under her scrutiny. "You didn't come here to check up on us, did you?"

Helena's gaze slid sideways, and she watched Milo as he ran in and out of the tables, so carefree. "Do you ever wish we could turn back the clock and go back to being Milo's age?"

"You are skirting around the question. I know that's part of your job, but not when you are talking to me." Penny squeezed Helena's hand tighter. "Tell me what's wrong."

"I think I'm going crazy." Helena kept her eyes fixed on the plate of pastries in front of them.

"Going crazy?" Penny asked. "Why do you think that?"

"Because..." She shook her head. "I don't know, it's stupid."

"No, it's not stupid. Whatever you think is obviously bothering you. So tell me. You know there's nothing you can't tell me." Penny's soft tone of encouragement was the reason Helena had traveled here to Wishing Moon Bay.

"You always were the best listener." A tear rolled down Helena's cheek and she dashed it away.

"You're not so bad yourself. I don't know how I would have coped if you weren't at the end of the phone every time I called and needed a shoulder to cry on or someone to listen to me rant about..." She glanced at Milo and stopped talking.

"That's what sisters are for."

"Then tell me, this is my turn to listen. My turn to repay the favor." She nodded as she squeezed Helena's hand again. "Come on."

"It's probably nothing..."

"You don't think it's nothing."

"I met someone."

Penny rolled her shoulders back, her eyes darting to the door leading to the kitchen once more. "You met someone. Is it serious? Did you come here to tell me you are getting married or something?" She covered her mouth with her hand. "Are you pregnant?"

"No!" Helena shook her head. "None of the above."

"Then what?"

"I met this guy. We bumped into each other outside work. I mean *actually* bumped into each other. I dropped the stack of files I was carrying on the ground and he helped me pick them up. Our eyes met..." She gave a lopsided smile. "No, I didn't think it was love at first sight. That doesn't mean that I wasn't attracted to him. I'm a single middle-aged woman and he was cute, dimples, nice smile."

"That's a healthy response." Penny nodded. "What happened?"

"He called and asked me to dinner the next day." She looked down at her hands. "I thought it was romantic that he went to the trouble of tracking my number down."

"Romantic would be one word to describe it. But I'm guessing that's not how it turned out?"

"At first I'd call it romantic. We dated for a couple of weeks. I liked him a lot."

"You never told me you'd met someone."

"You were in the middle of your divorce. It felt wrong to tell you I was happy when you were in such a dark place." Helena shook her head. "I know what you're going to say. I know that you would have been happy for me, I really do.

But it was a call I made. I figured that if the relationship lasted, I'd tell you about it when things settled down for you, if not then it made no difference."

"What happened?"

"He was a very sweet guy. He treated me nice. With respect. He never pushed himself on me, if you know what I mean." She sighed, recalling their dinner dates, of dancing in his arms, resting her head on his shoulder as he held her close. "I really thought I'd found a good guy. Someone with whom I could make a future. He had a good job in a similar field to me. We were a good fit."

"Okay, so that's the good, what's the bad?" Penny asked.

"He wore this expensive cologne." She inhaled and closed her eyes. "A mixture of exotic spice and musk. Very distinctive."

"What happened?"

"The day you were due to arrive..." She put her hand over her mouth, her face pale. "After you called, I went home..."

"Honey, what did he do?"

"Nothing." She shook her head. "Not to me."

"Tell me."

"I think he'd been in my apartment."

"You *think* he had."

"I could smell him. His cologne." She shook her head. "I'd never invited him back to my place. We never got that intimate."

"Do you think he let himself into your apartment?"

"Or maybe I just imagined it, in the same way I imagined that horse today." She took a shuddering breath. "What if I'm going crazy? What if I'm losing my mind like Mom did?"

"Oh, wait, no. The horse, I'm almost certain you saw." She glanced over her shoulder to check on Milo. "As for the guy, is there anything else about him that makes you think he would go into your apartment like that? Was there anything missing?"

"Not that I know of." She shook her head. "I could have just imagined it. But the smell, it seemed so real."

"Okay, well, you're here now, you're safe here in Wishing Moon Bay." Penny nodded. "And when you go home, I'm coming with you."

"No, you've already said you want to stay here. I don't want to get in the middle of what you have with Logan. A real chance at happiness."

"And that happiness will still be here waiting for me when I get back. Although, I suspect that Logan will want to come with us." Penny got up and came around the table to hug Helena. "You're not in this alone, I promise."

"Thanks, Penny. I don't know who else to turn to. I couldn't call the police, they'd laugh at me if I said I can smell an intruder in my apartment." Helena leaned on her sister. "I'm just scared I'm going crazy like..."

"Like Mom. I understand. But I don't think Mom was crazy. Not really."

"She used to believe in monsters in the closet and all that crap."

"I think she just saw things differently." Penny sighed heavily. "But that doesn't mean what she saw wasn't true."

"Now you believe in monsters and magic?" Helena pulled away from her sister. "Where did that come from?"

"There are things about this town that I need to tell you," Penny said cryptically. "But for now, let's just drink coffee and eat these delicious pastries. The rest can wait."

"I don't think it can, Penny." Helena was just about ready to bundle her sister and nephew in her car and drive out of town. But as Penny poured the coffee, Helena had a feeling she was right where she was supposed to be.

32

DARIO

"The horse lord returns." Logan entered the hotel kitchen where Dario was devouring a plateful of Ivan's food. He'd traveled all over the world but there was nothing like his brother's cooking.

"Logan. I came as soon as I could." Dario placed his plate down on the counter and hugged his brother. "Congratulations."

"Thanks, Dario." Logan patted his brother on the back. "And are congratulations in order for you, too?"

"Have I missed something?" Ivan's sharp inquiry was met with a sheepish grin from Dario. "I have missed something." His dragon shifter brother looked from Logan to Dario and back again. "One of you needs to tell me."

"Dario, this is your news." Logan let his brother go and stepped back.

"I have found my mate."

"You're joking!" Ivan shook his head. "You aren't joking."

"He's not joking." Logan's eyes narrowed as he stared at his brother.

"Ivan tells me there was some trouble with a witch who

kidnapped your mate." Dario scraped the fork across the plate and glanced at Ivan. "Any more?"

"I'd forgotten how much you eat." Ivan fetched a covered plate from the fridge and set it down on the counter. "Help yourself. It's leftovers from last night."

"Oh, leftovers, my favorite." Dario peeled back the aluminum foil from the plate. "Spaghetti." He inhaled deeply. "Smothered in your famous tomato and basil sauce, with just the right amount of garlic."

"Dario," Logan said sharply. "Explain."

"Explain?" Dario heaped the spaghetti onto his plate. "Your tone hasn't lost its sharpness."

"Not when the subject concerns my mate." He drew in a shaky breath. "And this does concern my mate, doesn't it?"

"How does Dario finding his mate affect Penny?" Ivan recovered the plate and stowed it back in the fridge, his tone hostile.

"I'm sorry." Dario set his fork down on his plate. "I am being insensitive."

"Just explain." Logan ran his hand through his hair. "Please."

"Logan..." Dario nodded. "I was coming back here to meet your mate. Ivan called me and told me you had found her, and I dropped everything to come back. It's a big occasion."

"Get to the point," Ivan told him.

"I was outside of Wishing Moon Bay this morning when a car came by and I got this feeling." He rubbed the back of his neck. "It knocked the wind out of me. Then I realized that whoever was in the car was special to me."

"You are the horse Helena saw." Logan rubbed his chin and turned away.

"Helena?" Ivan leaned back against the fridge. "Penny's sister, Helena?"

"She is your mate's sister?" Dario asked.

We had no idea, his horse told him. *No wonder Logan is in shock.*

But why the hostility? Dario asked.

Maybe he's afraid we won't take this seriously. We spend our days traveling the world. Running wild and free. A mate means settling down. A mate means family.

"Yes, she's my mate's sister." Logan glanced toward the restaurant.

Dario could sense his mate, she was close, she was safe. That's why he was in the kitchen eating, because she wasn't going anywhere. The moment she did, he would follow.

He would follow wherever she went. They were bound together.

"And you are afraid I will…what?" Dario rolled his shoulders. If Logan planned to come between Dario and his mate, he was ready to fight his brother just as they had fought as children.

Grow up, his horse told him.

Logan believes I am not serious about this. He thinks I won't do right by my mate. He's wrong! Dario clenched his fists, then immediately relaxed.

"I'm afraid if we don't handle this well that Penny and Helena might both leave Wishing Moon Bay."

"Handle what well?"

"Penny had no idea that shifters or magic were real. That was a shock, and then Penny was kidnapped by a witch. Not exactly the best new experience of life here in town." Logan went to the back door and pulled it open, sucking in the fresh air.

"That must have been traumatic. And now you are worried that Helena might freak out when she finds out about shifters?" Dario asked.

"I am." Logan turned back around. "We planned not to tell Helena since we figured this was a fleeting visit."

"I am not going to hide who I am and what she is to me," Dario replied hotly.

"That's not what Logan is suggesting." Ivan tried to smooth over the situation. "Listen, this isn't like you. Either of you. You are not enemies. I suspect the nearness of your mates has elevated your testosterone. So just calm things down and let's work this out together. Like brothers."

"Ivan is right."

"As always," the dragon shifter muttered under his breath.

"We are in this together. We both want the same thing, for our mates to be happy and stay in Wishing Moon Bay." Logan held his hand out to Dario. "Or wherever it is that you are living these days."

"I have no fixed home." He pressed his lips together. "I've spent the last few years exploring the world, joining with the few remaining herds that roam wild and free. I lost myself to that freedom. But now it's time to start a new life."

"So, you're agreed. The plan is to make sure that Helena accepts that shifters and magic are real without freaking out." Ivan looked up, at the same time Logan took two long strides toward the door leading from the restaurant.

"Penny's coming." He half-turned to face Dario. "We need to tell Penny about you and Helena."

"No!" Dario shook his head. "When Helena finds out about us being mates, I want it to be from me. I certainly don't want her to think we were plotting and scheming behind her back."

"And I am not going to lie to Penny." Logan's shoulders rose as his muscles bunched. "Trust me, Dario."

"Logan." Penny burst into the kitchen but came to an abrupt stop when she saw Dario. "Hi. Sorry, am I interrupting?"

"This is Dario," Ivan said quickly.

Penny's eyes widened. "The horse shifter?"

Dario inclined his head. "It's good to finally meet you, Penny."

"And you." She pointed at him as she drew closer. "It was you."

"What was me?" Dario got the feeling no one needed to tell Penny about her sister being his mate.

"Helena said a horse suddenly appeared in front of her and steered her toward Wishing Moon Bay. She'd driven up and down the same stretch of road a half dozen times and never saw the turnout and then you..."

"And then me." He inclined his head.

"You're her mate?" The question was direct and one he could not deny.

"I am."

"Oh." She glanced over her shoulder toward where her sister was still seated in the restaurant.

"Oh, what?" Logan placed his hand on his mate's arm. "What's wrong?"

"That's what I came to tell you." Penny eyed Dario, not with suspicion, but with sympathy. "Helena is in trouble. At least I think she's in trouble."

Dario stepped closer to Penny, but Logan inserted himself between them. "It's okay," Dario told his brother. "I just want to hear what Penny knows. If my mate is in danger, then I intend to do whatever it takes to ensure her safety."

"I know and I understand, but give Penny some space." Logan patted his brother's chest. "This is all new to her, remember?"

"I'm sorry, Penny." Dario stepped back, his hands curled into fists. "This is all new for me, too. Having a mate. When I felt the connection to Helena in the car, it was like being hit by a freight train. It's like being a teenager again when my first shift was close and the hormones in my body were out of control."

"I understand." Penny pressed her lips into a thin line as she switched her attention to Logan. "I assume that's how you felt, too, Logan?"

"When I saw you walking down the street, I just knew you were the one. Then panic took hold. And my head filled with all these thoughts, what if you didn't like me, what if you ran away and I never found you again. After so long waiting for my mate, it kind of makes you crazy."

"Okay. Well, you're gonna need to deal with that crazy and fast." Penny's firm tone alerted him to the presence of danger. Not here in the hotel, but somewhere danger threatened his mate. That was the reason for Penny's sympathetic gaze. Her sister's problem was now his problem.

"What's wrong?" Logan asked gently. "Did something happen to Helena other than a wild stallion jumping out in front of her car?"

"I think so. Before she came here, a man...he seems to have inserted himself into her life."

"Inserted himself into her life?" Dario frowned.

"He literally bumped into her on the street. He then called her at work even though she never gave him her phone number. She's a grown woman and had no reason to be suspicious of him. She figured it was a cute gesture. She really liked him..." Penny placed her hand on Dario's arm. "I know this isn't easy for you to hear."

"If you're expecting me to celebrate my mate being in love with another man, then no, this is not what I need to hear." He shook his head and turned from Penny, pacing the kitchen.

"She isn't in love with him if that's what concerns you," Penny told him. "If anything, it's the opposite."

"The opposite." Dario spun around to face her, his feet planted hip-width apart as his anger simmered below the surface. "What happened? Did he hurt her?"

"No, he never touched her." Penny's forehead creased as she shook her head. "And maybe it's nothing but Helena doesn't scare easily."

"She's scared?" Dario headed toward the door leading to the restaurant. "I should be with her." Every part of him wanted to hold his mate in his arms and tell her it was all going to be okay now that he was here to protect her.

"Slow down a second, Dario." Ivan grabbed his brother by the arm and spun him back around to face Penny. "Let's hear the rest of it, shall we?"

"A couple of days ago, Helena went home, and her apartment smelled like this guy's cologne. Expensive cologne." She locked eyes with Dario. "And before you think...*those* kinds of thoughts, the guy had never been back to Helena's apartment. There's no way the place should have smelled of him."

"On her clothes?" Logan asked. "Expensive cologne can linger."

"Since when did you wear expensive cologne?" Dario asked.

"I don't. But we have guests who do, and the scent can linger for days. So what if Helena went on a date with this guy and it rubbed off on her clothes? It might have been on her coat or her purse." Logan spread out his hands in defense as the others looked at him. "Hey, I'm trying to make sure we check out all the alternatives before we unleash a territorial stallion on the world."

"She isn't my territory, she's my mate," Dario told his brother.

"Believe me, when you have a mate, anywhere she is *is* your territory." Logan inclined his head toward Penny. "I try to keep it under control, but when I first found out you were my mate, it was hard not to rip the head off any man who so much as looked at you let alone talked to you."

"I'd say I didn't notice but I'd be lying," Penny answered smoothly.

"So what happened now?" Ivan asked. "We can't just dismiss what Helena believes happens."

"Does she have any idea why he might have gone to her apartment?" Logan asked.

"No, she had never met him before he bumped into her. And while they were dating, he never acted unusual, never questioned her about anything that raised her suspicions."

"Could it have to do with work?" Dario asked.

"She doesn't have any information on anything that would warrant anyone going into her apartment."

"What if it's not about Helena?" Ivan asked. "What if this is purely about the apartment itself? Perhaps there was something hidden there that the guy needed. He might have wanted to gain access by dating Helena."

"She didn't take him back there. That's what she said, and she has no reason to lie. We tell each other everything. If she took a guy home for sex, she would tell me," Penny insisted.

"What if he had access to her keys and got one duplicated?" Logan asked. "That way he could get in and out without arousing her suspicions."

"Stop!" Dario held up his hands. "This is a conversation we need to have with Helena present."

"Dario is right." Penny hugged herself as she turned back toward the restaurant. "You should come and say hello, Dario. And then I suppose we should tell Helena all about shifters and all the other magic that exists in the world."

"How do you think she'll take it?" Dario asked.

"That I don't know." Penny half-turned to face him. "Our mother never told us the monsters under our beds didn't exist. If we were scared of the monsters in our closets, she'd put up a talisman to ward it off. That's probably why I thought I recognized the talisman Milo found in the attic."

"Your mom knew magic and monsters existed?" Dario asked. This might be easier than he'd feared.

"Maybe she did. But we just thought she was a little crazy." There was that sympathetic look in Penny's eyes. "If anything, our mom's behavior made Helena resentful toward anything supernatural. She even hates watching fantasy shows or movies."

Dario's heart grew heavy. This might all be a lot harder than he'd ever expected.

But Helena was his mate, and they were destined to be together. Somehow, he'd make her understand that magic was wonderful and shifting was a gift.

And that he would love her to the end of time.

Now, doesn't that sound like something a stalker might say? His horse chuckled.

Growing up, Dario had learned to be strong. He'd fought and played with his predator brothers, never giving in or backing down. But nothing had prepared him for the challenge his mate posed.

And the stakes could not be higher.